TO THE SKYLINE

GISSANE SOPHIA

For my late father, I would've never been a writer without your faith in me. Whatever I create, it's for and because of you.

AUTHOR'S NOTE

This story is a work of fiction that's largely inspired by my love for the second chance romance trope as well as the real stories I heard growing up. As the child of Immigrant parents at a time with no smartphones or simple means of communication, I was constantly hearing about families that were split apart while leaving their homes and finding each other later in life. Some happened quickly, others took time. The point is these things happen. They aren't just tropes that make up beautiful love stories, they're an inexplicable part of our messy, complicated real world, and I felt that addressing this was important for this novel.

TRIGGER WARNINGS: grief, past deaths of parents (off page), verbal and physical domestic abuse (ex-spouse, on page. please skip chapter 27 if this is triggering for you), mentions of and on-page anxiety attacks, depression, divorce, infidelity.

If any of these topics are too much for you, please take care of yourselves, first and foremost. It takes time to get to our happy ending, but we get there eventually.

PART ONE

PARIS
16 YEARS AGO
JULY 2004

1

VIOLET

"Welcome to English Airlines," Violet said for the sixty-seventh time that day.

Violet Wedlake hated nothing more than midday international flights on Thursdays. Something about losing time felt more drastic during a bizarre thrust toward a Friday. It put her body clock off in a way no other day managed. Sunday came too soon. She couldn't explain it logically. It was just *off*.

She especially hated flights to the west coast of the United States—they always felt longer and more dreadful in the summer.

She was used to delays and used to turbulence. Used to unruly passengers.

She was also used to the plane feeling too big and simultaneously too small.

She wasn't used to being stunned.

An impossibly handsome man stepped in front of her, nudging her to look down at a badge in his hand. "Ben Williams, MI6. Could you take us to your pilot, please" he whispered. These were the passengers Sam paged them about from the gate as boarding began, though if she were being fully transparent, Violet wasn't exactly paying attention.

Two agents will be approaching at some point. They need to speak to Eric.

Sam hadn't specified that the men would be from MI6 or that they'd be attractive. Granted, that might not have been a good idea, but still. And to be fair, she was only half listening at the time because she was trying to calm a fussy toddler scared to come aboard.

Suddenly, the concept wasn't something she'd seen solely in the cinema.

Violet signaled to Henrietta at the other end of the plug doors with a head bob that she was leaving. She led the men through the first-class cabin toward the cockpit, a flame of nerves subtly crawling into her chest.

What was happening? Would this flight even take off? She wouldn't mind a cancelation if she were being frank, though she also hoped that whatever they were here for wouldn't be too dangerous. But they were MI6, for crying out loud. Didn't that mean international operations as opposed to U.K. based?

She wasn't entirely sure; everything she knew about MI6 was because of James Bond, specifically the Daniel Craig version.

If Ian Fleming hadn't written the novels years before, Violet would've sworn that Agent Williams was the inspiration for the secret agent. He had to have been in his early thirties. Lean and ridiculously attractive with sandy brown hair pushed back, a flawlessly groomed short beard, and eyes so blue she could swear the sky began and ended there.

But beyond it all, there was something inexplicable about the way his eyes bore into hers. Something she'd never seen in another person before. Something she couldn't understand. She'd seen a vast number of attractive passengers as a flight attendant, so much so that she lost count by the end of her first week.

But this—*him*. He was something else.

Eric was standing at the front of the cockpit, waiting for them. Violet smiled politely and walked back to the doors. This scenario was new and terrifying. As the rest of the passengers entered and the doors closed, Violet, Yana, Christine, Henrietta, Sam, and Sally were called back to the cockpit.

"Ladies, while something like this hasn't happened before, and we haven't trained for it, I need you all to act as if nothing is amiss. We will be making an abrupt stop at Charles de Gaulle under the guise of engine troubles. We will remain seated, as will passengers, for as long as the agents need to apprehend the man they're looking for and ensure the circumstances are safe before taking him into custody. Should this take longer than two hours, we will look into changing planes," Eric said.

He looked to Violet then. "Do you feel comfortable helping out the agents if necessary?"

Violet came to a halt then—"Uh," she started. God, she was too tired today, and the bloody heatwave made her feel mad. "Yes, sure," she blurted, unsure when her lips decided to betray her tired mind.

"They're trained professionals. Most of this should be quick," Eric clarified.

"Of course."

It would turn out that now they'd be two flight attendants short to accommodate the extra passengers on an already full flight. Sam and Sally, two newer hires, were sent home by Eric. Violet envied both of them.

The other agent turned to Violet and quietly whispered. "Keep your eye out for a white, jet-black-haired man with brown eyes, average height, and a large scar on his wrist." She was supposed to ensure he was on the plane while making her rounds before the agents conducted any other business.

This plan should be simple, ensuring passengers' seat belts were securely fastened and chairs were upright could make it easy to spot a scar on someone's wrist. So long as they weren't wearing a long-sleeve. The world was on fire outside, so who'd be doing that anyway? The agents would clandestinely sit on opposite ends of the galley, toward the doors, while Violet and Yana would join them during takeoff. The women would still be the ones to face the passengers.

Violet came across the man in question toward the end of the plane, seated beside a child, remembering then that she watched them board together. *This couldn't have been part of the plan. Did the agents know there was a child with him?*

She smiled sincerely at the girl. "Could you move the teddy bear so I could check your seat belt, sweetheart?" Violet asked, bending over just a little.

"It's fastened," the man barked back.

"It's precaution, sir. We must see it ourselves," Violet said with an overly enthusiastic fake smile. He moved the stuffed animal just barely, showing Violet the seat belt and, at the same time, the scar on his wrist.

As she made her rounds to the end of the plane, keeping a regular routine up, terror started to creep up again. This wouldn't end as quickly as they thought it would. If the agents knew there was a child, they would've mentioned her.

She walked over to Agent Williams first, standing at the galley away from the passengers' eyes, pretending as though she were taking something from the overhead bin above them. "There's a child with him," she whispered.

"What?"

She nodded anxiously. "A little girl. Maybe ten or eleven. He walked in with her."

"And you're sure it's the same man?"

"There is no one else with that description on the plane. And I saw the scar on his wrist."

"Shit," Agent Williams bit back with a whisper, taking a moment to recalibrate. Agent Adams sat beside Yana, and they were about to take off shortly.

There was nothing they could do now.

Agent Williams stood up, moving closer to her to ensure she could hear his hushed whisper. "We're going to try something if you're okay with it."

"What is it?"

"Cabin crew is going to serve drinks as quickly as possible. Once you get to him, you'll accidentally spill something on him. If we're lucky, the kid will ask for a sugary drink," he paused, looking at her as though to make sure she was okay before he continued. "Hopefully, he gets up and goes to the toilets to wipe himself off. When he leaves, you'll ask the girl about her relationship with him. We have to find out if she's a hostage or if he's using someone he actually knows."

"Okay," Violet replied. "And what if he doesn't move? What if he stays there?"

"In that case, we move to Plan C immediately, which is making ourselves known once we stop the plane. I'd rather we not go there. It could get ugly if we know nothing about the hostage. Knowing how he'll react depends on her relation to him. We need to get to him without hurting anyone else. That's the goal."

"Got it," she said with a hint of unspoken bravery rising in her chest. At some point, she'd start freaking out, but some of this seemed relatively simple for now. Wild, dramatic shootouts didn't happen in real life; those were reserved for films.

She sat beside him and fastened her seat belt, staring straight toward the aisles ahead.

Agent Williams turned to her. "I'm sorry, by the way."

"For what?"

"All of it. The disturbance. But also, he's not going to be kind to you during all this."

"Ah, well, many men are seldom ever kind here, so that'd just make for an ordinary Thursday."

"I'm sorry," he said again. This one sounded different and more personal—a look of genuine remorse piercing through his eyes. There was something achingly sincere about his tone and every move he made, including how he'd draw near to her when necessary—meticulous and gentle. And she was right back to the start of it all—the something she couldn't quite understand.

Violet smiled and nodded. "So, how many times has something like this happened?"

"On a plane? Not in my time."

"Where do these things usually happen?" She caught herself quickly. "Wait, am I even allowed to ask that? Do I have to be put into witness protection afterward?" She was sure she sounded twelve, but fear crept up again at the realization of upending her entire life, never seeing Nan, her best mate Simone, or Aunt Helen, Simone's mum...

He probably couldn't answer her questions; he could lie. He had no obligation to tell an outsider the truth. She wasn't sure why she asked, but these seats were generally close in proximity, and he was larger than Henrietta; if either of them moved an inch, their thighs would be touching. Violet was already in a daze today, what with the heatwave and her exhaustion.

There was also the minor detail that she'd been thinking of quitting in the next month or so. The stress of wondering how she'd do it or what she'd even do without securing a teaching job first weighing on her. But she was tired of tight compartments, time changes, and shitty men gawking at her.

She had only planned on doing this for a year, but that

somehow turned into two. She was twenty-two then, fresh out of university, and she had turned twenty-four a few months ago. It was time. It was *definitely* time. She wanted to go home now more than ever.

He let out a low chuckle, closing his mouth so no one else could hear. "You've watched too many spy films, yeah?" he whispered.

"Or not enough," she replied.

"It could happen anywhere, really, but it's generally a quicker process—a lot of times, we're able to find the person we need at their place of work, making it that much easier. We haven't dealt with someone like this guy or the operations he's a part of in the states. He's our first in a lot of areas." Agent Williams responded, cutting Violet loose from her thoughts.

"Wait, is this manageable? Can you guys handle this?"

He smiled again. "Yes, we can. We're trained for much worse."

Weren't MI6 agents supposed to be stoic or something? How was this man so kind? She hadn't watched that many spy dramas, but they always seemed either unkind or the James Bond type, overly cocky and full of themselves. Agent Williams didn't seem anything like them. There was a softness to his edges, a soothing rumble she could catch in his voice even through the whispers.

She took a deep breath, catching a trace of what must have been his cologne—bergamot, musk, and *unbearably hot*. The idea of getting up and spilling a drink on a criminal sounded much more effortless than sitting beside Agent Williams while trying not to drown in him. She was far too attracted to this man for her own good, and she didn't know how to handle it.

"Hey, Violet," he said softly. She turned to him slowly. "I promise we got this, okay? The kid just took us by surprise. My partner and I will ensure that no one else will get hurt. But with a potential hostage, we need to know what we're dealing with."

She nodded in understanding. "He can't hurt her, can he? Surely, security picked up on any weapons," Violet asked.

"There are ways to hurt people without a weapon."

"Right. Jesus. Is he capable of that?"

"Unfortunately," he answered.

"Good lord."

"Yeah. He might be the biggest case we'll ever have. At least, I hope."

"I do too."

"So, whomever he's working with is in Los Angeles then?"

"Yes, that's what we believe."

They were silent for a few beats as the plan began to move forward. A baby's cries filled the corridors immediately.

When the seat belt sign blinked off, and the pilot finished recapping the flight duration to "Los Angeles," the flight attendants got to their job. Violet started from the back where she'd be closer to the man.

She should be nervous. Of all the stories her mother had told her about her time as a flight attendant, *nothing* came close to this. She wondered how her mother would've handled it. Would she be the one chosen to operate from the inside? If that's what this could be categorized as. Or would she be like Yana, Henrietta, and Christine, in on the operation but entirely off the turf?

As she got to the man and quickly asked what he would like to drink, he dryly replied with, "nothing." Then she asked the girl what she would like, hoping she would ask for a drink. She did. And after a silent prayer, Violet spilled it on his lap, landing it all over the tucked-in part of his shirt and trousers.

"Jesus Christ, you twat!" he yelled, turning the entire plane in their direction.

"I'm so sorry, goodness, my hand slipped." Violet tried to

sound genuinely apologetic, not like she joyfully wanted to punch the teeth out of his head.

"You fucking idiot, what are you, new? Move over!" he bit, heading to the toilets. *Thank heavens. It worked.* Violet leaned over to the little girl, helping her open her tray table. "I'm sorry about your father's trousers, sweetheart," she said.

"It's okay. He's not my father," she replied quietly.

"Oh, I apologize. Is he a relative of yours?"

"No," the little girl said, dipping her head then, realizing perhaps that she had said too much.

"How do you know him?"

"I can't say," the little girl answered. That was that. Violet needed to hurry along before he came. She would speed up the process of handing out drinks now. She placed the cart back in its secure spot and hurried to where Agent Williams was sitting, signing something to the other agent.

"He's not her father, and he's not a relative. When I asked how she knew him, she said she couldn't say."

"Shit."

He continued signing to Agent Adams, presumably the same plan she had heard. Her nerves were increasing again, setting something subtly ablaze inside her while she tried to remain calm. Violet was an anxious person by nature, but perhaps, because of some otherworldly means, being in a plane helped her feel comforted by her mother.

As sounds on the plane grew louder, Agent Williams tried distracting Violet throughout the flight, asking questions about where she was from and her favorite color. Silly questions, really. She learned that he was seven years older than her and spoke four different languages, English, Welsh, French, and British Sign Language. Not counting the few Armenian words she knew courtesy of her Nan, Violet was only fluent in English.

He didn't have a favorite color, but his mother was Scottish, and his father was Welsh.

"Ah, yes, seven-year-old Violet would appreciate your mother's heritage. She stuffed a mini luggage full of toys and biscuits in order to, and I quote, 'run away and live with the fairies' on the Isle of Skye." She laughed at herself. "There was a documentary airing that morning. According to my mum, I got up, quietly packed my bags, and said I was leaving. I reached the end of the street before walking back to say I was tired and someone should take me."

He moved his head to the side and laughed. She could hear him trying to conceal the noise, turning back to her with a massive smile that sparked a delirious one of her own as she shook her head at her little self.

There was a comment or two about how much they both hated the heat and wished summer would be sent straight to hell where it belonged. And a companionable silence followed for the last fifteen minutes before Eric called the emergency landing at Charles de Gaulle.

AGENT ADAMS WAS SUPPOSED to stand at the passenger boarding bridge, ready to detain the criminal, George Lind, stating it was merely a cautionary customs examination. However, he quickly understood what was happening instead and hastily took the little girl in a chokehold. Lind threatened to snap her neck if anyone came near him. Agent Williams was still on the plane, standing by in the galley, waiting for the "opportune moment," as they'd called it.

Violet didn't think the situation could get worse until George Lind realized she was in on the operation with her little stunt, hurling insults at her left and right with every vile word one could think of.

It didn't faze her as much as the pool of anxiety watching the little girl's face in terror. She had to be safe in all this. Agent Adams tried to reason, denying that he was anything but a customs officer. It was a distraction—a means to buy time. And then, Agent Williams moved so swiftly when Lind was still facing Agent Adams that Violet was sure she imagined it. He knocked Lind from his feet, thrusting the girl forward into Agent Adams' arms. He cuffed George Lind's hands, and they immediately removed him from the plane.

The entire, horrifying affair felt as if it lasted mere seconds, but it had been minutes. Twelve, according to Yana, who was obsessively looking at her watch. Hours from when it all began with the start of a regular shift and days from when it would truly end. As Agent Williams and Adams took him away, George Lind shouted aggressively about how "none of you are getting away with this! I have more allies than you think!"

Agent Adams instructed Eric that no one should leave the plane until authorities gave them the go-ahead.

Agent Williams' eyes held Violet's for an evanescent beat before they hurried through the doors. This was all far more than she had ever signed on for, yet she couldn't help but hope that maybe, just maybe, she'd see him again.

2

VIOLET

Because of George Lind's threats and the revelation that someone on the plane was involved, the entire flight crew needed to be relocated to a hotel and investigated. There was also something about more targets, but they had very little information about them.

Though Violet and Yana were cleared on the first day, as witnesses, they needed to stay put. They were told it'd last a day, but one became two and two turned into three and three to four, five, and six. What was happening with the other girls? Were they okay? How was the little girl George Lind had taken as a hostage?

In truth, Violet probably could've used a few days off, but being stuck in a hotel room instead of roaming the Parisian streets was far from how she imagined it'd be. Agents guarding each of their doors were anything but comforting.

And on day six, she was feeling trapped, anxiety rising in her chest, nausea creeping through, and sitting smack dab in the middle of her throat. If she didn't leave this room...she would have a panic attack.

She felt the waves rise momentarily when she spoke with Nan, lying about how she needed to do overtime due to another flight attendant getting ill. She called her best mate, Simone and made her promise to check in on Nan a few times while being truthful about the fact that she couldn't say much, but they were in Paris, waiting on news daily.

She pushed the nerves away then, willing herself to look at the bright side.

But the waves were back and coming in strong now. Violet had showered earlier, feeling a bit better at the rising tides, but after learning that it could still be a few more days of this unconventional confinement, nausea and dizziness came rushing in full force. She walked over to her bag, searching for gum. How had she not realized she was out?

"I need to get out of this room," she nearly cried, pacing quickly throughout the limited space. It was one of those hotel rooms with a small window that could only be cracked slightly open. If she could at least open it more, she might be able to breathe better.

"We can't leave, Vi. You know what the agents said." Yana rose to meet her friend where she stood. She placed her hand on Violet's shoulder. How was she handling this so well? Why was Violet the only one who felt like she was going mad?

Since going off of antidepressants a year ago, Violet found the means of dealing with her anxiety with the help of her therapist, Jane. Deep breaths were key—and the outdoors. The outdoors had been a saving grace since she was a child; open spaces outside of tight compartments made a world of difference at times.

She placed her hand on Yana's to wordlessly thank her but set her mind to walking out of the room. She needed to get out. "I can't. I just...I need air."

Violet swung the hotel door open so rapidly that she walked straight into a man's back.

Agent Williams. Of course, it was Agent Williams.

It couldn't have been the other, older man who reminded her of an uncle or a neighbor, not the man she was most certainly attracted to in a way she didn't want to be.

"Agent Williams, I'm sorry," she said, not recognizing the chaos and fire in her voice.

"Is everything okay?"

"I—I need some air. I know we can't be out, but I'm very close to an anxiety attack, and being in an enclosed space for days isn't helping." She couldn't believe she was telling him the truth, but there was no use in lying. If she wanted a means to leave, this was perhaps the only way to ensure it.

"Shit. Okay. Hold on," he said, the look in his eyes stirred with a recognition that she found comforting.

He nudged another agent standing by to trade positions. "I'll be a few. Room 813 still has someone inside," he told the man.

"Come on. I'll walk out with you," he started to say. "I know you'd rather have space, but it's a risk we can't take right now. One of us needs to be in proximity. We don't yet know who would've been tracking Lind's whereabouts and if anyone's close by," he finished.

"It's okay. I get it."

They were quiet as they walked into the lift and down eight floors. Violet closed her eyes, repeating *You're okay* in her head. Followed by *five things you could see. Four things you can feel. Three things you can hear. Two things you can smell. One thing you can taste.*

She knew the tactics. None of this was new.

Picture a place you feel comfortable and safe, her therapist Jane had told her. *Go there. Remind yourself that you're okay. Repetition is a good thing. Deep breaths in and out. Grief won't ever fully go away, but you can choose how to grow around it.*

In those harrowing moments, she was always with her parents—Hyde Park in the autumn, stomping on every leaf she could manage, her mother's laugh, her father's hideous olive-green poncho. Reds, golds, and amber hues all around them—the crinkling sound of leaves at their feet.

You'll see them again someday, Violet would always tell herself. *You are not alone,* she repeated in her head.

Breathe.

Autumnal shades in the crisp morning air, waking up to the smell of brown sugar waffles. Their quaint kitchen was always full of what an average person might think were one-too-many flowers. Her mother humming the lyrics to what was almost always a Queen song—her father grunting over the latest debacle in the newspaper.

No one could be unhappy when autumn is in the air, her mother would say.

Those were the places she went to—the vivid corners where the leaves danced and fell.

The lift dinged open. Agent Williams' hand hovered over her back in a phantom touch as he led her out.

Reality hit. It was still too hot. Autumn was nowhere in sight.

Breathe, she repeated in her head.

His nearness was almost making it worse. She'd never shown this side to others. The only one on the job who knew about Violet's anxiety was Yana, and for that reason, it was a blessing to be stuck in the room with her instead of someone else. Violet wasn't ashamed of her anxiety; she'd lived with it for so long that it was second nature, but it was still very much something that made others flinch.

"Do you take anything?" he asked in a low whisper while

they made their way out the sliding doors toward cobblestone steps that led to an empty garden area.

"I used to. I've been off medication for a while. It's usually manageable, but it sneaks up now and again. I chew gum for nausea, but I'm all out."

"I could get you some. What flavor?"

"Oh, that's not necessary, Agent Williams. Thank you. I just… I really needed the air."

He was looking at her with a softness that made her heart clench. She'd never seen such transparency in someone's eyes. It was a look that made her feel safe in a way that was both terrifying and relieving.

"Please, call me Ben. And it's no problem, Violet. I can have someone bring it. Tell me." His tone sounded like an ardent plea.

Ben. The idea of calling him that, of familiarizing whatever this madness was…felt oddly right.

"Last I checked, your job didn't include managing a flight attendant's bouts of nausea."

"We've put a load on this particular flight attendant. She deserves gum if that's what she wants."

Violet smiled. God, he was so kind. So bloody kind, it could wreck her if she allowed it.

"I appreciate it, Ben. Thank you. But really, it's fine."

He cocked his head to the side. "Either you tell me, or I'll get every flavor that's on the shelf. I'm afraid there's no way in which you win this round."

She chuckled then, guilt taking a momentary holiday. "I could've outsmarted you if I were in a better headspace. Mint. Or peppermint. Just nothing fruity. They'd make me even more nauseous."

"Oh, I don't doubt it. I'll have it to you soon," he said, resounding empathy evident in his voice.

"Thank you."

"Of course."

Ben wasn't judging her. She gathered as much through deep breaths. And the air was helping, too. But heavens, she missed her flat. She missed Nan. She wanted her bed.

She decided to change the topic from the attacks happening inside of her. "You probably can't say, but do you know who was involved on the plane?"

"Your co-pilot," Ben said quietly and abruptly at the same time.

Violet clasped her hand to her mouth, "*What*?" she nearly screamed.

Ben looked around then, a *ssh* sound coming out of him.

"I'm sorry," she said, returning to a whisper.

"Why would he ever get involved?"

"There's a lot I can't say. And you're safer not knowing, believe me. But people like your co-pilot are offered large sums of money to help men like George Lind carry on the operations they're meant to."

"So, uhm, just to clarify what I clearly only know from films. But if you're MI6, that means his ties outside of the UK are much bigger than some average case, is that correct?"

"Yes, our involvement usually occurs with larger and foreign threats. Lind isn't working alone."

"Jesus! If I quit now, can I go home?" Violet asked, serious and genuinely contemplative.

"I wish I could say yes, but you must remain under our watch for your safety. We're close, Violet. They've apprehended a few more people in Los Angeles now. You'll be home soon. I promise."

Violet wasn't sure why she could trust every word out of this man's mouth, but she did. It surprised her that Joe was involved, but not entirely—not when he was known for dating female flight attendants regularly. Not when he was sleazy and moody at times. It might be why he requested for Sally to leave immediately. He cared about her more than others. He would rather she be safe, Violet supposed. Or, maybe he didn't want her to realize he wasn't the suave, smooth-talking man she knew. Violet didn't care anyway.

She was going to quit the moment they were free to go.

It was time.

Ben's voice broke through her thoughts. "What would you do if you quit?"

"Teach or something in administration. I have degrees in both fields," she replied.

"What year?"

"Primary school, ideally, but I don't have a year preference."

He smiled at her, and a strange look of knowing flashed in his eyes as though he expected as much from her. "Aces," he stated.

She wanted to ask what he would do if he weren't here. If he could also leave it behind, but it wasn't her place. Not here. Not now.

Her heart rate was finally back to normal. She didn't want to scream anymore. It was best not to push.

"I think I'm ready to go back inside," she said, looking up into the kind eyes holding hers.

He nodded.

"Sorry to…" she started.

"Violet, no. Come on. Don't apologize for anything," Ben declared, a delicacy intermingled with the gravity of his tone.

"Thank you then," she managed.

"Anytime. If you need a few minutes every day, let me know. And if I'm not around, ask for me. Someone will come get me."

"That's awfully kind of you."

A slow, compassionate smile curved on his face. "We did get you into this mess."

As they turned to walk away, they caught sight of Agent Adams sitting far off on a chair alone, appearing to wipe away tears while on the phone.

"Is he okay?" Violet asked Ben, knowing that he likely wouldn't say anything. Why did she even ask?

"Being in a relationship in our line of work is a fucking shit show," Ben began, looking at his friend with an empathy that stung. "But they're lucky. They're both in it. And she rightfully worries about him. A lot."

"You're certain he's talking to his significant other?"

"Edmund's an only child, and both his parents have passed. Plus, Nina's the only one who can bring all that out of him." Something equally painful and haunting dawned in his eyes.

Edmund was just like her, Violet thought. An only child with no parents. Except she didn't know what having a steadfast partner was like. She could imagine how hard it'd hit, heightening the lingering fears she already carried with more horrid questions of what-ifs.

"Am I stealing you from someone you should be speaking with?" Violet asked, kicking herself for it. *You don't need to know this information,* she reprimanded herself.

Ben shook his head. "You're not. Some days, it's hard to keep in touch with my family, let alone a significant other. Plus, it'd put more people at risk, and that's not a cross I can bear."

Weirdly, she understood it. "I shouldn't have pried," she replied.

"You can ask whatever you want—no need to apologize. But fair play, is it not?" he added with a sneaky smirk. "Is there someone waiting for you in London?"

"Nope," she said firmly.

He cocked an eyebrow, making her smile and prompting his

own in tandem. "I'm glad that smile is back on your face," he replied with a genuine glimmer of warmth.

Ben dropped her off at the door, promising to have gum for her soon.

One pack was what she imagined; two months' worth was what she got.

3

BEN

The air was thick and muggy.

This bloody case shouldn't be taking so long. Cyber blocks on the intel they continuously tried gathering made every day trickier. George Lind had multiple contacts, yet he was smart enough not to carry anything incriminating with him. Any ties to the people he was working with were far from sight.

Still, they were closer than yesterday.

Only it was half past eight, and all he could think about was Violet.

His head throbbed.

He realized sometime during another painfully grueling interrogation that he couldn't wait to see Violet. Hoping she'd send for him again. Like the last three days, which were perfunctory but lovely still.

Her courage in the congested plane emitted a flare to the parts of him that wanted to be better—braver. These quiet nights underneath the embrace of stars were quickly becoming a familiar tranquility.

Space was imperative to Ben, and bringing someone into it

on more permanent grounds felt like an invasion he didn't know how to handle. His best mate and partner, Edmund, had found love early in their career as agents. Nina Jones was head of their treasury department and the one person who could keep Edmund's head out of the clouds and his impulses at bay. She was home to him in a way Ben couldn't comprehend. He also couldn't fathom the arguments and the pain—he watched her weep for Edmund the two times he was hospitalized. And all this was after she had rejected him repeatedly because she had a strict rule concerning dating within the field. They were an exception to all the rules in the end.

His head continued to pound as he thought of it—the possibilities and the what-ifs. If he were a different man, if the circumstances were different, if she was interested, perhaps he could try with Violet.

But not like this. Not when their jobs could lead to days or months without seeing each other.

He beelined to the lift without thinking after he was released from his duties for the day, leaving paperwork for another time. He pressed the button for the eighth floor, and the normally cold metal was clammy too—everything was too hot—too frustrating.

He bobbed his head to Agent Green, prompting the older gentleman to move aside for Ben. He knocked placidly on the door. If Violet hadn't sent for him, perhaps she didn't need to. Perhaps she was fine.

But today, he needed her. He wanted her company. He wanted this to be a routine—ending the night together.

Yana, the other flight attendant, opened with a look of concern on her face. "Agent Williams. Hello," she said.

He smiled courteously. "Hi. Is uh...Violet in?"

"Yep. One second," she turned, closing the door just slightly before walking away. "It's for you, Vi," he overheard.

He held his breath for the entirety of the seven seconds he must've waited. "Oh, hi," Violet greeted him. A shy, surprisingly understanding smile made its way onto her face. "Give me a second, please."

Ben bowed his head. "Take your time."

She walked out shortly after that, a small smile on her weary face. He hated what they were putting these women through. They should've been allowed to leave. They should be in the comfort of their homes, never worrying about this case again. The guilt taunted him for a moment.

"You alright?" he asked, allowing his hand to hover over the small of her back instinctually. He didn't know what he was trying to protect her against. These grounds were safe.

She nodded with an expression that felt like a punch to his chest. "Is your friend alright? Would she, uh...does she need to be out on occasion as well? I could arrange for it if so."

"I've asked. She says she's fine. Yana's an introvert; some time away from the bustle and noise is doing wonders for her. Or so she claims. She's asked for a notebook, and she's been scribbling stuff in there constantly. I wouldn't be surprised if she writes an entire manuscript by the time we're out of here." She giggled slightly. It made his insides melt.

Coming to her was indeed the preeminent remedy.

They were quiet in the lift, filling the silence with brief glances and faint smiles.

She walked over and sat at a bench facing a scattered bloom of poppies, glowing from the fluorescent lights planted in the soil. Ben followed suit, sitting close enough to talk comfortably with her but far enough that no parts of them touched.

Violet turned to him. "How was your day?"

"We've had better," he replied, sounding more tired than he wanted to show. He leaned back with an exhale.

He caught the slow movement of her hand in his periphery.

Violet placed it delicately on his forearm and gave a gentle squeeze. He turned to face her, bringing his other hand atop hers and traced her knuckles with his thumb.

It was an unfamiliar sort of comfort. Neither said a word for a beat. Their stillness floating in the heavy air delivered a momentary respite.

"Does your family know?" she asked, drawing his attention back to her pretty face.

"They do, yes. My father was in the agency," he replied quickly, careful not to stare too long.

"Oh, and it doesn't bother your mother?"

"I'm sure it did. It's why he left it behind when they married."

"And how do they feel about you being a part of it now?" she asked.

"He's not too chuffed, but he bears it." He wanted to mention his mother, but it was always a bit awkward to do so indirectly.

"And your mum?"

"We uh...we lost her at childbirth when she was pregnant with my sister," he said, looking down and feeling a little relieved that she was now one of the few people in the world who'd know about the gravest loss in his life.

A reckoning coupled with what seemed like guilt flashed in Violet's eyes when he raised his gaze back toward her. She dragged her thumb against his forearm. "Ben. I'm so sorry. How old were you?"

"Ten."

"Goodness, that's so young. The baby, did she?"

"Yes, my sister made it. It's a true shame she never got to know her. She's a carbon copy of our mum in every way."

Violet shook her head, a flurry of sadness suddenly engulfing her. "My God, that's so awful."

She was so sincere—so full of heart that it brought him some semblance of comfort to tell her. She repositioned herself, sitting criss-crossed on the bench. Violet lifted her hand from his forearm and set it down on her lap—the loss of the weight of her touch palpable in its absence.

He wanted her touch back.

She swallowed. "I know the feeling too well. My parents died in a car crash when I was eighteen," she confessed, an awkward tilt formed against her lips. It was a look he recognized in his own movements when his mother would come up. An odd sort of expression between a frown and a smile, often geared toward the person receiving the news than the one declaring it.

Eighteen.

Both of them.

Ben's heart plunged instantaneously into the pit of his stomach. He assumed she was being nonchalant when she said no one was waiting for her back home in London. So much about Violet abruptly made sense—the sadness in her eyes that matched his own was due to the tremendous loss she carried like her very own cross.

"Jesus, Violet. I'm so sorry," he started, shaking his head as he closed his eyes. "I can't imagine."

A faint, grief-stricken line curved on her lips. "We all have something tragic looming over us, don't we?"

He gulped down a stubborn, immovable lump in his throat and sighed.

"I wouldn't wish it on my worst enemy," she said quietly, averting her gaze toward the cobblestoned ground.

They were quiet again for a few moments. The companionable silence took them to an ocean of heartaches—waves rising, and the aftereffects of treading through grief enveloped them closer.

"Do you have any siblings?" Ben asked, wanting to reach over and hold her hand—to do something, *anything* to have her closer in case the answer was what he feared. But what if she moved her hand for a reason? What if this was too much for her?

She shook her head with a somber, lonely smile. "Only child," she replied.

He remembered the look in her eyes when he told her of Edmund. He pushed it aside then as empathy pouring through, realizing only now that it was a profound understanding of scars that never quite stop aching. The thought of how lonely she must have felt in this world shattered him. The lump in his throat grew sharper and more rigid.

She was so much like Edmund that it haunted him; only Edmund, at least, had Ben and his family, along with Nina's.

Who did Violet have? Was there honestly no one waiting for her? Who was the emergency call she was granted when they first got here? He wanted to ask. He wanted to know every detail and somehow etch himself into her circle, stay there in the mutual familiarity they'd uncovered for however long she'd let him.

Before he could ask, Violet changed the subject. "Why did you join the agency, if you don't mind me asking?"

"It was Edmund's idea. So when he suggested it, I went along with it."

"That's why?" she asked, clearly trying not to laugh at his reasoning.

"I have a degree in forensics, but barely managed it cause I hated school so much," he replied. His sister was the one meant for university and medicine, not him. "Plus, I think Edmund looks up to my father like his own and thought it'd make him proud; instead, we're scolded every time we go back home like we're teenagers again and not in our thirties."

She tittered. "It's a solid reason. I'd have done the same if my best mate had asked me to. I'd follow her to the ends of the earth. But the brilliant thing willingly chose to become a heart surgeon. I'd have been a lost cause."

Good. Violet had a best mate, at least. He released a faint exhale.

She tilted her head again. "Do you plan on doing this until the age of retirement?"

"That's a loaded question," he said with a chuckle, wanting her questions never to end.

It was a fascinating kind of curiosity. He'd answer anything she wanted.

"I'm sorry. I get chatty when I'm nervous."

"Why are you nervous?"

"I'm not sure," she bit back quickly, trying to draw the attention away from her.

She shouldn't be nervous when it was her scintillating eyes evoking something tenderly comforting in him. The man was ready to do anything she asked of him—throw everything out the window. He would stay right here all night until she begged him to leave.

She shouldn't be the one who was nervous because he was sitting with a woman entirely out of his league and whose intrepidity floored him to the point of no return.

"If it helps, I'm nervous too," he said with a faint smile. "And to answer your question, hopefully not, but I'm not entirely sure what I'd do now. As damaging as this job is, it's steady."

Violet smiled, looking into his eyes with a regard that said she was trying to read between the lines—searching for the words he wasn't saying aloud. It was thrilling and agonizing to be on the receiving end of her gazes. "There's something else I want to ask you," she started to say, "but it's more personal."

"You can ask me anything," he replied promptly.

She opened her mouth and then closed it. She traced the edges of her fingernails with the pads of her thumb again. "You seemed so calm that first night when I was anxious. Many people, men especially, don't know how to react when someone's in that state. They either brush it off or shut down from what I've experienced. But you seemed to understand it. Was I wrong in that assessment?" she asked.

If he sat here and went back to his childhood, the fears, and the darkness, he wouldn't be able to pull himself out.

He sighed, surprisingly content about telling her a small part of the truth. "You're not wrong. I'm familiar with what an anxiety attack looks and feels like."

She nodded, the expression in her eyes threading together another form of familiarity they'd uncovered. She didn't need to say more when the silent conversations said everything. Her eyes continued to study him.

He wanted to hold her hand.

He wanted to take her in his arms, sit here for hours while he held her close.

He did none of those things.

After a few beats, Ben spoke. "You said you wanted to teach or go into administration when we first spoke. What stopped you from going into it immediately after you finished your programs?"

"My mum was a flight attendant. And I was fighting a lot of depression, so I wanted to walk in her shoes a bit and see the world before settling into a more permanent job. I...uh, stayed longer than planned."

It made complete sense. "How long has it been?"

"A little over two years, and up until the last few months, I loved every minute of it, but the rotations are more taxing now. I've certainly overstayed my welcome."

"Where's your favorite place you've traveled to?" he asked, wanting to lighten the atmosphere.

"Mykonos, Greece. It was only for three short days, but it's a different life than ours. Warm and wild and comfortable. There's something ineffable about the Mediterranean, really."

"Would you live there?"

"I'd love to, but I think I'd miss the English rain too much. I'll take it over wind any day."

"A fan of storms, then?"

Her eyes lit up. "Oh, massive. Thunder and lightning shouldn't be calming, and yet they are."

"I agree. My sister used to fear them, but I'd take her to our garden and tell her it was Mum trying to water the flowers. The storms were to remind us that she missed us."

She smiled with such humility it broke his heart again. "Oh, I adore that. Did it help?"

"It did. We'd built forts when storms hit, and Emma would pick a film to watch."

"Brilliant. You did well there," Violet acknowledged with a big, sincere smile.

"I'd like to hope so."

The binding cords between them continued to work overtime.

He might never understand the strength of the tethers pulling him to Violet, but he was certain in this very moment that the ease he felt while around her could never be replicated. He'd never subject her to the life of uncertainties his job was riddled with, but heaven help him, he'd do anything for the chance.

One night. One kiss—a taste to hold him over for the rest of his life. Those pretty pink lips drove him to oblivion. The way her eyes always seemed to be searching for something more made him want to break open every closed part of him and find ample ways to fulfill all her desires.

"Do you wanna talk about whatever's made your day such rubbish?" she asked gingerly.

He swallowed. "Haven't we put you through enough with this case? I won't subject you to the bullshit we're dealing with on the inside."

"Are you sleeping?" she said, charting her expression with such reverence it wrecked him.

"As much as I can," he replied. "Is that your subtle way of telling me I look knackered?"

She pursed her lips as though she were debating something. "Sort of. But more than anything, you seem off today. I want to make sure you're taking care of yourself, even if the job doesn't allow much room for that."

He closed his eyes for a beat. "I know I said you should send for me if you needed anything. But let's set the time, yeah? I'll come get you, same time, every day. You won't have to ask."

"And how does that factor into you taking care of yourself?"

"Well, for one, I'd much rather hear about your day, however uneventful, than end my night going over this bloody case in my head."

She bobbed her head in understanding, uncrossing her legs back to the ground. "Deal. Maybe by tomorrow, I can update you on whether Yana has figured out if the room's remote is haunted."

"Wait, should I be concerned?"

"Absolutely. If the verdict is a yes, I'm requesting a room change."

He laughed heartily, leaning further back into the seat. He'd get up soon and walk her back. But for a moment, he wanted nothing more than to be still with her.

4

BEN

The lift came to an abrupt halt, internal mechanisms jerking underneath them with an audible clang. Ben and Violet were already standing close to each other, his body facing her mid-conversation. He locked himself in place but instinctually moved his arms around her, stopping himself without actually touching her to ensure she'd have a place to land if she came forward.

She moved slightly, finding her balance as quickly as he imagined someone used to turbulence would. Still, she was mere millimeters away from his face. *Christ. If he simply moved his lips, they'd be on hers.* Their gasps came in hard and fast, both looking at one another for a beat before uttering a word.

She swallowed hard. "Are we...stuck?"

He confirmed with a nod, stepping away from her to walk the short step forward to push the emergency call button.

"Bonjour, quelle est votre urgence?" said the woman's voice on the other end.

"Bonjour, l'ascenseur s'est arrêté," he replied.

"À l'Hôtel Lavande? Nous travaillons à la résolution de ce problème."

He thanked her and turned to Violet. "They're working on it. These things shouldn't take too long. How are you feeling?"

"I'm fine at the moment, but ask me again if it lasts longer than a few minutes," she answered.

He stood in front of her, resting his hand on the metal railing. "Think of something better. Somewhere more exciting. What's your favorite part of flying?" he asked, partially to distract her and selfishly to continue getting to know her more.

She leaned her head against the steel behind her, her eyes contemplating.

She sighed deeply. "It's usually during the longer flights, anything five hours or more. But the lull right in the middle when you look out the window, and all you see are clouds, the sky, and the possibilities. You're far from where you were and not quite close to where you need to be, but you know with utmost certainty that you're headed there. That moment right there. I try to catch it as often as I can. The immensity of the in-between is always so comforting and oddly beautiful."

He said nothing for a moment, searching her gaze intently for the place where those thoughts had fallen from.

"What is it?" she said, almost diffidently now.

He shook himself out of the daze. "I'm sorry—I think you broke me there."

She took a deep breath as though she wanted to laugh, to dispel any awkwardness. As though she wanted to draw attention away from how he was looking at her, except he couldn't stop. Ben couldn't break himself from looking at the parts of her he could physically see, and every layer pleated underneath.

He wanted to understand the depth of the in-between she believed in. He tried to say something profound, but all he could do was stare.

She snapped him free from his thoughts by speaking next.

The anxiety, he thought. She must still be anxious, often echoing his questions with ones of her own. "What about you then? What's your favorite part of the job?" she asked.

This case, he wanted to say—*meeting you,* he wanted to affirm because nothing and no one had engrossed him so completely. There was no beauty in this job. There was no beauty in his whole mundane life. It was clear as day now that he felt he had no purpose, nothing that made him want to give himself to the novel remnants of the in-between.

He blinked, trying to will himself to return to a more rational state of being. "There's no part of it that I love. I suppose we do the right thing here and there, but there's no beauty in any of the quiet moments or even the shitty loud ones," he replied, hating himself for sounding so pessimistic.

"You'll find it someday, then. I think we're meant to," she said, smiling with such pleasing certainty that it made Ben's heart plunge with a flip.

He slid down and sat on the clammy floor. He didn't expect her to follow, but she did. *Did she realize the hold she had on him? Did she understand what she was doing to him with her mind?* He dreaded to think of the day he had to say goodbye to her.

He turned his head ever-so-slightly to face her. "Your light continues to amaze me, Violet. I don't know how to be around you sometimes."

She blushed. *He was going to melt into this floor.*

"I could say the same about you and your kindness," she replied.

They could not be having a moment like this in a bloody lift of all places. It was getting substantially hotter, more humid, and the lack of air was growing uncomfortably heavy. This was the last place on earth he wanted to be stuck in with her.

Ben and Violet sat in silence for a few beats. *Did she desire him in the same way? Did she want him as desperately as he needed her?* And then her breathing began coming in faster, a bit more shallow than usual. *If he took her hand, would that make it better or worse?* He wasn't sure, and he hated that.

"God, it's disgustingly hot in here. Where are they?" she said.

He was probably just as uncomfortable, but he couldn't show it. Not here. "How can I help, Violet? How can I distract you?"

"I was fine until I realized how hot it is, and now that I'm aware of it, I swear it's getting worse by the second. How on earth do people say summer is their favorite season? What part of this is cheery and wonderful?" she complained, releasing a deep exhale and leaning her head back further.

"I'm afraid I don't have the answer to that one. Though, it is a little funny how much your name says about you. Violets don't do well in the summer."

She chuckled. *Good.* "My mother must've known exactly what she was doing with that choice."

"Are you named after anyone?" he asked, his curiosity now piqued to learn more about her family again.

"No. My mum just really adored it. But my middle name, Eleanor, is for both my grandmothers. Coincidentally, yes, they are both called Eleanor. I didn't know my father's parents well; they both passed when I was fairly young, but I love having that small connection to her and my Nan, who's the closest person to me now."

Her mother was right to adore it. It matched her gorgeously.

She tilted her head a bit, looking at him with an expression he'd never be able to resist. "Can I ask you a question?"

"Always," he answered.

"Are you really called Ben Williams? Or is it a code name?"

The query amused him, even if his answer might not do the same for her. If he was going to give anyone his real last name, it might as well be Violet Eleanor Wedlake. He'd give her anything. That much was painstakingly apparent now. "I am, yes. But my actual last name is Grant. Not so much a code name, more of a precaution," he replied.

"I like that. It matches you," she said.

He smiled. He would give anything to hold her—right here at this moment. He heard noises come from the other side of the elevator doors, so he rose to his feet and held out his hand to her. She took it, allowing him to pull her up.

They stood there for a beat with her hand in his, eyes locked on each other. He didn't want to move. He couldn't even avert his gaze. He wanted to lace their fingers together and walk out with her close to him. But they couldn't have any of that—not out there. These moments were theirs and theirs alone.

He loosened his grip just barely, and she moved her hand back and then dusted off her clothes.

The metal doors slid open, with two people standing outside. Ben acknowledged them with a simple greeting and placed his hand on Violet's back, initiating for her to exit first.

She turned to him when they got to her door. "Let's take the stairs tomorrow?"

"Sounds like a plan," he replied with a smile.

He tapped the key card to its designated spot and opened the door to his room.

Edmund was sitting at the small desk, head deep in paperwork before he looked up. "That took longer than usual," he commented.

"We got stuck in the bloody lift on our way up."

Edmund raised a brow. "With Violet?"

"Who else?"

A sly smirk made its way onto his face. "And how was it?" he asked.

Ben shook his head and rolled his eyes. He walked over to his bed and unclasped his watch, setting it on the stand before he turned to face Edmund again. He was tapping his foot, waiting for an answer.

"I don't know what you want me to tell you, mate. It was the same as always, minus an uncomfortable fifteen minutes in a lift."

Edmund's lips quirked up. "And you're still going to wait until the absolute last second to ask her out?"

"And when do you propose I do it, Ed, right this second? She deserves better than that."

He agreed with a nod. "Not saying she doesn't. I'm just saying you should put it out there sooner rather than later, see how she feels about you and whether she'd be interested. I can't imagine why she wouldn't be, but still."

He scoffed. "And what if she doesn't want to go? It makes the time left more awkward. This way, if she doesn't want anything more, she's free to go home, away from the four walls she's been trapped in."

Edmund swung his head from left to right. "Alright. But don't back out, okay? Or so help me, God, I'll do it for you. I'm not about to spend the rest of our days with you moping over the one woman who's managed to get through those walls of yours."

"Yeah, okay, enough of that. Anything new in there?" Ben asked, bobbing his head toward the papers.

"Absolutely nothing," Edmund replied.

Ben sighed. "Take a beat. I'll have another look in a minute."

Edmund nodded and walked out.

Ben went to the toilets to wash up. Edmund wasn't wrong. He'd talk to Violet right away if he could—do everything in his power to ensure that the rest of their time in this mess was more pleasant, but he couldn't. He couldn't bear the thought of not seeing her because he somehow scared her away.

It'd be different when there was a goodbye in the picture.

He was prepared for that much.

Or so he thought.

5
____

VIOLET

Evenings with Ben became a perfect respite, quiet moments with just the two of them and all sorts of conversations. Yana would make offhanded comments about knights in shining suits. Violet was crushing hard, and it was becoming harder to deny. But she had to.

He made it perfectly clear during the first night that dating in his line of work was a nightmare. She could tell how horrible he felt watching Edmund and Nina on the phone—two people who understood the job closely. If that were the two of them, complete opposites in their chosen careers, it'd be hell.

No matter what she was starting to feel, she needed to be smart. She learned early on how cruel life could be to ordinary people, driving home from the shop. It took two years for her to sit in a car again. Another four for her thoughts to stop venturing into dark places every time someone went somewhere. And she knew that the pain could come rushing back at any time because grief was a bloody unpredictable beast.

She'd be miserable, tirelessly wondering if he'd come back home or...worse. She couldn't subject herself to the painful possibility of brutally losing love, too. And she'd never tell him to leave the agency for her. They weren't his parents.

She'd never force another person to dwell in the cages of her trauma.

Yet, while every hour seemed to pass slower than the one before, time with Ben flew quicker than a plane's trajectory. She, of all people, would know—she was all too aware of the beginning and end. As much as they grew closer, she'd never allow herself more. She wanted so desperately to hold him—to reach forward and cup his cheek, kiss the worn-out glares away from his eyes.

She didn't do any of those things.

And by day seventeen, they were free to go.

THERE WAS a knock on their door as she and Yana were just about packed and ready to leave tomorrow morning.

Ben.

If he hadn't shown up at her door, yesterday's conversation would've been their final exchange. She would've hated that. Those bright blue eyes would've been a distant memory, interlocked with hers as they talked intently about Man City's season. In the upheaval of preparing to leave, she hadn't even thought of goodbye and what that'd eventually mean.

He was a bit winded, like he had raced over here. He took a deep breath and smiled.

"Violet, I know this isn't the ideal situation," he started, his voice tinted and warm. "But...can I take you out for an early dinner before we leave? A proper goodbye that way."

Her brain shut off for a moment, replaying his words in her head to make sure she heard correctly. She blinked once, twice, three times, nearly catching Yana's indistinct gasp from her side of the bed.

A proper goodbye.

"Sure, I'd like that. What time is your flight?"

"It was supposed to be in an hour, but now, ten-something," Ben brushed off. "How does four sound?"

Did he change his flight *for* her? He couldn't take the train? Agents didn't have private transportation? She looked at her watch. She wasn't even sure what time it was.

"I'll be ready," she replied with a smile.

There had been a lot of men who'd asked Violet out on the plane or impulsively at airport bars. One too many. But she never once said yes to any of them.

Was this even a proper date, or merely a goodbye between friends who'd grown close through unexpected circumstances? As a woman whose mother met her father on a plane, people always assumed she'd be more open to the prospect. Yet, the seventies were a different time. And this would certainly make matters more complicated, but something about his eyes took hold of hers in a way she might never find the words for.

Something about his gentleness and the inexplicable spark she couldn't quite understand were worth giving into for a few hours.

When she turned, Yana was smirking with her arms crossed. "The knight in a tailored suit strikes again!"

"Oh, bugger off. It's not like that."

"Ah, yes—fit men merely take fit women to dinner because they want to be friends."

Violet tilted her head. "He wouldn't date in his line of work. He made that much clear the first night he came out with me when I was anxious. Did you also not hear the part about a proper goodbye?"

"Doesn't mean it's not a date, babe. We've had a shit storm of a few weeks. You bloody well deserve a night out with the hot agent," Yana shrugged.

She leaned against the drawer. "He is so damn kind that it's astonishing. Most men hear about an anxiety attack and run for the trenches. He was the one who suggested heading outside every day and asking for him, you know?" Violet said.

Yana tittered. "Yes, you've told me, which is why it's a date. Now, please tell me you have something nice to wear?"

Violet bent down and opened her luggage back up. Excluding her uniform, all she had with her except the gift shop t-shirts they'd rewashed four times by now was a red dress, a pair of denim jeans it was too hot for, and a plain white shirt. She thanked the heavens for the red dress because this heatwave in Paris would be the very thing to murder her.

Violet held the dress up to Yana.

"Oh, it's perfect. The fit agent won't know what hit him," Yana declared.

Violet rolled her eyes. "He has a name, you know."

"Eh, I prefer the fit agent. You say his name and then drive him wild the way it does to men in historical romance novels when the woman uses his given name for the first time."

Violet chuckled loudly. "I've already used his name in conversation."

"Ugh, you're no fun," Yana shrugged.

"He insisted."

Yana's jaw dropped sardonically. "And that's not something you felt you should disclose to me? We were out of our wits here, Vi. This could've been just the entertainment I needed. You would come back every night and tell me the most random facts but fail to mention a romance-heavy moment like that?"

"You're ridiculous. It wasn't some magical moment. We were talking about gum. And you've heard me call him Ben."

Yana shook her head. "Ah yes, the monthly supply that he

got you. Perfectly normal behavior from someone who's certainly not into you. Well, I want every detail about tonight."

"Fine. You'll get it all," Violet replied.

Violet wasn't sure why she agreed to this date without thinking about it further. She grew more nervous as the time drew closer. Maybe it was the heatwave after all—perhaps the weather deluded her a bit, forcing her into this.

Yes, it was the heatwave.

She was more than happy to blame the insanity of it all on it. It was also partly Yana's probing.

She got ready and went to the hotel lobby with five minutes to spare.

Ben was already there, waiting.

"Hi," he said, an easy smile forming on his face.

"Hi back."

They stood in the chandelier-covered lobby for a few moments. Silence and soft smiles added dancing hues to the light purple walls. "So, where to?" Violet asked.

"Whatever you're in the mood for. I have a few options, but tell me what you'd like first." His gaze was fixed on hers.

"Well, if I'm being frank, I'm not so chuffed with France right now...So, Italian? Indian? Japanese?"

He let out a husky laugh. "I know just the spot."

6

———

BEN

The Italian restaurant was shimmering in gold and shades of warm crimson. Violet's vibrant red sun dress brought the blues out from her eyes that the navy uniform and night skies had tucked away. She was transfixing in the sunlight as they made their way over and bewitching in the dimly lit room—the brightest part of it.

Ben had not asked out a woman on the job before. He'd never asked out a woman he hadn't known for at least a bit longer, either. But something about the woman sitting before him made his heart clench, and his walls shudder.

Violet was wittier than she knew, far more courageous than she believed, and so indescribably warm he couldn't put words to the comfort her presence infused in him. He watched her gaze flatten and question the responsibilities thrust upon her on the plane, but she agreed to them anyway. It allowed him to understand that she was someone who did things even while she was afraid, examining and probing where necessary and taking the reins when suitable.

He admired it, thinking about his lack of bravery everywhere else but during the job.

But there was something more in Violet as he faced her in a new light—the possibilities, perhaps.

Something that made him feel like he was both ten feet tall and so very small. Like he could start over in ways the world might not otherwise grant him.

He didn't know.

He might never know.

But for now, even if it only lasted a few hours, he'd take whatever chances he could find to hear her laugh in a place that didn't require the two of them to be on edge.

The restaurant had been passed down for generations, but the modern renovations integrated with the older features made Tesoro Amore a sight to behold. The brick walls never changed, but the chandeliers and burgundy armchairs were recent additions. Gold edges trimmed the mahogany-capped bar, and champagne hues shot through cage chandeliers.

Ben and Violet sat in a secluded corner, away from prying eyes.

"Congratulations on finding an Italian restaurant in Paris I hadn't heard of," she said, breaking the silence as they skimmed through the menu.

He smiled. "I can't take the credit. Edmund is half-Italian. He'll sniff out a spot everywhere we go. This one has always stood out from the others here in Paris."

Dancing with Violet's bravery were nerves that manifested in the form of gently grazing her fingers against the table. It was an intriguing back-and-forth he both understood and couldn't quite reckon. Her hands, he gathered from the first moments he met her, frequently kept themselves busy in some way.

She'd fidget with her neatly painted red fingernails, trace the edges or entangle her hands, spinning her thumbs around each other. If there was something in front of her, she'd graze her fingers against it, sometimes with her knuckles. She'd repeat the habits through meticulous, minute movements.

He wanted to know all her tells, observing as she smiled while ordering, never breaking eye contact with whoever she was speaking with.

Their conversations while they ate were surface level; she asked him to briefly catch her up on the case, how he could be confident they were all safe. And further, credit where it's due, Violet informed Ben he must thank Edmund personally because Tesoro Amore's chef had mastered the perfect blend of spices that made the tomato basil penne she ordered a delight.

"I swear, no one ever gets the perfect sauce to pasta ratio right. It's why I usually stick to pizza," she said with a stunning grin.

The compliment to the chef made Ben wonder if it was something he, too, could master someday. His mother, a former pastry chef, frequently made dishes from around the world, digging up old recipe books at the library to experiment at home with Ben and his father.

When he was younger, he sometimes wondered if he could follow in her footsteps but brushed the thought aside because no one had his mother's touch. And though he used to help her in the kitchen when he was younger, it'd never be the same.

There was a conversation, or rather, lofty complaints about the weather. When the waiter took their empty plates and left them to the devices of old-fashioned cocktails, it became easier to slip into something more.

There was so much he wanted to say.

But all he could do was stare.

She took a sip of her drink, leaned forward ever-so-slightly, and released a muted exhale. "Question for you," she said.

"Ask away," he replied.

"That first night we took a walk, when you were outside my

door—what were the odds of that happening? For six days, it was other agents. I had assumed you were long gone."

She was right. The odds had to have been a twist of fate strung together by the universe. He would've known, still, but it could've delayed her getting air, and he would've hated that.

"Agent Green, the older gentleman assigned to your door, wasn't feeling well that night. We could have one agent watching two doors, but we preferred two. It was quiet in the rooms where we conducted our investigation, so I came up instead."

"Ah."

"I would've known regardless. I was in charge of the operation, so any requests would have gone through me. And if I was told about it, I would've still chosen to come with you."

"I didn't want you to see me like that. But I am glad it was you."

He smiled. "It worked to my benefit. I wanted an excuse to see you."

A slow, shy line curved against her lips. She shook her head, almost like she didn't believe him. But maybe that was a good thing.

She'd run for the hills if she knew how desperate he was to get to know her more.

"Do you say that to all the flight attendants you meet?" she asked with an achingly sweet smile, her blue eyes sparkling with the curiosity that kept taking hold of him.

She was looking at him differently now, like the more ordinary parts of this date were over, and she wanted something more. Something he was terrified to give but would without question.

"Only the one sitting in front of me," he answered confidently.

Her cheeks turned scarlet.

She cocked an eyebrow, and an alluring smirk rose on her face.

He wouldn't make it the rest of the night if she did that again.

He took a large gulp of his drink, put it down, then quickly eyed the bartender. His gaze turned back to Violet, watching her take the final sip of her drink. His attention retreated to her long fingers.

He was going mad, staring again, marveling at her brown hair falling freely, taking in the sight of her in the red sun dress.

God, she was beautiful.

Her eyes were so achingly enthralling, and every story in her smile made him want to collapse. He wasn't sure how to liberate himself from the grip of her warmth. He couldn't let go of the weight she carried with her, eased by a belief in the possibilities she held on tightly to.

Violet was hope and promises and laughter personified, and the way she saw the world ignited embers within him. He was awe-struck beyond grasp.

"Ben," she called in a low voice.

His name had never sounded better, instigating him deeper into enchantment. He looked at her, attempting to dispel whatever fixed gaze he must've had. The sounds of a pianist playing a quiet melody echoed faintly throughout the restaurant.

She tilted her head slightly, a timeless smile forming on her lips. "You're staring."

"I'm sorry," he replied, blinking once, twice, willing himself to pull it together. "I'm sorry. You're just...so beautiful, Violet. In every way. Your mind, your smile—that look in your eyes when you get curious—*all of it*. I can hardly bear it."

A flush deepened the scarlet on her cheeks. She smiled, biting the inside of her lips, nerves pushing through her trembling hands. He saw them go from calm to shaking, taking the one closest to him in his hand. Ben meticulously traced her fingers with his thumb, hoping she wouldn't pull away, praying she felt every bit as overcome as he did.

"Thank you," she whispered, intertwining her fingers with his. He was unsure who was trembling more now.

They were both staring, equally transfixed by the other and searching for small treasures to hold onto after they eventually part. They were cut from their gazes finally when the waitress brought over refills.

"You're pretty decent too, you know?" she finally said.

"Decent, yeah?" he drew a slow, seductive smile.

"Would you prefer I tell you that you have the most ridiculously brilliant beard I've ever seen, and your kindness drives me mad?" she added, taking a sip from her newly filled glass.

He threw his head back, and a hearty laugh rumbled out of him. "I'll take it," he said. He'd never shave now.

With every look and every word she spoke, Violet was giving parts of herself to him that he didn't deserve—warm flirty edges, longing looks, and insurmountable depth with each glimpse into her mind.

He wanted to stop time, right here, at this very moment, with her hands interlaced through his.

"Good," she beamed, squeezing his hand gently. "Do you get to go home now too? Or another job?"

He sighed. "Home for seventy-two hours. I'll visit my father and my sister, then onto the next gig."

"I bet they miss you a ton."

"I certainly miss them so I'd hope so. Have you gotten the chance to speak to your grandmother?" he inquired.

Violet lit up almost instantly. "I did! It was almost brutal to hear her cry from joy on the line. I cannot wait to see her."

"Give her my most sincere apologies for putting her through that, yeah?"

She smiled at him. "I'm certain you'll forever be in her good graces if I tell her you didn't mock my anxiety."

His vision grew dark for a beat. The thought of someone doing that to her made him profoundly uncomfortable. "Has anyone ever done that to you?"

She shook her head. "No. The only people who know about it are the people I trust who wouldn't use it against me. The girls I work with are all very lovely, but Yana's different; we got close quickly when I was first hired, so I feel very lucky that she was the one beside me. I don't know how I'd explain it to someone else."

The fact that this was something that concerned her broke him. Yet simultaneously, he felt so damn proud to know he was someone she felt she could trust. They might never see each other again, but he'd carry this with him, always.

She made his heart palpitate far too many times than an average person's probably should.

But, he didn't care. He didn't want this night to end. The private plane wouldn't leave without him.

They could wait.

"I'm not ready for the day to end, but I want to get out of here," he said.

He wanted to see her in the dimming sunlight and hold her hand through cobblestone streets.

"Well, we are at the heart of Paris. Take a walk with me to see the gargoyles?" she asked, a childlike elation stirring on her face.

He nodded, taking euros out of his wallet, he secured them underneath a glass. "Lead the way."

7

VIOLET

It was like floodgates had opened after their dinner. Walking to the hills of Montmartre, they talked of every little detail that came to them.

"When I start teaching, I'm breaking the curriculum just to give kids a whole history on gargoyles," she said, looking up at the hill awaiting them.

He chuckled. "So, you plan on traumatizing them?"

"I plan on *educating* them," she specified.

Ben squeezed her hand in his. "You're really going to quit the moment you're back home?"

"Yeah. I've already drafted a note. And especially after this dreadful experience, I don't want to get on a plane for at least a year." She looked at him, catching guilt in his gaze. "You and this moment, excluded," Violet added.

"Do you mean that?"

She held up their entwined hands in front of them. "I wouldn't want to melt in the humidity with anyone else right now."

His smile grew tenfold. "Don't tell me that. It'll go to my head."

"It should. You and that ridiculously perfect beard are special. I also wouldn't have suggested coming here with anyone else, Ben. The last memories I have at Montmartre are with my parents," she admitted.

"You're going to ruin me for everyone else, darling. How am I ever going to take a case here again and not lose myself thinking of you?"

She smiled, but her heart broke thinking of their eventual parting, intimate glimpses of themselves spilling freely like water from springs. They were shedding their armor, quietly giving each other pieces for safekeeping.

Violet caught herself wishing it didn't have to be this way, hating that she was allowing him to see the parts of her that felt too vulnerable to let another see. Details about her parents, fond memories, and her open, earnest attraction to him.

These were the pieces of her she hoped she could one day give away to someone else but not like this. Not to the man she'd never see again.

His lifestyle.

Hers.

It'd be too messy. Violet would soon settle into a routine profession, and Ben would be gone, somewhere with a new case that could be even more dangerous than this one.

Perhaps the clock ticking against them made trusting somehow easier. Perhaps it was believing that someday they'd be distant memories to each other. Perhaps it was Violet knowing that, no matter how intensely she wanted to protect the good things in her life, they'd be taken from her anyway.

That had to be the case.

The sunset kissed the sky with purples and pinks that made her heart swell. This view was the only part of summer she loved—the sky at every moment, every shade more captivating than before.

They stopped at the base of Sacré-Cœur. Side by side, their hands still clasped tightly together.

Heavens, she adored the gargoyles. They made her feel like a kid again—comforted and so very safe.

Maybe it was a silly means of hoping for a discernible sign from above, God and gargoyles nudging her toward something that'd take the perpetual ache in her heart and allow it a sabbatical. She wouldn't have suggested coming here with anyone else. She would've waited until she was alone to revisit. But somehow, sharing these memories with Ben and her parents felt right.

She wanted this.

She shouldn't want this.

It would hurt and sting, and she'd find new ways to deny that these feelings were real. It could break her when it ends. Her headspace was muddled.

From the moment his eyes bore into hers on the plane to the mellifluous tenor of his voice bringing her back to reality in the hotel, it felt right.

It was the end in sight. *It had to be.*

It was the temporary, fleeting bliss of it all.

Maybe it was knowing that if he were to judge her eventually, she would never see him again.

It was the heatwave and his laugh and the ever-growing kindness in his eyes.

It was the end in sight.

It was two old-fashioned cocktails and weeks of anxiety in full force getting to her head.

It was the heatwave.

It had to be.

"Oh shit, did I tell you I took karate for a year or so when I was twelve?" she blurted. She was nervous beyond comprehension again as Ben held her hand steady in his.

"You what? My shoulder might have been a lot less sore for a few days if you had disclosed this information when we first met. Could've helped me take down that bloke."

She chuckled. "It completely escaped me until now. I don't think I remember much. A few self-defense tactics here and there. I humbly apologize to you and your shoulder," she said, looking up at the side she now remembered he slammed into, then gently traced her idle hand across it.

"We forgive you if you answer another question."

"Go on then."

He was looking up at the creatures in questionable antipathy. "How on earth do you not think these things are creepy?"

She laughed—loud and boisterous.

"Because they're aces. Come on. Look at the architecture alone. And to ward off evil spirits? They're marvels. It's a shame we don't have them on top of all houses."

He shook his head, openly laughing at the sentiment, which pleased her thoroughly. "You're mad."

"Oh, I'm sure. But you shall not mock my gargoyles."

"I absolutely will."

She tsked. "And here I was thinking you were a nice man."

"I am a nice man. I'm also a normal man who isn't fazed by rocks."

She squared her shoulders, released her hand, and stood in front of him. "Ben Grant. Those are not rocks. They're *art*."

A transfixing glow flashed in Ben's eyes. He stepped forward, wrapped an arm around her waist, turning her and pulling her into him. "That's art," he said in a low whisper, nudging her chin upward gently toward the sky. She was pressed firmly to his chest, his arms encircling her closer from behind. "You're *art*," he drawled, a hair's breadth away from her ear. It sent piercing tremors down to her bones.

The day's heat was engulfing her viciously now; chills and embers were dueling for control. She took a shuddering breath at his nearness and the galvanizing delicacy of his hand tracing her cheek. She could hear his heart thumping as rowdily as hers. The sense of his body against hers was too much too soon and still not enough to last a lifetime.

His breath hitched, catching fire alongside hers. "Can I kiss you?" Ben whispered with an astonishing tenderness that made Violet's knees crumble. If he didn't, she would lose her balance entirely. She was sure of it.

"Please," was all she could mumble.

He turned her to face him with another swift, waltz-like move. His fingers idly traced her collarbones, her shoulder, and down to her forearms. He looked at her for a beat, the same attentive gaze piercing through to her core as though she was indeed a work of art, and he was examining every brushstroke.

His eyes fell to her lips decisively. Ben traced the curve of her chin with soft strokes, cupping her cheek in his hand before his lips followed suit. She trembled as though she'd never done this before. Except she hadn't. *Not like this.* Never with a man whose entire presence sent electrifying jolts through her whole body.

His lips were finally on hers with a warmth that lit a fire to her bones. Violet enfolded her arms around his neck, the weight of him a perfect anchor for when he picked up the rhythm.

She'd laugh if she weren't so intoxicated. His deliciously hot beard made her want to scream. His other hand slid up and down her back as he deepened the kiss, allowing their tongues to dance with fine caresses. His lips moved then, scattering from her cheek to her jaw, then down to the juncture of her neck, elic-iting a low groan brimming with unbridled need from Violet—and thus, provoking his own.

This was the perfect in-between—this moment, tucked behind walls with gargoyles atop them.

He pressed up against the wall behind them, holding himself still and pulling her body closer. Violet's hands traced his shoulder before her fingers found his hair, tugging at the strands as he licked and drew from her pulse point, taking whatever she'd allow. She trembled and bit back a gasp. If he were to leave a mark, she never wanted it to fade. She wanted the memories of him buried in her neck, with her hands in his hair, to dance in her mind forever.

She wanted him to stay there all night.

She wanted his lips to roam all over her.

Ben's mouth was on hers again, one hand on her jaw nudging her closer to him, the other nestled in the crook of her back. A needy groan rolled through him as she deepened the kiss with her tongue, his head falling against the wall as her fingers stroked his beard.

She'd compare every kiss to this, and they'd all pale in comparison.

Her desires for him were foreign—wild and more demanding than anything she had experienced with her exes. She decided it was her turn to take in more of him, to find the spot where his heartbeat would drum through her lips and travel all over her.

She tiptoed a little, peppering kisses along the corners of his eyes, cheeks, forehead, nose, and strong jaw. He wrapped his arms around her waist and let her wander in his grip. She kissed along the column of his throat. Teasing and tantalizing with achingly thoughtful movements—she giggled, nestling her face deeper in the crook of his neck. His arms tightened around her and squeezed. "You're going to destroy me, you know that?" he said, a subdued, heavy groan emitting from him.

Violet hummed at the force of his body against hers. She placed her lips at the column of his throat, lingering for a moment just to feel him tug at her waist—a sign that showcased his desperation matched her own.

"*Violet.*"

He called out her name, and she nearly lost it—low, hoarse, and laced with every ounce of his desire for her.

They were sticky and tangled, but none of it mattered. The heat was far more intense, still fighting control over the chills as beads of sweat marked them both. She found his lips again—hot and wet and not enough.

It would never be enough.

Whatever this was, it would never be enough.

They were entangled against the travertine limestone in the quiet corners of one of the gaudiest expanses in France, both of their lips commanding for control in a desperate attempt to hold on for a little while longer. They were operating beyond what they could handle—their bodies speaking in a familiar language far outside what their minds could decipher.

Stay, begged the tug of his lips. *Don't stop,* said the dart of her tongue.

As they came apart, breathless and bemused, he fixed his eyes toward hers, warm and gleaming in the shadows. His hands found hers with effortless ease, and he laced their fingers together.

"I wish you could stay," she started, hoping to God that this wouldn't be a time when she'd lose all sense of self and do something ridiculous like cry in front of a man she'd only known for a few weeks. "But I know you have to leave, and I won't ask you to."

"I would if you meant it. I might be mad enough to do so if you asked me," he replied with his lips tracing her fingers interlaced with his, anchoring himself with a delicate kiss on her wrist. It sent shivers to every hollow cave in her body.

"Just hold me a little longer, and then you can leave," she said, wishing she could be selfish enough to ask him to stay—to find her when they're back in London, to hold her like this forever. To never let go.

Ben spun her body, mounting his arms securely around her torso. He nestled his face in the slope of her shoulder. "A little while longer won't ever be enough," he whispered.

She was sure she imagined that part.

She was certain she imagined nestling herself closer as they watched the afterglow darken.

SHE WAS sure she imagined him saying, "I'd miss you even if I had never met you."

She was certain he couldn't have possibly meant it when he said, "Your laugh is the most wonderful sound I've ever heard."

She was so sure that she imagined him turning and tipping her back in some slow, dazed dance down the hill.

And she was most definitely certain that when he walked her to the hotel door, he didn't kiss away her silent tears, wiping them gently with his thumb and following with the trace of his lips.

She could swear she didn't taste salt and whiskey on his lips.

She was positive he wasn't as devastated as she was when he whispered, "I can't bear the thought of you walking away from me right now."

How they parted ways and who left whom, she blocked out entirely. She could only taste his lips on hers and the touch of contentment that he left with every piece of her.

She opened the folded paper he'd slipped into her hand as his lips trailed her face.

Violet, if you ever need me, please reach out. Wherever you are, I'll come to you.

—Ben

He'd given her his email.

She might always need him—might always want him, but their paths likely weren't meant to cross again. She wouldn't deny her feelings any longer. She couldn't continue blaming them on the heat or the alcohol. It wasn't the artistic or poetic corners of Paris either.

It was the man holding her in his arms.

It was his spacious heart and his gentle soul.

She hadn't felt this safe in a long, *long* time.

She'd never tell him to leave the job for her. Their chapter was destined to end here. That had to be the truth she would cling to.

Ephemeral and once in a lifetime, not evermore.

She had to let him go.

The world always took from her, just as it did today.

But he was her in-between below the skies, and no matter how hard she wished, she couldn't continue orbiting around him.

PART TWO

PRESENT DAY
BATH, SOMERSET
16 YEARS LATER
END OF AUGUST 2020

8

VIOLET

Violet slid the diamond ring and matching band from her finger, placing them on the manila folder set atop the black wooden table. She exhaled deeply, trepidation and relief interlocking within her. She should've taken them off over a year ago when she first learned about Dean's infidelity. But they were still putting on a show.

She glanced at the two large, fully stocked suitcases in front of her. She would no longer be anyone's perfect puppet, forced steps and conversations to the yanks of Dean's strings.

One step closer to freedom, no matter the odds stacked against her.

Violet's phone pinged with a text message from Simone's mum, Aunt Helen.

Almost there, love. 10 minutes.

She gulped down hard. This was it.

Violet walked down the winding hallway to the guest bedroom that had been hers for the past year. She had packed all the belongings she needed. Whatever else remained wasn't hers—it was part of the role she played. Sparkling sequined gowns and stunning satin ensembles were only beautiful when worn joyfully and by choice.

Of all her decisions, leaving Dean Colborne eight years after being with him and nine years after knowing him was both the wisest and most terrifying. She would have never known who he'd become when he first introduced himself to her. The bloke lied through his teeth better than any secret agent could have.

And she had met secret agents in her lifetime. She supposed it was a claim she could vouch for.

But Dean was a conundrum she wasn't psychologically equipped to understand. He wasn't always vicious. He could be so sweet in public that every head would turn at his actions. And isn't that what mattered in this world, actions over words?

At times, Dean Colborne was a walking saint—every woman's dream husband. Until she knew better.

Violet initially met him at an administrative conference. He'd been there to attend a gala, only sitting in on the conference as a representative of his law firm. He claimed to be utterly fascinated by Violet's questions regarding how severely underfunded the London primary schools had been. Dean stopped Violet afterward to speak with her, asking her which school she taught at, followed by offering to buy her dinner. She politely declined, uninterested in dating at the time. And well, if she was being frank with herself, despite Dean's charm and undeniably handsome looks, she wasn't attracted to him.

The following week, Violet's place of work, Briar Primary School, along with the neighboring secondary schools, each received charitable donations of twenty-five thousand pounds, courtesy of Dean's firm, Colborne and Martin.

She knew exactly what he was doing and wouldn't buy it. She located his number on the firm's website and called to thank him sincerely on behalf of the entire staff but, as expected, declined another offer for dinner.

She was the Year 4 teacher at Briar at the time, chosen to attend the conference by their Head Teacher, Nora Hendricks. Since Violet had been the one to push for various fundraisers and community programs, Nora and the rest of the administration team believed she would be perfect for the assignment. She had been honored then and loved every minute she spent at the school, which made leaving it now sadder.

Dean had been persistent. After the call, he swore he wasn't going to give up on her. *"I don't know—I just feel it. You and I could be great together. You're worth waiting for,"* he had told her.

She was flattered, sure, but simultaneously, she hated it. *You just feel it? We haven't even spent five minutes together,* she'd thought. Hell, she felt *something* when she first met Ben Grant, too, but she wouldn't go so far as to say that she knew he was the one for her on the plane. No, it was the first night they went for a walk, during day six of isolation, when he looked at her like he understood the many heartbreaks she was always hiding from. And even then, she'd deny it if someone asked.

A year later, at thirty-two years old, Violet became head teacher at Briar—everything she wanted was finally hers. It was a tremendous accomplishment that she counted all her lucky stars for. Yet, the prevailing solitude she frequently felt turned colossal after Nan passed away and her best mate Simone moved to Edinburgh with her husband.

Slowly, her strength fractured. One day at a time, her anxiety would worsen, resulting in the decision to go back on antidepressants. Some days, it felt manageable, but the blasted loneliness would probe and sting in a way that was sickening. She might have been an only child, but Violet was never lonely as a kid. She had mishaps as a teen, sure, but she had friends all around her—outspoken and loud despite the damn anxiety.

But things changed, and people grew older, following their dreams to the places in the world where they were meant to be.

Violet had her dream job.

She just had no one to share it with.

One day, she went to a local pub after work, too tired to cook for herself, desperate to be around people her age.

It was the wrong place, wrong time. It was a horrible day after three agonizing nights of feeling like the walls were caving in on her, forcing her to believe she'd never know what it was like to breathe again.

Dean was at the pub with his colleagues.

He bought her a drink. She mistook it for a sign.

Perhaps if she hadn't hit such a low—if she hadn't felt so bloody lonely, devoid of breath, and so desperate for a reprieve, her life would've been different today. If she didn't believe with every aching bone in her body that she was only ever destined for second best, she wouldn't have said yes to him that night.

Except she did, and one date turned into three, then five months later, he introduced her to his family—a mother, father, brother, and a sister—all wonderful and so welcoming. Maybe the relationship wouldn't be second best, she had thought at the time. Maybe she was destined for an average sort of respectable and pleasant life without the explosive romance.

It'd be fine. She had her moment—years ago in Paris— seventeen days, kind eyes holding her steady, soft lips anchoring her home. The sparks Ben Grant detonated inside her she would never experience again, not even with Nick Higgins, her last boyfriend whom she adored deeply, but sadly not enough to pack up her entire life and move to Los Angeles.

But that was a different Violet—she wasn't scared of the dark or the quiet nights alone; she was brave and full of conviction. She would wait or stand firm on her own two feet, hoping that the best was yet to come.

She would have *never* settled.

She broke and settled, praying that the flames would ignite later. She confused the moments when she missed Dean's presence as desire for him when it was merely the loneliness inside her searching for anyone who'd reach forward.

The fire never came, sinking Violet deeper into a cold trench, hardening every fiber of her being that believed in something bigger—better.

Please don't do this, Vi. I know waiting is a bitch. I know how harrowing doubts can be. But there's someone better out there for you. Dean's...well, I don't really know him. He won't allow that. But something's off with him, and I don't want to see you throw your life away. Simone had texted her days before her wedding.

It's too late now. I've already agreed. I care for him enough, Simone. I'll be fine. But thank you. Violet had replied, hating herself for it momentarily because she knew Simone was right. But she couldn't listen to her. Not now, for as closely as Simone knew Violet, she couldn't understand how she felt. And a part of her was always grateful for it. She wouldn't wish her experiences on her enemies, let alone her best mate in the entire world.

Tears shot through Violet as she walked back to the living room, remembering the first day they had moved into the house and the fact that she spent the entire night crying in the loo, claiming she felt ill.

It was too large—like her doubts and her regrets. The house felt even bigger now, but she didn't feel as small as she had before.

She wasn't its prisoner anymore, bound by the confines of her own heartaches and his emotional abuse. She was fragile still, and maybe she might always be, but she was ready for a fresh start.

On the eve of her fortieth birthday, when Dean was working late, Violet rang Simone sobbing. *I can't do it anymore, Simone. I can't*—was all she could say. Her best friend stayed on the phone with her for what felt like hours before Violet finally mustered up the courage to tell her about Dean's infidelity, the gaslighting, the one-time physical outburst, and the threats he had made if she dared to mention divorce.

I'm going to get you out of there, Violet. If it's the last thing I do. I swear it. We're going to figure this out, Simone had promised.

For the past two years, Dean was invited to consult on cases in America. They could take weeks or months at times. Coincidentally, or perhaps this was the *real* sign, one of Aunt Helen's tenants would be moving in July—the house would be ready when Violet was, one month before Dean was set to depart at the end of August. During the five weeks Violet had to remain with him, she privately hired a solicitor to draw up the divorce papers. She gave her notice to Briar, thanking the heavens for trustworthy co-workers who wouldn't publicize her departure outside the school. She got a new phone under Simone's family plan and packed up her most prized possessions to leave London for Bath.

There was a knock on her door.

This was it. One step closer to the woman she used to be. Or, hopefully, better.

Violet threw herself in Aunt Helen's arms, crying quietly in her warm embrace. In an unpredictable, horrible flash, it felt like she'd just learned about her parents' accident. Nan had been inconsolable. Violet's granddad had passed away two years prior, and then she lost a daughter. Violet's Aunt Robin and her husband Nolan stepped in to support Nan.

Violet lost her mother that evening, and Aunt Helen grieved her best friend—the women met when they brought the girls to daycare, bonding instantly and never looking back. When she closed her eyes, she could always see Aunt Helen's heartbroken face approaching her in her bedroom. She and

Simone sat with Violet on the floor while she sobbed hysterically in their arms.

Aunt Helen, like Nan, had been like a mother to Violet. Since they were young, whatever she purchased for Simone, she also got for Violet. However she would treat her own daughter, Violet received the same attention, lectures included. She was a petite Persian woman who always filled every room she walked into with unfailing warmth. Violet was taller, a grown woman now, but around Aunt Helen, she would always feel like a little girl—safe, happy, and deeply beloved.

I've got you, love, she had said then and repeated now. Violet was terrified that Aunt Helen would be disappointed in her after she married Dean, but like Simone, she knew that all she ever wanted was to see her happy. She had said as much, even while she was actively angry that Violet was throwing her life away.

Helen squared her shoulders and placed her hands on both sides of Violet's cheeks. "Seeing you cry is one of the worst things in this world. It's over now. We've got you," she said with a hearty tone.

Violet gulped and took a deep breath, nodding her head. "Ah, Uncle Thomas, I'm so sorry—hi!" she exclaimed and went in for a quick hug.

"No worries, you," the cheery Black man said with a pat on her shoulder. Violet adored her Aunt Robin, but they lived in France and hardly visited since Nan died. Regardless, she had always felt closer to the Henrys. In every way, Aunt Helen and Uncle Thomas were her family. They offered to drive over and take her to Bath themselves, not wanting her to drag luggage around in a train station.

"Freddy's waiting in the car. Let's get you home," Aunt Helen said, nudging Thomas to take her luggage. Freddy, the Goldendoodle. Ugh, Violet missed the pup. No pets were allowed in the

Colborne household; whether Dean was truthful about the severity of his allergies, Violet didn't know.

Thomas picked up the large pieces of luggage. "Are these all you're bringing?"

"Yep. I've got all the important things in there," she said, pointing to the beige carry-on. She could always buy new clothes and shoes. She had what she needed: the three photo albums from her childhood, the blanket mum knitted for her, dad's ugly old poncho she secretly adored, and the jewelry pieces Nan had passed down.

"How am I ever going to repay the two of you?" Violet asked in the air.

Aunt Helen grimaced. "For starters, no more marriages unless I fully approve of the man."

Uncle Thomas chuckled. "She's not a child, Helly."

"Hush you."

Violet smiled at them. She and Simone were so damn lucky to have parents who adored each other. And she was so glad that Simone found a partner as brilliant as Peter.

This moment was Violet's second chance to make life right again.

It might never be as magical as she hoped, but it would be better than the lonelier web she found herself spinning in with Dean.

Violet swung her bag crossbody, then looked back at the house once more. Her eyes darted toward the envelope and the rings, then she locked the door shut, turning the nob thrice to ensure it was closed.

This chapter in her life wasn't over quite yet, but as she walked down the five steps toward the gate, for the first time in nine years, she could breathe a little easier.

9

———

VIOLET

"What the hell!?" Violet said aloud, jumping from her sofa. She was not referring to the TV suddenly shutting off but to the blaring noise coming from what sounded like an alarm. She had settled in the night before, unpacking her clothes and toiletries before crashing. She planned on familiarizing herself around the house today after sending out applications, but the storm had been a pleasant excuse to give herself a lazy day on the sofa.

Aunt Helen didn't warn her about an alarm system, which was odd considering she'd given her the rundown on every nook and cranny in the house, including the broken garden roof. It could've been the perfect spot to sit and watch the rain fall.

Violet picked up her mobile phone to ring Aunt Helen; at forty-four percent, she'd have to do her best to keep the battery from draining in case the lights didn't come on for a while.

She texted after the call went to voicemail:

Aunt Helen! The alarm's gone off after the storm cut the power. Is there a code? Thanks! 😬

Violet walked through the house, finding the alarm at the front near the door. "Ugh! What would a code be? Simone's birthday?" she said to no one in particular. She entered the numbers 0218 before the alarm momentarily paused, only to scream again. A culmination of Simone and Steven's? *Fuck.* When was Steven's birthday? July nine or nineteen? She'd completely forgotten and was about to utter another grunt before a knock on her door jolted her.

Jesus! She jumped again.

Violet opened the door, expecting either the police to have already made their way over or a miffed neighbor who was probably soaked and hating her for it. But the ocean-blue eyes of the man she believed she'd only ever see again in her dreams were the last on the list of prospects.

"Ben," she said in a whisper. Her eyes darted and froze on his drenched form. Her heart raced at an obscene, likely unhealthy, rhythm.

His eyes were stilled and blazing with disbelief. "My God. Violet..." Her name on his lips stirred a frenzy from which she didn't know how to push forward.

Ben Grant.

After all these years.

Violet couldn't speak. She only stared, questioning the alternate dimension she must've entered after the alarm, wanting to pinch herself to see if she'd fallen into a deep slumber on the sofa.

"Five-two-eight-nine," he said, pointing at the blasted thing still howling at them. His voice somehow burst through the agonizingly loud thoughts in her head and clamorous heartbeat.

How Violet walked over and entered the numbers through her trembling nerves, she'd never know.

When the shrill halted, she turned to face him again. "Would you like to come inside?"

He nodded calmly. "Sure."

He dried his shoes on the outdoor mat and spoke again before entering the house. "I installed these alarms about a year ago. The woman who lived here before was a bit older. Mr. Henry and I thought it'd be best since she was alone."

Had Ben Grant been Aunt Helen's neighbor all this time? For a year, at least? She'd been so close to him, yet...so achingly far, trapped in a loveless marriage in London.

"They must've forgotten to tell me that," Violet replied, walking over to her kitchen. "Tea? The water reached a boil right as the power went off."

"Sure," he said. His skin had lost color, and Violet imagined she didn't look that much different than him at the moment.

How? When?

"How do you take it?"

Stop asking him about tea, Violet, she thought to herself, wanting to rip at the seams from the shock still moving inside of her.

"Milk, no sugar." She wanted to look back at him, turn to face him again, but the sight of the tea kettle was less alluring. It didn't release a flurry of butterflies inside of her.

She wanted to say "same," note a silly comparison, but remained silent. She was thankful Aunt Helen filled the kitchen for her.

He was quiet.

She was in shambles as she poured the tea into matching striped mugs. Violet turned and placed the drink on the table.

Ben's gaze never left hers as she came closer, taking a seat only after she sat down. He blinked, once, twice, and closed his eyes for a beat.

"What brings you to Bath, Violet?"

"Divorce," she replied bluntly.

She couldn't believe she said the word out loud; she might as well spill her guts out to him right here. *Wanna know just how miserable I was and wished he was you every day?*

"I'm sorry," he said sincerely.

She shrugged. "I'm not, but thank you."

"Is this a permanent stay, then?" he asked, a glimmer flickered in his eyes like a distant lighthouse.

She nodded. "If my ex doesn't make things difficult. Yes, I'm hoping it can be."

"Why would he make things difficult? Isn't he Dean Colborne, the barrister?"

Violet cocked her head slightly. Had he searched for her as she had for him? Had he ever been involved in one of Dean's cases? "Ah, so you've heard of him," she replied.

"I might've searched for you a few years ago," he answered earnestly.

A slow line framed her lips. "I tried to. But you're like a ghost on the internet."

He chuckled.

She took a sip of her tea before speaking again. She wanted to know every detail now. If someone told her she'd see him again, she'd never have believed it. With every year that passed, she had convinced herself he was a dream.

She smiled at him. He was watching her closely with his hand encircled around the mug. "How have you been? No more MI6, I gather?"

He took a breath. "No, those days are in the past now. You teach, right?"

"I do. Or I did. I was the head teacher before I left Briar."

"And now?" he asked, taking a sip of his tea.

"I've applied to the primary school here. We'll see how it goes. How's Edmund?"

Ben smiled. "Well as can be. He's in Boston now with Nina and their three kids."

"Boston? There's a distance. No MI6 for him either, then?"

He sighed deeply, and a protruding look of sadness dawned in his eyes. For some reason, the question cut him deep, digging into a place it didn't seem he went to often. "No, uh...he was injured, nearly died. That was the end for him. Nina got a job as a financial director there, and the rest was history."

Violet swallowed a heavily. The words "nearly died" took up every space in her senses. She couldn't imagine it—not for Nina or Ben. The impact would've been utterly devastating.

"I'm glad to hear he's safe, even if far away. I can't imagine how that time must've been for you," Violet finally responded.

He agreed. "Thank you. Yeah, it gives me ease to know that he can't hurt himself as a software engineer."

Ben paused for a beat, looking at her like he had at the dimly lit restaurant. *Staring.* "Why Bath? Of all the places in the UK. The world, really," he asked, taking another sip of his tea, keeping his eyes locked on hers.

"Aunt Helen. Mrs. Henry, as you know her. She is my best mate's mum. Once the former tenant said she was leaving, she called to tell me. Plus, I loved it here as a kid."

He chuckled. "Simone's your best mate?"

Violet smiled almost sheepishly, still swimming in disbelief that this was happening. "Since we were four years old at daycare. We made our mums schedule a playdate immediately after that first day, apparently. They got super close, too. She's my whole heart, actually."

She knew he'd understand what it was like to have a friend for whom you'd give your life. "I met her briefly a few times. Her husband more so. They're great people. All of the Henrys are," he said with a sincerity that made her heart happy. "Her family have owned these houses for generations, yeah?"

"Yeah, but Aunt Helen and Uncle Thomas moved here when

Simone and I were nineteen. What about you? What brought you to Bath?"

He swallowed. "My dad had a stroke. I came here to take care of him. When he passed, I don't know, I couldn't move. I stayed."

Violet's heart sank. Every time she heard that someone had or would be losing a parent, it crushed her. Understanding the pain profoundly, she hated every bit of it. "Oh, Ben. I'm so deeply sorry," she said. She wanted to reach forward and place her hand on his, but she couldn't bring herself to.

He nodded. "Thank you."

They were quiet for a moment. The two of them in a place where the aftereffects of grief simmer and unfurl. A place where comfort can only be found in the memories people hold onto— each in their own way. A place they'd been in before.

Violet broke the silence with a query, waiting for a moment where it felt it'd be okay. "What do you do now?"

"I'm the head chef at The Crooked Branch."

She gaped at him. "That's...different, but somehow fitting?"

He chuckled. "My mum was a pastry chef. She wanted to do more; I used to help around the kitchen when I was young," he replied.

She smiled at him, picturing a tiny Ben trying to bake and cook at a young age. The thought delighted her. "That's lovely," she replied.

Her phone rang then. It was Aunt Helen. "Ah, finally, I can tell her I didn't resort to drastic measures to shut the bloody thing off."

"Aunt Helen, hi."

Helen was frazzled on the other end of the line. "Oh, love, I'm so sorry I forgot about that alarm. Have you got it settled?"

"Yes, your neighbor Ben was gracious enough to come by. It's a good thing Mrs. Bradley hadn't changed the code."

"Oh, thank goodness he was home. Sorry again. You alright?" Helen asked.

"All good now. Thank you."

"Good. Back to work. See you in a bit."

"Bye," Violet said before hanging up.

She faced Ben again. "Seriously, I'm glad you were home. I'm pretty sure I would've smashed this thing in half to shut it up."

"I'm happy to have been of service. And more so, to see you again."

Violet bit the inside of her cheek. "Of all the people in the world, I never thought our paths would cross again."

"Thank you for the tea," he gestured to his cup, rising to walk it over to the kitchen sink.

She sighed, watching him and still kicking herself internally at the reality of what was happening. Ben—*her Ben,* the man of her dreams, standing in her kitchen, eyes heavy and still the most handsome human being she's ever known.

God hadn't abandoned her yet.

She rose from her seat and placed her cup in the sink as well. "I'll see you around, yeah?" he said, walking over to the door.

Violet nodded. "I'll be here," she replied. He looked back at her one more time; his eyes bore into hers just as they always had—warm and kind and so deeply understanding.

10

———

VIOLET

Falling asleep with Ben Grant so near wasn't an occurrence Violet had thought of since she was twenty-four.

Sixteen years ago.

After a few months, she gave up on the idea of ever running into him on the streets of London. The bloody town was too big for advantageous outcomes of that sort. But it wasn't too big to lead her into the arms of the wrong man.

She shook it off, wondering why Simone hadn't responded to her texts since last night. She had called a few minutes before Ben knocked on her door, confirming her itinerary for the next day's arrival. It was both unlike her and just like her simultaneously. Simone could be the world's worst texter at times, but she'd always pick up Violet's phone call if she needed her.

Still, a text like: "OF ALL THE PLACES TO SEE BEN AGAIN (YES, MY BEN), I DIDN'T THINK IT'D BE RIGHT NEXT DOOR TO YOUR MUM'S HOUSE!! CALL ME," would've gone answered.

That was no matter now because today, Violet needed

Simone more than ever, and she counted her blessings tenfold to have the kind of best friend who'd take time off to see her.

Simone rang from Uncle Thomas' car to note that she was fast approaching and joked that she expected to see Violet standing on the street with her arms wide open. She'd oblige. It would be like the old days, waiting for each other on their doorsteps when they were kids without phones.

They bolted toward one another the second Simone strode out of the car. She could hear Uncle Thomas chuckle while he walked away toward the Henrys' home.

"God, I've missed you," Violet declared, a small tear leaving her eye as Simone's grip tightened around her.

"Not as much as I've missed you." Simone maneuvered toward the house, lugging her weekender bag on the ground as though it weighed a ton.

"Feels a bit odd coming to Bath and not staying with my parents." She turned and winked.

Violet laughed. "As does living in one of these houses after so much time spent here."

"I'm sure, especially since the last time you were here was, what, ten years ago?"

Violet's breath hitched. She knew Simone wasn't trying to make her feel guilty about the fact. She hated it, too. She had visited Simone somewhat frequently in Edinburgh, but it was true. Violet hadn't been back to see the Henrys; catching up with them when Helen and Thomas were in town was all she had done. And in the last two years, none of that happened either. Only phone calls.

"I'm s..." she started to say.

"What, no. Don't go where you're thinking. You know I didn't mean it like that. I just meant shit's changed since we were younger. And we're about to change things again for the better."

Simone pointed to the living area, covered in rustic shades

of browns and creams, with pops of color in pillow form. "I swear, Mum should've gone into interior decorating. She loves this sort of stuff far more than she does making tea sandwiches."

"And she's good at it. But you know your mum; she loves being around people more than anything."

Simone chuckled. "Like mother, like daughter."

"She did hit copy and paste on you, height included."

"Missed making fun of my height, have you? I'll remind you again that Phoebe's got her dad's genes, and one day, she'll be taller than you."

"And I'll be the proudest godmother when that day comes."

Simone shook her head playfully. "You would. I need a quick shower, and then we'll get this bash started."

How was Simone not commenting on Ben? "Wait, quick question: are your texts working properly?"

"Have you sent one since yesterday? This bloody thing needs a fix. I've been trying to send messages all morning, and it wouldn't budge. Peter said he'd take it to the shop when I got home. What's up?"

She pointed toward the house next door. "Ben...uh...he," Violet tried to say.

Simone looked confused. "Mum's tenant? What about him?"

"Yeah, he's..." Simone's big brown eyes seemed to connect the dots, filling with zeal as her jaw dropped.

"Wait, he's *the* Ben? Is that what you're trying to tell me? The one you'd never shut up about, including, and I quote, 'those bloody beautiful lips,' Ben?" Simone added, nearly screaming.

Violet scowled. "I never called them 'those bloody beautiful lips.' And keep it down, you heathen! He could be home."

"Didn't see his car out. And you so did!" Simone shook her head quizzically. "Jesus, Violet, the man you've compared every single person who's ever shown interest to you is now your neighbor? How? Still, go on; tell me everything. What happened?"

"Well, your mum forgot to warn me that there's an alarm system set up, and yesterday's power outage set it off. He heard and came over. He was the one who installed them. I invited him in. We had some tea and talked a bit. And that's it. He left."

"Bloody hell. Sixteen years after a night like the two of you had, and you drink tea and send him on his merry way?"

"Yes. But listen, I don't want to talk about him or any man right now. I only need girl time."

Simone smiled promisingly. "And girl time you'll get because I have a brilliant idea."

"Let's hear it."

"We get on a train to Cardiff, go to our favorite gin bar, and get pissed like old times."

"Tomorrow morning?"

"The tickets are already booked."

"I adore you, you know?"

"Oh, you damn well better. It's all on me too."

Violet shook her head. "You're not doing that."

"You turned forty, and that fucker did nothing to celebrate you. I haven't seen you properly in the last two years. You best believe I'm doing it."

Tears welled in Violet's eyes again.

"None of that, babe. You know you're the only person capable of making me cry, and we're not doing that today. What we're going to do after I shower is put on *Mamma Mia* and scream at the top of our lungs until we lose our voices. And we'll also be eating all five bags of the sea salt and pepper crisps I brought."

Violet sighed. "You're my angel."

"I am your bloody soulmate is what I am. Ben could fight me," Simone declared.

"You'd let him win."

She shrugged. "Begrudgingly."

NEITHER OF THEM had normal voices the following morning. Helen, who'd rang to see if they were dying, was certain that their obnoxious sing-a-long would've merited a complaint or two.

And Ben must not have been home; otherwise, seeing him this morning would've been a lot more awkward.

He looked like he was about to get into his car when he spotted them walking out—a slow, incandescent smile formed on his face.

"Violet, Simone. Morning."

"Hi," was all Violet managed, silently praying he hadn't heard her high-pitched, ridiculously dramatized renditions of ABBA songs. If this was his car, Simone was right; it hadn't been here yesterday afternoon.

They weren't supposed to think of men during this time together, yet here she was.

"Where are you ladies off to?"

"Cardiff. Booze is better there," Simone answered.

"Train station, yeah? Need a lift?"

"It's all right, Ben, you don't have to," Violet said.

"I want to. It's no trouble."

Had he heard her unholy shrills?

Violet shook her head. "Is it on the way to wherever you're headed?"

"Sure."

"That's not..." Violet started.

Simone looked at Violet then, cutting her off. "Better him than some prick on the bus trying to talk to us."

Ben opened the passenger's seat and the one behind it for the two women without another word.

Simone walked straight to the back, and Violet smiled faintly. His nearness was as intoxicating today as it was when she was twenty-four.

Simone popped forward the moment he started the engine. "Hey, Ben. I have a question for you."

"Oh, God. No, you don't," Violet replied, rolling her eyes.

"Last I checked, you're not called Ben. He can tell me if he doesn't want to answer my question."

"What's your question, Simone?" he replied, looking at Violet with an expression that said *it's okay.*

"Well, it's a bit personal."

"Go on then."

Violet eyed her best friend, who was now too close to both of them.

"Biscuits—the Jammie Dodgers. How much of my soul do I have to sell to you for the recipe?"

He laughed. *Heavens, she missed his laugh.*

"Your mum has it," he said.

"Shut it. Does she really?"

"Yeah. I gave the jam recipe to her a while ago."

"Bloody woman kept it all to herself. I swear I'm disowning her."

Violet and Ben laughed in unison, looking at each other, then at Simone.

"I didn't know you were such a fan of biscuits, babe," Violet noted.

"Pretty sure you'd collapse and die if you had these, Vi. They're magic."

"Thank you," Ben responded shyly.

"You're very welcome. I'd also like to add, which I'm sure you've gathered by now, that I love Violet a little bit more than my own husband," she made a gesture with her thumb and index finger. "I wouldn't hesitate to murder on her behalf."

"Why are we contemplating murder now?" Violet chimed in.

"I'm always contemplating murder on your behalf, babe."

"I'm flattered," Violet responded.

"You should be."

Ben chuckled. "Noted."

Thankfully, they weren't far from the train station as he pulled over. Violet might've lovingly murdered Simone if they had stayed in this car longer.

Ben turned to face the women. "Be safe, yeah?"

"Thanks for the lift," Violet said. Simone agreed.

"Anytime," he replied. The sincerity that flashed in his eyes took her to a scalding and humid place, gargoyles atop them, encircled beneath afterglows. None of this would feel real, at least not for a long while.

Simone spoke when they were far enough from him. "Well, that man would shag you in a heartbeat if you let him."

"Simone Mina Henry, for the love of God."

"I'm just saying. I've known him for years now, and all he's ever said to me were three bloody words. '*Hi. You alright.*' Dry as fuck but hot as shit. He might've spoken to Peter a few times, but just barely. All of a sudden, he's laughing and offering lifts?"

Violet shook her head. "It's only because he knows me, I'm sure, and we will not speak of him for the rest of this trip."

Simone winked. "You're right. He knows how you kiss."

"Ssh."

"Ugh, you're boring."

Violet swung her arm into her best friend's elbow and pushed her into the station. Yesterday, today, and tomorrow would be only about them.

They were quieter on the train for a few beats before Simone spoke again. "I wish I had known he was *your* Ben, Vi. Why couldn't he have a rare name? How many blue-eyed bearded Bens exist in the world? Thousands, I'm sure. It never even crossed my mind that he could be the same one. I didn't even think it was a possibility. Plus, what if I was wrong and I got your hopes up."

"What? Simone, you're fine. Like, you said, how would you have known?" she started, then whispered. "Plus, I don't think your mum knows he's a retired MI6 agent."

"She doesn't. Or at least, she would've told me if she knew. Or, rather, why would she? I know his dad was ill, and I believe he moved here to take care of him."

Violet was quiet then. "Yeah, he told me the other night."

"He has a sister too, though I've never met her, but I reckon you also know that."

"Yeah. But seriously, Simone. Don't go there. Even if you had known, it wouldn't have changed any part of the last few years."

Simone reached forward and squeezed Violet's hand. If Violet dared to think about the what-ifs, she'd spiral, and no one needed to be subjected to that. Her best mate included.

THEY HAD DROPPED their bags off at the hotel concierge, and Simone insisted they immediately head over to the bar.

"Why are we headed to the bar now? It's only fifteen past noon. It won't be open."

"We're just walking by. Like old times."

"Then I'm getting my avocado toast?"

"Yes, then you'll get your avocado toast, which your goddaughter is also mad for, might I add. I swear that child will grow up entirely American like her father, and I will have to disown her."

Violet smacked her shoulder. "You will do no such thing to my Phoebe. She can be as American or as British as she'd like."

Simone made a gagging sound, followed by a not-so-appealing indication of the act. As they got closer to the bar, The Gin Land, Violet noticed a few people sitting outside on the patio, already drinking. When they got closer, she recognized the back of one of their heads.

Friends recognize each other's heads everywhere, don't they? Violet turned to Simone. "What's happening—what is this?"

The group turned then, screaming like they were teleported back in university with obscene reactions. Violet lost track of who was crying in her ear while rocking her back and forth after Valeria. The people she loved most in the world—the ones she barely got to see in the past decade—were all suddenly beside her.

Simone, Eddie, Valeria, Kevin, David, and Louisa. How on earth were they all here?

People warn you about many things, but no one ever tells you how devastating it is to constantly miss your friends.

"What are you lot doing here?" Violet said with tears streaming down her face.

"You didn't think we'd let you celebrate your freedom alone, did you?" David remarked, taking her bag and setting it down beside his chair.

"I'm not divorced yet," she replied.

"But you will be. And the world will be better now that your fire's returned," Simone added.

"I can't believe you goons managed this."

"Simone texted the group and told us her plans. We were available to crash and make a trip out of it," said Kevin.

"You went through a lot of hellish shit with us when we were in school, Violet. And life got hectic for us all at one point, but we couldn't pass up being here with you today," Valeria finished.

"Ted is still one of my mates, thankfully. I rang him a week ago and told him of our plans. He opened the bar to us and only us," Eddie retorted. "Come here, you," he added, putting Violet in the gentlest headlock.

"What are you drinking? The usual?" Louisa asked.

"*Yes*," Violet said, a little too loudly. *Dreamland.* A purple, hazy cocktail with lime tonic and elderflower syrup—*the drink of deities,* she was sure. And bless them all, avocado toast from another restaurant nearby was already waiting for her.

When drinks were on the table, Violet raised a glass first. "First things first, we're toasting to our Louisa, whose animated film is on its way to winning a bloody BAFTA and an Oscar in the winter!"

An explosion rumbled from all of them. Louisa was pinker than when she would spend five minutes in the sun.

"Will you thank us all in your acceptance speech?" Kevin asked through glasses clinking together.

Violet had missed her friends deeply. They used to be like this all the time. They used to talk constantly. The distance sucked, but it was manageable until she got it in her head that she couldn't burden them with her pain. Plus, life was different when they all lived in London. It was better. Easier.

She missed their souls. She missed Valeria's loud laugh. She missed Louisa's grace and kindness. She even missed David's obnoxious, on-purpose burps.

Eddie now lived in Amsterdam. Valeria was in Liverpool. Kevin and David were in Manchester. And Louisa was in New York.

Near or far, these were the people who made her the luckiest woman in the world.

. . .

TIME TURNED one drink into three and brought appetizers galore.

"Guys, Violet has something she needs to share with the class," Simone blurted.

"We weren't going to talk about that," Violet responded.

Simone rubbed her temple rhythmically. "We have talked about Kevin's flat renovations for forty-five minutes. If I have to hear about curtains for another minute, I will sit with those kids over there at that restaurant and show them photographs of my children covered in dirt. Spare me."

"Well, excuse me; my Victorian curtains and I take full offense," Kevin said.

"Good, you should," David replied. "I told you to go for the linen."

"I'll take your opinion seriously when you stop falling asleep to reality shows on the telly every night."

"Can we go back to bullying Violet to tell us her news?" Louisa said.

"Fine. I hate you all, but you more than others," she pointed to Simone. "You lot remember Ben? The man I met on the plane back when I was with English Airlines?"

"The one you made out with at the Sacré-Cœur like some bewitching siren?" Valeria said with a laugh.

"It wasn't *at* or *in*; it was *next* to. But yes. Him."

"Honey, you'd never let us forget him. We asked you if you liked kissing Dean, and your response was: 'I guess, but not if I compare him to Ben.'" Kevin said.

"Well, he's my neighbor now."

Some variation of "*WHAT*"—"*NOW?*" came from all sides of her. Simone was grinning from ear to ear. Kevin was blinking so rapidly that it was concerning.

"*Ben*. The man you've basically been pining after for years is your neighbor, and that's not the first thing you started with?" said David.

"I didn't want to talk about men. No offense," she gestured toward him, Kevin, and Eddie.

Eddie gulped down a drink. "Offense taken. Bloody hell, woman. Have you spoken to him?"

"Briefly."

"When you say neighbor, do you mean like *right* next door... the same street?" Valeria asked.

"Right. Next. Door," Violet answered, pausing after every word.

"Bloody fucking hell, Vi!" Kevin said.

David threw his hands up in disbelief. "I've got nothing for you, mate. I would've shagged him right then and there."

"I'd like to. Because if twenty-four-year-old Violet was attracted to him, it's a whole new level for forty. The man's greying at the temples a bit, and his beard—it's wildly unfair that he's still so bloody fit."

A roar of screams came from the table again.

Dear lord, she had missed them.

"Violet, what are you going to do? This is massive," Louisa said

"I don't know. I really don't. It was different back then. It was easy to give in to our desires because we knew we wouldn't see each other again. At least, I think that's what it was."

Simone cut in. "Mind you, the man is clearly pining after her, too. He's been Mum's neighbor for years and never talked; suddenly, he's up for giving rides."

"Simone is biased. She doesn't get a say," Violet said.

"I think I'm the one who was staring at the two of you in that car ride—the man stole glances at every turn."

"'Stole glances'? What is this, the bloody cinema?"

"With your wild love story, yes. Definitely," Simone confirmed.

"Somewhat unrelated to this conversation, but Vi, does Dean not check on you when he's away—like, at all?" Kevin asked.

"Nope."

"How is that possible?" David added.

Violet took a sip of her drink. "Just like that. He's in 'work mode' and doesn't want any distractions. Hell, if I know anymore. I just need all the prayers that he doesn't retaliate when he comes home and is served the divorce papers."

"But he probably will, won't he?" Louisa noted with a tinge of fear in her voice.

Valeria shook her head. "I don't get it. How do you not divorce someone if you're cheating on them with other people? Wouldn't you want the freedom to do as you please?"

"Not if you're a prick who's looking out for his own reputation. Plus, one of his selling points as a shitty barrister is the loving and loyal husband front he puts up," Kevin said.

Violet was quiet then. They didn't know of her internal battles as closely as Simone and Eddie did. She told the others about the cheating recently, but that was as far as she'd disclosed. She trusted them completely, but talking about her loneliness, breaking that dam, and revealing how much it pained her was never a truth she could fully disclose.

"I will genuinely never understand how such a monster was born from two amazing people," Violet noted suddenly, thankful for Dean's parents, who could've never known what their son had done to her.

His mom wept for days after she'd told her he almost raised a hand at her, stopping just at the wall he punched. She cried and begged Violet to forgive him—to believe that he could change, that the stress of the job made him this way. She begged Violet to stay with him because she was "the best thing that ever happened to him." She cried for Violet to remain hopeful because this could not have been the son she had raised. He was better than that.

Violet knew she could trust her because she asked her never to tell Dean of their conversations, and she hadn't. His family was the only blessing to come from their marriage. His parents and two siblings had been utter joys to have around, even as she hid every moment of his darkness from them.

Even his siblings had distanced themselves from him in the last four years. Matthew, his brother, had explicitly told Violet that once he learned of the cheating, he told his brother to stop, or he'd cut ties, too. Christmas dinners had become that much quieter when Matthew would spend them with his wife's family instead of coming home, visiting only when he knew Dean wouldn't be around. Anna was fortunate she lived in the States with her family, making her visits even more infrequent.

"Well, nurture only takes you so far, doesn't it?" Louisa said.

"Plus, as much as he was a cocky bloke when you first met him, he wasn't *this* bad," Valeria finished.

"No. It was losing the Granger case that set him off more than anything. I do think he would've eventually cheated—Dean's never fully satisfied with anything, but the viciousness, I would've never imagined," Violet said.

David sat upright. "What happened with that case anyway?"

"I don't think I'll ever know the whole story. He's never told me. I asked him to go to therapy because I could tell how much it impacted him, but he pulled the man card on me."

"Look, I get it. I don't like discussing every little thing either. But if I went through something that stressful, I'd run for help," Eddie said.

"Right, but you've also known me, and I've been in therapy longer than I haven't. To some, it's still taboo."

"Still, you might think he's changed, but I feel he's always had it in him, Vi," Kevin said. "Men like that could never be trusted."

Violet nodded. "Maybe. And maybe if I didn't mistake his persistence as an admirable trait of sorts, then I wouldn't be in this mess. But that's neither here nor there."

"Been there," Louisa confirmed. "But now, all that's behind you. And whatever comes after, you've got us. You know that, right? No matter how far we are?"

Eddie smiled. "I wouldn't be living my dream in Amsterdam if you hadn't gotten on that plane with me. You say the word, and we'll all drop anything for you."

She knew they would. She believed every word. But it was *so hard*. It was too much to take them up on it. Valeria's husband, Jesper, was so gracious with the kids; he never had difficulties taking care of them. Louisa's job was wild and unpredictable, but she'd make a way. Kevin and David would stop at nothing to spend time with her. Eddie, God, Eddie. She knew how grateful he was for everything she did. She knew he'd do anything for her.

And Simone. Well, Simone would turn the world upside down.

But she couldn't. She could ask for help in the form of therapy, but the horrendous guilt of burdening these brilliant, beautiful people made her bones ache. They were her people. They'd always be. But they each had their person, too—the one who'd take precedence every time.

When Eddie finally packed up the courage to leave his abusive home, he met Clara shortly afterward in Amsterdam. Clara would've been here, too, if it weren't for their newborn twins.

This horrific, suffocating pain brought on by loneliness led her to Dean. It was the fear of burdening her friends when she was tired and sad and wanted people around her.

She sat at her computer hundreds of times, drafting emails to Ben but never sending them.

What if he had a wife and kids, and she caused trouble? What if he was merely being nice by offering it in the first place?

"We should do karaoke tonight. Like old times," David blurted.

"No, we shouldn't," they all said in hearty unison.

And they all laughed because they knew they'd end up there anyway, underground at The Crow's Head, just like old times.

11

BEN

He was going to murder Billy. Right here, in the kitchen, with a pan.

"I'm just saying, boss, if we bring in more pumpkin-flavored things, it'll attract all the American tourists. There's a store that apparently has pumpkin-themed food starting in September. It's all over social media," Billy continued.

"No."

"C'mon. At least think about it."

"No," Ben repeated. This is what he got for hiring an overly enthusiastic twenty-two-year-old aspiring chef who had offered to create social media accounts for The Crooked Branch to attract more business. The new logo alone had done wonders, but Ben wasn't going to agree to every nonsensical idea Billy had.

"Okay, but you approved pumpkin cheesecake; why not add a few more things? The restaurant is called The Crooked Branch, for crying out loud. We're a walking autumn advertisement."

"If you don't stop talking, you're going home."

Billy chortled. "What's got you riled up today, boss?"

"I'm not riled up. I've had it with you and pumpkins."

"I bet if I post a poll that asks our customers what they'd like, most of them will vote yes on more pumpkin."

"If you run that poll, you're fired."

"So, we went from sending me home to firing me? And you say you're not riled up. How would you know if I ran it or not? Not only are you not on social media, but you have no idea how to use it."

"I know how to use social media. I *choose* not to. Now, shut up and start unpacking the avocado shipment."

"It just doesn't make any sense. You're always up for new things during every other season, but I bring in pumpkins, and it's like I'm asking you to start experimenting with dirt."

"Billy, if you don't shut up, this pan's coming straight for your head, eggs included."

Billy muttered something incoherent under his breath. It sounded like he called Ben, Oscar the Grouch. He was right. Typically, Ben was more than willing to accommodate. But his father died in September. His mother died in October. He was always on edge this time of year.

Autumn was beautiful but cold and murky, and every bone in his body broke down to remind him of the hills he couldn't climb over. The losses. The long approaching winter.

And yet, autumn brought Violet back to him.

Sixteen years later.

He should be thrilled about it—ecstatic, rather. But what did any of it mean? She was in the middle of a divorce. He wasn't the man she remembered that night in Paris, yet every part of him wondered if her return was somehow tied to the light he'd repeatedly been searching for.

As though every leaf that fell since their parting scattered through time to lead them here.

The world—*his* world, had been brighter since the two-day

storm. He should credit it to the natural cycle, but it hadn't been the case.

It was Violet.

It was knocking on his new neighbor's door, wanting to shut off the blaring sound, and instead, the most incandescent dawn he'd ever known plucked him out from perpetual midnights.

The last person in this wretched, cruel world he believed he'd see again.

The woman he'd left behind in Paris, standing before him, stray pieces of hair falling effortlessly on her face. Striking blue eyes jolting life straight back into his heart while simultaneously robbing him of breath.

I'd miss you even if I hadn't met you.

Had he actually said those words aloud to her that night?

Did she miss him the way he ached for her?

Had she lost sight of herself the way he had, lying awake at night since those summer days, wondering for whom she had reserved her most boisterous laugh? He wanted to move mountains to find her again. Did she still have panic attacks? How did her ex-husband comfort her through them? Did he know which flavor of gum to buy? Mint, she preferred, nothing fruity.

She seemed fine during tea. And in the car, laughing heartily with Simone, a woman he saw yearly during the holidays, never knowing he was so close to the best thing that ever happened to him.

But then again, she seemed okay in Paris, too. She held herself with a grace and serenity that coexisted with the fire in her, trying to conceal the sadness from her eyes by finding something to laugh about. He knew some of her heartaches back then, but what had she gone through in the last sixteen years? Who was beside her during those days?

She stumbled into his life accidentally and stayed somewhere deep inside through his refusal to let go. And now, he wanted nothing more than to be beside her, to take down whatever stood in her path—kiss her pretty lips senseless and hold her through the nights.

A chipper voice cut through his thoughts, "Okay, hear me out, pumpkin Welsh cakes," said Billy, holding his hands in front of his face to swat away anything Ben would throw at him.

Ben squared his shoulders and took a deep breath. "*That...is a maybe*," he stopped in front of his wide-eyed co-worker, who was grinning like a buffoon. His hundred-watt smile would win any argument simply because, and that was the only reason this was happening right now.

"We have a maybe, lads!" Billy blurted through the kitchen. Jeff and Leo laughed on the other side of the island. Jeff sliced a box open, making a satisfying swoosh sound before looking up.

"Let him have it, Chef. The chap knows what he's doing."

"And traffic has been better than before," Leo finished, looking up from the batch of cranberries he was examining for rotten fruit. Ben didn't reply to either of them. He knew deep down that they could be right despite his better judgment, but he wasn't about to completely reevaluate their seasonal menu for bloody pumpkins, of all things. Especially when whatever Billy was talking about sounded like an abomination to the fruit.

"If we keep going like this, maybe I can get him to try the pumpkin spice crisps I ordered," Billy said to Leo and Jeff.

Did he really say pumpkin spice crisps? Who in their right mind was eating pumpkin spice crisps? The absurdity of this fad wasn't lost on him, but if it meant his staff would be pleased with the increase in income, he'd grumble through accommodating.

Ben always understood that he was fortunate to land this job without an ounce of professional experience because Jason, the former head chef, worked with both his late mother and grandmother. When Ben started cooking for his father, Albert Grant claimed he had his mother's gift—a sentiment Ben would consistently ignore and disregard. *It's true,* his father would say. *Your sister can deliver babies, but she can't even follow a simple recipe.* Ben would ignore it all.

He figured Jason later pitied him, considering he was a forty-three-year-old man whose days with his father were numbered. Or, he supposed it was because the sous-chef at the time, Charlie, refused to take the promotion, thrusting Ben into the position of head chef after Jason's retirement, seven years after he started.

And the truth was, Ben loved the job far more than he ever appreciated his time with the MI6, except for the seventeen days and thirteen hours in a Parisian hotel.

This job made him feel far closer to his mother than anything else ever had, forcing him out of bed and into the world after his father passed. But like everything else, he didn't think he deserved it. He didn't deserve second chance after second chance because what had he done for it? Sure, he could follow a recipe, but did that merit the head chef position? Was this imposter syndrome or longing for a woman he shouldn't be thinking of right now? *Why wouldn't his mind just shut off for five minutes?*

Billy would someday deserve it when he was older, and hopefully, he wouldn't fight imposter syndrome as Ben did. The kid was born loving nothing more than the artistry of cuisine. According to his mother, who visited just last year from London, Billy would reorganize the food on his plate before eating it, and by the time he was four, he was begging her to let him help in the kitchen. He even went to culinary school, unlike Ben, whose supposed expertise was in forensics.

Yet, he was a lot like Billy when he was younger—he, too, would beg his mother to let him help in the kitchen. Sunday afternoons were reserved for baking sticky toffee pudding together after church.

The kitchen suddenly felt foreign to him, as though he hadn't been there for almost a decade now. It was astonishing he hadn't burnt the eggs in front of him. Imposter syndrome and longing shouldn't ever interact.

"Hey, boss," Billy said, as though he were repeating the words but much slower this time.

Ben tilted his head to look at him.

"I—I should probably wait to ask you this when you hate me a little less, but I've got to give an answer to my friends. Can I get next weekend off? My best mate's granddad passed. We're trying to get him out of the house for a bit. A friend can get us tickets to the Man City game."

Ben nodded. "Sorry about your mate's granddad. But yeah, that's all right. We'll manage."

Billy stood taller then. "Ah, shit. You really are the best when you're not threatening me with pans and fried eggs, you know?"

A smile crept up Ben's face. "Get back to work now."

If Billy wanted to stay here, The Crooked Branch would be his someday. Ben was sure of that. At the same time, someone with as much fire might want to move elsewhere eventually, and he'd never stop him. He was only twenty-two. Ben couldn't even remember what he was doing at thirty-two—the kid's potential was wildly brilliant.

"Ben, we're out of Jammie Dodgers and chocolate chip biscuits. Should we make a new batch or call it for the day?" Leo called out from the door.

He tilted his left hand to look at the time. It wasn't even late afternoon. How were they already out? "Uh, yeah, I'll do it."

"Cheers, man. Should I tell the customer wanting both to come back? A regular, too. One of the Harvey kids."

"If they're willing."

Ben placed the fried egg on the greens for the salad he was

prepping and hoisted it up to the restaurant floor. He moved over to the designated area for desserts.

He should make a batch for Simone to take home. And maybe Violet could try it, too.

Tomorrow morning, before he got to work. He'd do it then.

12

———

VIOLET

Simone would leave later today, and Violet didn't want to be without her. Granted, Aunt Helen would be right next door, but being near Simone again was wonderful. It was safe and comforting, and she felt like a little girl, wanting to cry her eyes out like when they were young and one of them would go home from a sleepover. She could never have another flatmate after Simone and thanked her lucky stars that she was able to afford a London flat on her own.

The Bluetooth record player connected to her tablet played The National's *Boxer*, with harmonies coming loudly from Simone in the shower. Violet took mugs from the cupboard and set them down, leaning against the counter, her eyes froze on the simmering kettle.

She always had Simone when her world came crashing down, and she'd have her to the end of time. She knew that much. But she wanted her closer.

Violet would have to start over at a new job with a new staff, and while she was pretty good at making friends, it felt like an impossible task these days. Like her baggage was too heavy to haul, and she just couldn't be her usual, loud self.

The days would pass with busy schedules, yet it felt like she was dangling from threads while the rest of the world moved forward around her.

I don't know how you do it. It takes strength to carry on after the losses you've lived through. You're so strong. If Violet had a dollar for every time she heard those words, she could buy strength somehow—be the beacon of fortitude the world thought she was. *What you've been through destroys people.*

And it did.

She had lived in the world without her parents longer than she had lived with them, but missing them never stopped.

Was she really strong if she could still feel the cuts burn?

Her therapist, Jane, knew them all, at least. If no one else, Jane was aware of the pain.

Violet would always say she had three saviors: Jesus, Jane, and Prozac.

When Violet vocalized her loneliness and how much she hated living in a world where it felt like everyone else was running a cross-country marathon while she was stuck on a treadmill without an off switch, Jane pointed out the things Violet could control instead of the ones she couldn't.

Unplug it from the socket.

Jump off.

Change the direction you're running in.

Some days, it worked. Some days, it was too hard.

And now, here she was, alone in Bath, living right next door to Ben Grant, the only man who made it seem like he could see all of her and still stay.

That was the thing about wanting love that made people say and do absurd things. It's what forced her to say yes to a man she wanted to say no to because she was so utterly desperate to have a love that was entirely hers. When she watched Simone find love after a massive heartache, she experienced profound happiness for the very first time. Her best mate would have someone who'd turn the world upside down for her, a partner who'd move across the ocean for her, without ever looking back. She'd have someone who'd be her first and last call of the day. She'd be his, and he'd be hers.

You're complete on your own, but love brings a touch of magic that makes every moment better, her mother would always say. She wanted to believe in that kind of love. She wanted it with every part of her, eventually settling because maybe her mother was wrong. Maybe that kind of love wasn't meant for everyone. Maybe she was just meant to be lonely, as though God were using her as an example of what *not* to do, like disregarding instincts.

The kettle finally boiled, and its loud whistle intermingled with a knock on the door. Violet turned off the contraption and took a quick peek at the mirror in the small foyer. Her hair, thankfully, wasn't all over the place, and she was wearing a white oversized Queen t-shirt with the *A Night at the Opera* album cover on it and black cycling shorts. It would do.

She opened the door to Ben, holding a large plate. *This man.* He wore a shy, unfamiliar smile. His hair was pristinely pushed back, and the familiar scent of bergamot engulfed her immediately. Someone would get to run their fingers through that hair. She wanted it to be her.

"Ben," Violet exclaimed, sounding far more chipper than she would've liked to.

His smile grew bigger as he mapped her ensemble out. It didn't feel invasive, never from him, even when she noticed his breath hitch at the sight of her dress in Paris. He pointed at her t-shirt then. "I still think this is their best album."

A proud glint flashed in her eyes. Violet would argue with anyone who dared to critique the album. She squared her shoulders proudly. "As the self-proclaimed president of the '39' is the Best Queen Song Fan Club, I wholeheartedly agree."

He laughed. "Not sure I remember that one as well as the others. I'm going to have to give it a listen in a bit," he said. They looked at each other for a beat, neither saying a thing.

He took a breath and inched the plate closer to her. "I—uh, these are for you. And Simone. The biscuits she wanted. They're right out of the oven," he said.

Her cheeks burned. "Oh, Ben, you didn't have to," she said, knowing her best friend would actually murder her in this very house if she dared to refuse these presumably God-sent biscuits.

He must've noticed the concern dancing on her face because an undeniable sincerity locked in his eyes. "Not a problem at all. Truly. If I don't make them at home, I'm making them at the restaurant. It's the easiest thing on my menu."

"Simone's in the shower, but I have no doubt she'll give you a kidney if you ask for it."

He chuckled. "Hopefully, I won't be needing one any time soon. But please enjoy them. And let me know if they're as magical as she claims?"

"Well, if they're as good as she claims, you might get tired of seeing me both in your back garden and place of work. So, for your sake, I almost hope she's a little wrong," she said, gesturing with her thumb and forefinger.

"Not a chance," he said, the enchanting smile she loved rising on his face. He stepped back, his eyes still locked on hers, before bopping his head in a goodbye.

"Should I shout the verdict at you? Or would you prefer I write it down and send a paper airplane to your door?"

"Depends how far you're throwing them from, and if you love the biscuits, I'll make them all week for you."

"And if I don't love them?" she questioned, arching a brow.

"I'll make whatever else you'd like to make it up to your poor taste buds that've been subjected to Simone's lies about magical biscuits."

"From my doorstep to yours," she said. "That's how far I'll be standing."

He smiled and nodded softly. "Cheers."

Violet turned her back from him and closed the door, biting her bottom lip as a bevy of nerves and excitement roped with the elusive warmth she had only ever felt with Ben.

She set the biscuits on the table, removed the tin foil, and took one from the top. They were massive and so neatly made that she could be astonished by the presentation alone. She took a bite, finally—the perfect balance between firm and chewy with a flavor that did indeed make her want to collapse and die. "Bloody hell! What'd he put in here?" she said to herself, hunched over with her elbows on the table.

"Who put what where?" Simone asked, walking toward her while spinning her hair into a high bun. Her eyes went wide. "Oh. My. God. Are those what I think that they are?"

Violet huffed, taking a larger bite this time. She moaned. Christ on a football pitch, she moaned over a biscuit. "You were right. They're magic."

Simone nearly ran to the table, grabbed one, took the most massive bite Violet had ever seen, and then laid her head on the table. "I'm taking these home with me," she mumbled with large chunks in her mouth. "You get to have these every bloody day of your life while I suffer in Scotland with store-bought wannabe shits."

She kicked her feet up on another chair. "Did he *just* make these because, good lord, they're so..." Simone didn't bother finishing her sentence, taking another massive bite and making some incoherent sound that sounded like a mixture between "fuck" and "me."

Violet threw her head back against the chair and slid lower.

"Simone, this is dangerous. What the hell am I going to do with this man?"

"Waltz him down to the church, say 'I do,' then serve these biscuits at the reception. We don't need cake. We just need these."

Violet laughed, imagining the entire thing for a beat. It would undoubtedly be a better wedding than the large, luxurious affair she didn't want but had to go along with because Dean had too many people to invite. The fact that their photographs were on the internet was something she'd always loathe. It's how Ben must've seen them; all he had to do was look her up online, and there they were. Perhaps, when all this was over, she could kindly ask the photographer to remove them.

She turned her attention back to Simone. "No, but honestly, what do I do?"

"What do *you* want, love?"

Violet took a breath. "There was no bloody way I'd ever let a man in after what I lived through. I could've sworn that vow and stuck with it. But he's the exception, Simone. He's always been. I want to know who he is today—how he's changed. Everything."

She looked at Violet for a moment, took a sip of her tea, then set it down and took her best friend's hands in hers.

"Then you take it one day at a time. You trust your heart. You believe in the fact that you are worthy of the love that you give to others, and you remember that you are not cursed or a shining example of what not to do. After everything you've been through, you are still here because you deserve to live a happy, good life—not a mediocre one." Violet swallowed, tears welling in her eyes.

Simone continued. "I don't know what this is. If I didn't believe in God, I'd sure believe in something right about now because God, the universe, fate, whatever it is, the world is conspiring to bring the two of you face-to-face again. And what that'll mean, only time will tell. But I need you to believe that you deserve not only all sorts of divine interventions but also good things and second chances."

Violet was in full-blown tears at this point. She nodded. She was going to hate this goodbye more than others, but she'd be counting down the hours until she felt her light again.

13

BEN

When he got out of the shower later that night and walked to his door, a white paper airplane sat on the doormat. He didn't even care what the verdict was; the fact that she landed it there was impressive alone.

He picked it up and closed the door.

He also didn't need to unravel it because she'd carefully written the words on the wing.

She was right. They are indeed magic.

You're magic, he thought to himself. Propelling paper airplanes to his home, straight into his damn chest—everything that he'd experienced with her—it was all magic.

He stood there for a few seconds, maybe minutes, staring at the projectile. It was fitting for her, of course, it was. He'd wager there was a story behind it, too.

If it wasn't for the knock on the door, he would've stood there longer, letting his mind wander where he shouldn't allow it to go.

Violet was standing at his door, her bright eyes gleaming

even after nightfall. She was carrying his bowl with what appeared to be a custard-like dish garnished with pistachios.

"My Nan was half-Armenian, and she always said that you should never return a person's dish empty," she declared cheerfully. "She never specified what you should give to an actual chef, but I figured I couldn't go wrong with Lebanese Ashta pudding. Hoping you don't loathe rose-flavored desserts and aren't allergic to pistachios? I always make some for Simone to take home for the family when she visits."

His eyes widened. "What else can you make? And are you sure you want to teach because I can get you a job right this second?"

She made a face. "Sadly, not much without mucking it all up. My patience in the kitchen is reserved for very few things."

"God damn," he replied sardonically. "Come in; I'll make us tea." He moved aside to let her in, hoping she wouldn't object.

"Sure. Also, don't try that in front of me. I can't bear a chef's live reaction."

He laughed sincerely. "I'm sure it's amazing, but I'll note your request."

He walked to the kitchen, placed the Ashta in his fridge, and took two mugs from the cupboard. He leaned against the counter and turned to face her. "Is there a story to the paper airplanes?"

"Yes, actually. My mum was a flight attendant, if you remember," she started. "Dad taught me when I was a wee thing, so I got obsessed with trying to fly them through all sorts of places, and well, not to brag..."

Of course, there'd be a sweet story attached to it. He should've expected that from her. And, of course, he remembered.

He remembered every detail she told him.

"Your childhood sounds lovely," he commented.

Her lips curved slightly. She nodded serenely. "I suppose if there is such a thing as destiny, perhaps that's why—maybe God knew their lives would be cut short, so there was very little room left for bad times."

The response made his heart compress. It was moments like this that confirmed Violet's light was the perfect shade for his darkness. She wasn't a newly changed lightbulb, a little too fulgent and jarring at first glance. He wouldn't even compare her to sunshine, overwhelming and necessitating safeguards.

She was the earliest sight of sunrise—or a brilliant sunset afterglow, like the one that enveloped them in Paris.

A perfect in-between.

He cast his wandering thoughts aside. "How are you not more jaded?" he asked, wanting to know how to preserve her light further, to ensure nothing and no one would ever take from her again.

She huffed. "Years of therapy, for one. But at the same time, ask me about anything else, and you won't get as much joy in every story."

Ben was quiet for a beat. He wanted to ask about her marriage then. His gut told him that it was worse than he thought, but he also knew it wasn't his place. These weren't things he should know, not now at least—maybe not ever, not unless she wanted to tell him.

Yet, with Violet, asking and answering came easy for them. They'd both been afraid of crossing lines, both entangled with nerves. Him, more than she'd ever realize.

He took a deep breath. *I just want to hear you talk,* he wanted to say. *I want to know everything about you—the good, the bad, and the impossibly hard moments you've never shared with anyone else.*

How have the last sixteen years been for you?

How are you here right now?

How is this really you?

How am I still so madly drawn to you?

Yet, if he asked her anything else—if they ventured into uncharted territories, it might lead him to a place of no return—a place he barely recovered from the first time around. "What do you think about pumpkin spice?" he asked, wondering if he'd have to suddenly become Billy's biggest fan or beg Violet to come vouch for him at The Crooked Branch.

She raised her brows and pursed her lips. "No thoughts, what of it?"

"One of our junior chefs is insistent I implement it in the menu this season. Something about Americans doing it."

She thought about it for a moment, looking up and crinkling her lips as though to really ponder the scenario. "Ah, yes, I've heard of the craze. I want to say 'no', but he might have a point. What are we talking?"

"Can't say. I tuned him out after he mentioned buying pumpkin spice crisps."

Violet wrinkled her nose. Good. She looked as disturbed as he imagined he did. "Well, that's a bit odd. Are they meant to be sweet or savory? What's the purpose?"

He huffed, pouring the tea and milk. "Hell, if I know."

"Thing is, the lattes aren't bad. I've tried them. But I'd much rather eat sweets than drink them. Though again, store-bought pumpkin spice crisps sound like a recipe for disaster."

He held the two mugs in his hand, a painted floral one and a red buffalo plaid one. He gestured her toward the sofa, nudging her to follow him.

She sat down.

"Has Simone left?"

"Yeah, she spent the last few hours with her parents, then back to Edinburgh," she said with a sad, childlike smile.

She missed her friend, and he understood the depth of it.

The world could be a lonely place without people to care for. People weren't used to it the way he was.

"Does Edmund visit frequently? Or do you?"

"Yeah, they fly home for the holidays, and if it's a good year, they'll visit in the summer, too. Nina's family is in London still."

She smiled reverently. "I'm happy to hear that. Distance can be shit when too much time has passed."

Had too much time passed since she'd seen Simone? She might not have visited Bath as frequently, but what about Edinburgh? Had Simone visited her when she was married? The idea of Violet's friends visiting in a future space they occupied together made his heart clench. He wanted so desperately to see what she was like around them. He got glimpses of her dynamic spirit with Simone—the confident, funny, brilliant woman who wrecked him when she cracked jokes or stood with her bare legs in the doorway, donning a Queen t-shirt.

Ephemeral moments of joy that flared through, fighting against the desolation in her eyes. He wanted to hold onto them, keep them consistently close by for her. He wanted to leave no room for sadness, even when it was apparent that there was far more of it today than before.

"Does your sister live far?" she asked, breaking him out of his thoughts.

"No, she's close. Bristol."

She took a sip of her tea. "That's good. It's nice to have family nearby."

"It is, yeah. I hate having to go too long without seeing my nieces."

Her smile grew wide. "How many do you have?"

"Two."

"What about Edmund's kids?"

"Three of them. Two boys and a girl."

Her eyes wandered somewhere, and a slow, hopeful smile

formed on her face. "It's comforting to know it worked out for them in the end."

"It really is. They truly deserve it after everything they went through."

"It's lovely, isn't it? When good people get what they deserve?"

He nodded. "Does that mean we aren't good people?"

"What is it that you want that you've yet to get, Ben Grant?"

You. Only you.

He chuckled. Her tone dazzled him—a perfect mixture of serious and flirtatious.

"I want a dog, but I'd feel terrible leaving it home alone too long," he answered.

She laughed, low and sweet. "I do, too. And a cat."

"What else do you want?" he asked, taking advantage of the opportunity.

She tilted her head slightly. "What makes you think I'm good people?"

"Because I know you."

"Do you now...what's my favorite season?"

"Autumn," he replied without a second thought.

She blinked, a glint flashing in her eyes when she looked back at him. "You remember that?"

"I remember everything."

Her expression changed. It concerned him that he'd said too much—scared her off, perhaps. *Why was he still clinging to those nights like a schoolboy?*

"Good to know I'm not the only one cursed with good memory," she added.

His memory was rubbish. But when it came to her—sharp as a blade, new, and strong as steel.

He wanted so desperately to know if she was okay. If she was safe. But what if that pushed her away? What if it closed the dam between them, making things awkward and weird?

"What would you call the pets if you had them?" he asked.

"April Ludgate for the cat. And Leslie Knope for the dog."

Ah. *Parks and Recreation.* He'd seen it. Once.

He laughed. "The cat's spot on."

"She hates everyone. Why would I choose anything else? What about you?"

"I haven't thought that far ahead. I'll leave it to you."

"That's a bad idea. I'll just choose someone from *Parks and Recreation.*"

"I'd be perfectly fine with that."

"And what if I said Ben Wyatt?"

"Then we'd be Ben and Ben."

She smiled. "Sounds like a perfectly chaotic duo."

"It certainly would be. How come you didn't have any at home? You had a cat, didn't you?"

"Lola was fifteen at that time. She died at nineteen. It was hard after a while to get a new one. Then Simone and I shared a kitty when we were flatmates. I had him until I got married and had to take him to Edinburgh because Dean claimed to be severely allergic. But Steve Rogers is perfectly content with the kiddos. It worked out, I suppose. I still get to see the menace when I visit."

Dean Colborne sounded like the biggest tosser any time he heard about him.

"Violet, you're not in trouble, are you?" He hated himself for asking, but Christ, he couldn't bear it any longer.

"You're referring to why I'm in Bath, aren't you?" she clarified.

Ben nodded, wanting to apologize for being so bloody intrusive. He shook his head. "I'm sorry, you don't have to answer if that's too personal."

"No. It's fine. Not in the traditional sense, I suppose. There's a prenup, but Dean's...a difficult man. We should've never married."

"Did you love him?"

"I liked him enough at the time," she replied.

He hated himself for wanting to ask more—for being so invasive, remembering the bright-eyed woman he sat before in a dimly lit Italian restaurant who wasn't afraid of anything. This felt different. They weren't the same people they were then. Still, he wanted to know.

He took a deep breath. "I'll reiterate: you don't have to answer it if you don't want to. But why'd you marry him if you didn't love him?" he finally asked, abhorring himself for doing so.

She looked down for a moment before meeting him at eye level again. "Because sometimes you get really tired of nothing working out in your favor, and you think that second best is all you're ever going to get."

She looked the same way she did in Paris before they parted. Staring into the night sky, a pool of sadness cascading from somewhere deep inside of her. He caught that look multiple times throughout their time together, and it nearly killed him. He wanted to take the perpetual desolation in her eyes and sprout stars into them instead.

It was the type of sorrow he knew might never actually leave her, just as it'd never leave him. It was grief that left permanent marks. He hated everyone, the world especially, for taking so much from her and making her feel like second best was all she could have.

"Violet," he said.

She shook her head gently. "Please don't look at me like that."

"Like what?" he asked, imagining what the look on his face said.

"Like I'm a lost puppy in need of rescuing."

He'd never. The beautiful thing about Violet was that she didn't need rescuing, and he knew as much from the moment he met her. She was brave, even when she didn't realize it, but she deserved to have someone hold her through everything—someone beside her to remind her of her strength. Someone to be worthy of her.

Her eyes were glistening. She swallowed and took a sip of her tea. He watched as her hands cupped one of his favorite mugs, an amber-colored ceramic with painted wildflowers—lustrous red poppies, mums, corn marigolds, harebells, tansies, forget-me-nots, and scattered *violets* in all the creases. It belonged to his mother.

He remembered asking her to name them all, promising to build her a garden when he was big. He remembered her cheerful hazel eyes gazing down at his, telling him that when he was, in fact, big, the first thing he should ever do was learn what a girl's favorite flowers were and to always take them to her when he got a chance.

Not everyone loves roses, my sweet boy. I do, but your Aunt Bea loves lilacs.

He wanted to ask about Violet's favorite flower. He wondered if Dean had known, if he'd go out of his way to purchase them if they were something that couldn't be found at a common market.

If they'd been at home instead of Paris, Ben would've brought them for her in a heartbeat. He would've asked. He would've remembered.

He hadn't even realized that he'd given her his mother's mug. It was one he wouldn't ever allow anyone else to drink from. He and his father kept many things for when Emma was older. She was insistent Ben take the floral mug, and she'd keep the one with orange tabby cats on it.

He finally spoke after realizing he must've been silent. "I don't think that. I just hate that you believed second best was all you'd ever get," he finally said, watching her carefully put the mug down on the coaster as though she knew of its value.

"I suppose I could ask you the same question then, a form of it. Do you not have someone because you aren't interested in love? Or?" She paused; a mischievous gaze made its way onto her face—the same brilliant look in her eyes from the night at the Italian restaurant. "What's your story *today*, Ben Grant?" The hard emphasis on today was both precious and nauseating.

Today, he was the same man as he was sixteen years ago—still trekking through life, giving only twenty percent of himself to the world.

"It's harder for me to be around people than it is to be alone. My last serious girlfriend was great, but she sort of figured out I wasn't in love with her and broke up with me." He surprised himself with the words that left his mouth after. "I thought you and I were a bit alike in that sense."

She looked at him inquisitively, taking in his sentiment and thinking about it. "It's true to a degree, and it's strange, really, but I think something broke inside of me before I agreed to marry Dean." She took a deep breath and watched Ben's reaction.

"How so?"

"You don't think about your loneliness until your best friend finds her soulmate. Or, at least, I didn't as much. Simone and I dealt with nearly everything at the same time. It was bonkers. And I knew that wouldn't be the case forever. Someday, our paths would diverge. Then, one day, she was married, moving to Edinburgh on a prestigious fellowship, with a brilliant man like Peter by her side. I was so fucking proud of her. *So* happy I wanted to explode. You could write a novel about those two," she said, her eyes gleaming with a love he admired. The same fire he imagined he held inside for his sister or Edmund. It was a true, transcendent joy and no hint of jealousy or anything of the sort.

She started playing with loose hair then, twirling it through her index and middle fingers. "But then one day, I don't know, I sort of just...well, you're going to have to get me drunk if you want the rest of it. It's quite a road to venture down to," she said with a sincere laugh.

"Can I offer you a stronger drink then?" he asked quizzically.

"I wish, but I have an interview tomorrow, and I should be in a better headspace to prepare; plus, I already had too much this weekend. I don't need more."

"You have an interview tomorrow?"

"Yeah, at Knightley Primary School. Hungover second morning in a row might not be a good look for a Year 4 teacher," she replied.

"Oh, you've got this in the bag."

"They're going to ask questions. It's a bit concerning, but I'm hopeful." She paused and smiled.

He bit his cheek, wanting to know more about it all—he wanted to take her loneliness, fill it with biscuits and tea and whatever else she needed. But that wasn't his place. Not here. Not yet. Not when there was still so much she was holding back. It might've been long, but there was more; he knew as much, and he'd sit here and listen to every word she spoke.

Ben wasn't opposed to love, not then and not now. But he was adamant that it be with someone he wanted to share his space with. Someone he could trust with all of him instead of the mere twenty percent. He often wondered if maybe it was a good thing he hadn't loved as profoundly because if he experienced a loss the way his father had, he wasn't sure he'd survive it.

Yet somehow, Violet fit into his space seamlessly. Today and back then. She didn't feel like a mere witness during the Lind case. She was something else. An enigma he couldn't quite understand. She fit into his home, too, leaning gracefully on his sofa, floral mug in her hand.

Ben had looked for Violet in every woman he met, searching for the comforting sense of ease her presence filled him with. His last girlfriend, Hannah, was kind and funny, too—a lovely woman in every way, but the enigmatic magnets that drew him to Violet, the ease in talking to her, were missing in others.

They were quiet for a beat, a comfortable silence taking control of the helm, and then she laughed, guffawed, actually. It was a sound he could drown in—intoxicating, brilliant, and so fiercely infectious. He turned to her with a stunned look that said, what?

"We met on a plane sixteen years ago, had one incredible date, and now we're neighbors. I could've sworn these things only happened in the cinema."

She was the most adorable thing he'd ever seen at that moment. There was a flare in her eyes that set his entire being ablaze. She was right. No one would believe it. He still didn't. Not at this moment when she was sitting in front of him, not this morning when he took biscuits to her house, and especially not last night when he dreamed of her.

"Someone out there has a thing for theatrics."

She nodded. "You know, I always say God's got the best sense of humor. I stand by that, *especially* now."

He took a calming breath and leaned forward, resting his elbow on the knee he had crossed over his leg. He idly stroked his beard, then picked up his mug and raised it toward her. "Better late than never, then?" he suggested.

She leaned her mug in his direction with a soft, almost shy smile. It was a look he hadn't seen from her yet, and he wondered how many of these smiles were tucked behind her lips.

"I should get going. Thank you for the tea. And the biscuits."

"I owe you them for a week, remember?"

"The paper airplane. That's right." She rose to her feet then and took the mug with her. She gently placed it on the kitchen counter. "I look forward to them then. Though, let's not test my self-control with an entire batch next time," she smiled.

He walked her to his door. "I'll see you tomorrow then."

"Goodnight, Ben."

That was it. The way she said his name. It sounded different coming from her, and he'd do anything to continue hearing it.

14

VIOLET

Violet hadn't had a job interview in eight years. After quitting her position at English Airlines, she subbed for one year until she was interviewed for her teaching job, landing it almost immediately and working her way up to the head teacher's position.

She had gathered enough research on Knightley Primary to know the school's history, built in 1901 by Harrison Knightley and his wife, Mathilda. Mathilda was the Year 5 teacher until her retirement. And despite his qualifications to be in administration, Harrison coached football at St. James Secondary School. He loved the sport more than anything else, and their two children, Harrison II and Paul, both went into education as well, with Paul taking the reins as a coach when their father retired. The school had been in their family for generations, but their humility in hiring stood out among all things.

If she proved to them that she was worthy, Violet could potentially be promoted again to administration somewhere down the line. Still, she was mainly excited to teach again.

Violet stood in front of the long rectangle mirror that hung on her bedroom door to check her final appearance. Her hair was in a neat, low bun with wavy wisps hanging around both sides of her face. She wore a pair of rust paperbag trousers with a neatly tied bow—a skill she learned working at a small boutique shop while she was still studying—and a lightweight white jumper with cognac ankle boots.

The final touch would be her favorite red lipstick, a proven lucky gem she would use repeatedly and repurchase yearly. "Evermore Rouge" was a true, classic bright red. The lipstick was one of the first purchases she made with her own quid, wanting to mimic her mother's everyday look. Finally, she took her over-sized pleated blazer, tossed it around her forearm, and walked out the door.

Clouds were rolling in, and the weather app had signaled an incoming storm around six. She'd hopefully be home by then, but that was the least of her concerns at the moment. She walked out the door to a plate placed on a small wooden stool outside her door with a note attached.

She smiled to herself, a thrilling squall of butterflies taking over. She placed the smartphone she was holding in her bag and picked up the note tucked underneath the plate.

> *Early morning today. Didn't want to wake you.*
> *You'll do great at the interview! Cheers to day one*
> *of biscuit deliveries.*
> *-Ben*

He did not heed her advice by leaving her with one or two, but six. She was grateful, still. Simone would've been dancing in the streets from joy. She missed her again.

She walked the plate back to her kitchen, neatly took the first two peering out, folded them in a napkin, and beelined out. She also triple-checked the door to ensure she actually locked it.

Violet was thankful the bus stop was close to her new house. The tube station was often a bit of a walk from the neighborhood she and Dean lived in, so she'd drive closer to the car park, then take the tube almost everywhere. When she left Dean, she left the car with him. It'd probably come in handy in Bath, but she wanted nothing tying her to him—she'd eventually look into another one once she figured out a more concrete plan for her whole situation.

She rehearsed answers to potential interview questions the entire bus ride over, confident the ones in her head were far more eloquent than the words that would come out of her during the real thing. Isn't that how it always is for everyone? There should've been some sort of brain translator invented by now.

The school was stunning and fit beautifully into the city's timeless appeal. There were four large maple trees in front of the entrance—two of which were already sprinkling lambent orange all over, another shining with portions of deep reds, and the last one in its yellowing stage. Now she *really* wanted to teach here.

She walked to the front entrance and opened the wooden doors by their brass handle to a woman sitting behind the desk. "Good morning, miss," she said with a friendly expression. "How can I help?"

"Hello. I'm Violet Wedlake. I have an interview with Abigail James."

"Perfect. I'll give her a ring. I believe she has a teacher with her right now. Have a seat, please," she stated, gesturing to the three chairs set up in the corner.

Violet took a seat and waited, bouncing her knees as she always had when she was anxious. Thankfully, it took less than five minutes for the Head Teacher, Abigail James, to take her in. The receptionist, Nicole, guided Violet to the third room on the right-hand side. The door was left ajar, and Violet knocked faintly, entering only after she heard a cheerful "Come on in."

She smiled earnestly and walked over to the woman who looked as though she was only a few years older than her. Violet extended a hand to her, and Abigail took it with a strong grip. Both women had firm handshakes. "Violet Wedlake, a pleasure to meet you."

"Abigail James," she smiled, then motioned to one of the two forest-green armchairs. Violet needed these at her place, she thought. Abigail had excellent taste in décor, and Violet was already a big fan of that fact alone. Though her chair was more oversized and brown leather, understandably so as sitting for hours would require more leaning.

"I'm going to get to the core here, Violet. Your CV is thoroughly impressive, and I've rang your former school to ask about you." She set her hands down on the desk. "You have glowing reviews, which I'm sure you imagined you'd get," she confirmed.

Violet smiled sheepishly. She was never sure how to take compliments when it came to her work—or ever. Did anyone truly master this? She wasn't shy per se, and she knew she was good at her job, but taking compliments was seldom easy. A simple 'thank you' never felt like it was enough to convey the gratitude.

"But you are overqualified for this position, and I'm questioning what would make you leave a school with higher pay and rank."

She took a deep breath. At this point, she could only be entirely candid.

"If I may, I'd like to be fully transparent here." She waited for Abigail to agree before continuing. "My husband wouldn't even consider talking about divorce and wouldn't budge. He is currently on a business trip in America for two months, and I took the opportunity to leave while he was gone. I couldn't stay in London, and I was graciously offered a place to live by the closest woman I have to family here," she paused and swallowed convulsively.

"I sincerely do love teaching. And when I saw that there was a position open for Year 4, I couldn't pass it up. I taught for years before moving to administration. So long as I'm in a school setting, I'm perfectly satisfied with what I'm doing."

Abigail was quiet for a beat as she seemed to absorb Violet's response. There was an empathetic look on her face, one that many women quickly passed on to each other in situations like this. She believed her without needing the full story of what led to the divorce, and that was all that mattered to Violet.

"Could your husband potentially pose a threat to the school if he discovers you've left?" Abigail asked.

"No, I don't believe so. Uhm…" she paused for a moment. "You see, my husband, hopefully, soon-to-be ex, is a wealthy man and a recognized barrister in London. His reputation matters to him more than anything else. At Briar, he was known for his grand donations. He wouldn't withdraw the funds or do something publicly humiliating that would tarnish his name," she answered.

"Well, charitable donations certainly help," Abigail started. "But the school has also improved significantly in test scores the last three years, and that's often a reflection of the entire staff, which is commendable."

Violet smiled. She was proud of the work they'd all done at Briar. Her accomplishments were possible because of the team beside her, and she hoped that would be the case here, no matter what position she held. "The staff at Briar were truly phenomenal. The school is now in brilliant hands with Stella Jin."

"I also spoke to her, and she seems ready to take it all on.

One more question, Violet, I gather your stay in Bath is permanent, then? Despite complications that may arise with your ex-husband."

"Yes. And at the very least, I would not leave mid-school year or anything of the sort. Fate seemed to really intervene with his departure occurring in late summer. Once I knew the official date, I made the staff aware that I wouldn't be returning for the new school year," she replied.

"Understood. I appreciate your honesty. And I am sorry, I can't imagine any of this is easy for you," she said. Abigail rose from her chair then. "I know this is a quick interview, but I don't feel I need to know more based on what people have communicated about you. Not now, at least. I have one more candidate to speak with today, so expect a call from me either tonight or tomorrow."

Violet nodded then and stood up as well. She extended her hand to Abigail once more and thanked her for the time. Perhaps more than the interview, she thanked her for not judging the situation.

She wasn't sure if she'd get the position. Heck, she wasn't sure if she'd hire someone in her same situation, given what could possibly happen. What Dean would do when he came home to an empty house, rings on a table, and a mere note detailing that she'd left him, only time would tell. He was to be served the divorce papers the moment he returned home on October 21st.

Nevertheless, she wouldn't think about it for now. A storm was coming, and she had a new novel sitting in her bedroom, ready to be devoured over tea and Ben's biscuits. Or, rather, biscuit—she already had two on her way here. She shouldn't eat all six in one day.

15

———

BEN

There was a storm out, and he had almost an hour left on the clock. He wanted to go home immediately. Time often passed quickly for Ben on the job, but it had slowed drastically these days.

He thought of Violet all morning and afternoon. He thought of her in his house, on his sofa, and he thought of her in his bed, too.

It had been easier to take the chances they did when they knew they were agreeing to one date. It was easier to hold her hand and push against her body when he kissed her. It was all... easier. He wished Violet was staying with him. He wondered what it would be like if her house caught on fire or flooded, then loathed himself for such a horrid thought because it was a lovely little place. Plus, even if a disaster of some sort happened, she'd stay with Mrs. Henry, not him.

He had gone to the freezer room for something and completely forgot what it was, standing there like a bloody fool staring at peas while thinking of Violet. Ben threw a dish towel over his shoulder and hunched forward. Somehow, it wasn't cold enough in here. Still too hot, with every part of him catching fire. If he couldn't have her, he wanted to be near her—he wanted her everywhere. He wanted to be the first person she rang after leaving the interview to tell him how it went. He wanted to make biscuits for her every morning and drink tea with her every night.

She turned him into a blubbering buffoon, and he didn't care. He just wanted to be around her, convinced that even the ugly parts of her would be beautiful to him. He was convinced none of those ugly parts even existed.

He walked out of the freezer, not bothering to remember what he sought out in the first place. Billy was standing in his way with his hands in a position to receive the item.

Ben blinked, once, twice...*runner beans.* He was supposed to take chickpeas to the freezer and bring back runner beans for Billy. "Shit, sorry, forgot," he mumbled.

The boy's expression turned to concern. "You all right, boss?" He asked.

Ben blinked again. *What the fuck was going on with him?* "All good," he replied.

He could feel Billy's head tilt as he walked away. The strange part was he hadn't felt this way when he and Violet first met. He thought about her often, yes. He dreamed of her more times than he could count, but while working, the thoughts of her were mostly held at bay. Now that she was close, it was a battlefield he didn't know how to maneuver through. He walked in weaponless, and everything she did shot him point-blank to the heart.

He wasn't sure how the hour went by or how he dodged every look Billy, Leo, and Jeff threw his way. Florence passed him that concerned motherly expression that she'd usually follow up with, *are you sleeping enough? Have you had enough water today?* If he hadn't bolted out of the bloody restaurant, and if she wasn't with a customer, she might've stopped him dead in his tracks.

Maybe if there wasn't a storm out, he wouldn't have thought of her as intently. Since their meeting, the rain always reminded him of her. She had told him she'd miss the English rain too much if she moved somewhere else. Her love for it—he remembered it. It made him miss her. Back then, it might not have always rained for them at the same time, but that was neither here nor there.

He'd get home, take a cold shower, and then maybe pluck up the courage to find a way to ask her about the interview. It'd be the polite thing to do, after all.

A flash of lightning struck as he parked his car. *Fuck*, he couldn't shower now. He should've known better than to trust the weather app that said thunder would arrive far later in the evening. At the same time, his house keys wouldn't cooperate with him either, forcing him to let out a low grunt in agitation.

He walked into his house, hung the keys on the wall, and kicked off his shoes. Yesterday, he had plans to bring her biscuits until he remembered that he had the opening shift all week. He would only see her if he started delivering them late at night, which he would consider if she was interested.

The buzzing in his front pocket suddenly alerted him. *Sister*, the lock-screen read, with a photograph of a woman holding two little girls laughing in her arms. There was only one person in this world whose call Ben wouldn't ever ignore: his sister's.

"Emma," he said into the phone.

"Hi, brother, someone wants to talk to you," she said cheerfully. Emma only ever called him Ben in an argument—since she started speaking, he was only ever "brother."

"Oh?" he inquired.

A small squeaky voice came from the speaker then. "Uncle Ben?" It was Lily—his youngest niece.

"Yes, little light," he replied, smiling into the phone.

"I'm watching Miss Piggy. What are you doing?" she said eagerly. Miss Piggy, otherwise known as The Muppets.

"I just came home from work. What's Miss Piggy up to today?"

She dodged that question quickly. "What's work?"

"The restaurant. Remember the one you had the big ice cream waffle at?"

"Yeah!" Lily replied with intense enthusiasm. "Can you make again for me?" She forgot the "it" in the sentence, and it was the most adorable damn thing ever. He missed his nieces.

"Of course. The next time you visit, I'll make it even bigger this time."

"Okay," she said, handing the phone to her mother, who returned with an "And me again."

Ben chuckled. "You lot free next weekend? It's been a while."

"Should be, yeah, nothing as of right now. Although, during the third week of October, Luke and I have a conference in Glasgow. Any way you could watch the kids?"

"Of course, yeah," he replied. "What's the other peanut up to?" he asked, referring to his eldest niece, Catherine.

"She is in the garden with Luke. He's planting tomatoes. Anything new with you?" his sister asked.

"Nope," he replied dryly. "Tell 'em both I say hi, will you?"

"You got it. And don't think I didn't notice how quickly that 'nope' came out; I'm not buying it," she responded. Emma might've been younger than Ben, but she knew him better than anybody else. When she first moved, she would call him on his worst days, claiming she felt something was off and forced him to talk.

"You're going to have to cause that's what I'm selling," he said, now staring at the drawer in his bedroom, forgetting, once again, what he came in here for.

"If you had a bad day at work, you could just say you had a

bad day, and I won't push it. But don't lie to me, brother. I know you."

"Yeah, a bad day at work."

She sighed into the speaker. "I'm not going to say the thing because I know what you'll say, but know that I'm thinking of you. You can't come by this weekend?"

The thing she was referring to was telling Ben that she wished he would talk to someone again, hinting that he should go back to therapy, knowing he'd deflect by saying he had no time. Emma meant well; he knew as much.

"One of our chefs has the weekend off; can't afford two right now."

"That's fair. Then make next weekend happen, please. I'll see you soon, okay?" she said, wanting confirmation before she hung up.

"I'll be there," he promised.

"And you know you can call, right? After bad days? I'm always here."

"Yeah, I do."

"Good. Talk soon, brother."

"Cheers," he said and hung up.

He finally remembered what he was looking for in his drawer. Ben grabbed dark-heather charcoal joggers and a black t-shirt to change out of his wet work clothes. *Okay, this felt some- what better.* Yet now, on top of all the jumbled flutters he felt stir- ring for Violet, he missed his nieces. Today was determined to be a scathing batch of emotions he wasn't sure how to work through. Sure, therapy would help again, as it did when he was in the agency, but a therapist wouldn't fix the aching desires he had to pursue the one woman he was sure he could love.

He was forty-seven years old; many of his aches were manageable. Yet, when it came to love, he was a bloody lost cause.

He walked over to his drink cabinet, took the whiskey decanter, poured himself far more than two fingers, and walked to the kitchen. He took a big gulp, wishing it'd burn more than it did, then hunched over against the countertop. Some sort of a groan left him.

Every part of him felt...elephantine. It'd been ages since he had a panic attack, and this didn't feel like one, not as it usually had. Carrying his own weight felt like a colossal burden. He wasn't sure what to make of it, but he realized at that moment how often he had felt this crushing monstrosity at the end of each day.

He hadn't given much thought to it, but it was too loud and too demanding to ignore right now. It was shooting through every bone in his body. He was tired, furious for reasons he couldn't bother to understand, and desperate for something more. He would be fine—he had to pull it together.

No, he was breaking apart—the glued-up pieces of him were all loosening, and he couldn't bother to pick any of them back up.

He closed his eyes for a beat, trying to will whatever this was away, knowing damn well that wouldn't be the case. He wanted Violet. *He needed her.* Except she wasn't his and might never be. He couldn't burden her. He wouldn't dare.

A few moments passed. He emptied the glass with two huge gulps and strode toward the living room, filling it with another.

He could shoot her a quick text. There was nothing wrong with that—a simple message to see how the interview went—nothing more.

> **BEN**: Violet, hi, how'd the interview go?
> **VIOLET**: Hi! Well, I hope. And pretty short, though
> she seemed impressed with all the references she

spoke to from Briar. Said she'd give me a call
either tonight or tomorrow with the verdict.
BEN: Good. I'm glad. They'd be mad not to
accept you!
VIOLET: Thank you for saying that. How was work?
BEN: Eh, it was fine.

He hoped it didn't sound too bitter, hollow, or worn down.

VIOLET: Thank you for the biscuits, by the way. They
were divine.
BEN: You are most welcome!

He wanted to continue the conversation more than anything, sit here on his sofa, and talk to her through the night. It should be concerning how easily she calmed him.

16

VIOLET

A call from Knightley popped up on her phone right as she was ready to respond to Ben, a little thankful because as much as she wanted to carry on the conversation, she wasn't sure how. At least not like this. Not through text.

"Hi, Violet. It's Abigail," said the woman on the phone.

She seemed somewhat chipper, and Violet hoped this would mean good news. If she was going to give her a rejection, she might've sounded a bit more reserved. Or at least she hoped that was the case.

"Hi, Abigail."

"We met with our second candidate, and she seemed very lovely. However, I reviewed your application and the interview with other staff members, and we decided that you're the right woman for the job."

It took all her might not to scream. "Oh, does this mean...?" she tried to say.

"Yes, we would like to formally offer you the position if you are interested. As you know, you won't be starting for another seven weeks until Grace Wilson leaves," she began noting. "All I would need from you then is the official paperwork. I can email it to what we have on record if that works, and you'd simply need to fill it out and send it back to us," Abigail finished.

Violet was grinning from ear to ear. She had told herself she would've been okay with a rejection, but after meeting Abigail, she wanted nothing more than to work at Knightley. It felt right. "Yes, of course, I'm interested. And the email on record works."

"Wonderful. I look forward to speaking with you soon. I'm heading out for a conference at the end of the week, but when I return, we'll arrange a day for you to meet the staff and touch base with Grace as well about the curriculum."

"Looking forward to it as well. Thank you so much," Violet said.

"You are very welcome, Violet. Have a good night. We'll talk soon."

"Good night!" she voiced before hearing the click on the other end of the line.

She might've done some sort of a weird shimmy before immediately sending the text, "*I got the job!*" to Ben. It was strange how natural it felt to tell him this. She'd shoot one over to Simone as well, but this little back-and-forth, however small, was thrilling.

> **BEN**: "Never doubted you for a second! Congratu-
> lations!"
> **VIOLET**: "Thank you!"

For the first time, things were looking up. Violet also couldn't remember the last time she had a text conversation that made her feel like a teenager again. So much of what transpired with Ben felt new, even if she had done these things before with other men.

When she first kissed him in Paris, he was the only man she

had allowed to touch her freely—the only man she allowed to trail away from her lips. Before him, she'd had one boyfriend when she was in uni, and she wouldn't let him go beyond her lips. He tried, and she prompted him to stop instantly. It wasn't a religious choice or anything of the sort, but she didn't want anything more until she cared enough about the man to desire every part of him as well. In that sense, Nick was her first.

But she remembered wanting Ben in Paris more than she ever wanted anyone else. She didn't understand it then or now, for that matter.

It was frightening to think of how her feelings could grow if they had more time.

She sat on the edge of the window and carefully considered her next steps. But good news always made Violet feel bold enough to chase the delicate things in life—love and happiness.

> **VIOLET**: Are you free to come over? Have a drink
>   with me?

She couldn't believe the words that had escaped her via text. *Violet Eleanor Wedlake, what are you doing?* She could practically hear her mother's voice.

> **BEN**: I'm almost positive I have a better selection
>   here. You come!
> **VIOLET**: Are you doubting my taste in liquor? That
>   would also require moving from this spot by my
>   window, and unless you have a better view of the
>   storm, I'm staying put.
> **BEN**: Your back garden still has cracks in the roof,
>   doesn't it? So you can't sit outside.
> **VIOLET**: How'd you know about that?
> **BEN**: I was around when the tree fell.

VIOLET: Is your garden better?

BEN: You'll have to see for yourself.

VIOLET: I hate you a bit for making me move, but I'll
be there in a few.

BEN: The view will be worth it. Promise.

She wasn't willing to sacrifice a good hair day to the rain, so she donned an oversized hoodie, took an umbrella, and nearly ran for his place. Her hair was thankfully safe, and that's all that mattered now. Still, she wasn't nervous until she knocked on his door.

He wore the most gorgeous smile when he opened it, but as she caught sight of his eyes up close, it took everything in her not to react to the desolation breaking through. "Hi," he said.

"Hi," she replied. She had seen tired before, but this was something else. It was something recognizable but unfamiliar at the same time. His hair was slightly more disheveled than she'd typically seen, but not entirely a mess. Yet, it was the way he was carrying himself that made her heart sink.

His shoulders were hunched, and his tone sounded off despite how happy he seemed for her. She wanted to keep staring and understand what was truly bothering him.

He stepped aside, giving her room to walk in.

She didn't move.

She wanted to voice her concerns. She wanted to back away and take a rain check. Maybe tomorrow. Maybe he should sleep now. Maybe he shouldn't have company.

He arched an eyebrow. "You plan on staying outside?"

Shit, she was probably gaping at him. "Yeah, sorry." She left the umbrella by the front door and carefully removed her boots. She wanted to brush his arm, touch his cheek, do *something* —*anything*. But it wasn't her place.

Dean was always seemingly exhausted, always on edge, but

his eyes were also filled with pools of rage that made her recoil. Stay quiet, stay alert, and let him be. That wasn't the case with Ben; nothing about his edges unnerved her because even while she watched him take down a man, a gentleness still emanated deep within.

"What is it?" Ben asked.

Violet blinked, realizing that she was still staring.

"Nothing. I—You just...is everything alright?"

He was quiet for a moment, mapping out the look on her face as though he were seeing her for the first time. He blinked, once, twice.

"Yeah," he said with a nod and a warm smile, "just knackered."

"We could do this some other time then," she started.

"No, no. Please. Stay," he said, and she felt the final word down to her bones.

Stay.

I wish you could stay, she had told him. *I would if you meant it,* he had replied. She had meant it. She just couldn't risk it.

Those words tirelessly echoed in her head on the nights she spent lying next to another man. What would life look like if she had told Ben to stay? Where would they be if they had never said goodbye in front of her hotel room that night? He tasted like whiskey then; he smelled like it now. The smokey maple notes would feel like homecoming if she inched a bit closer and pressed her lips to his. They'd dazzle and intoxicate just as they had in Paris. But not here. Not now.

"Okay," she agreed, following him inside.

He walked over to stunning mahogany bar cabinet beside his kitchen and opened it. "What would you like to drink?"

"I'll have whatever you're having," she said.

"You sure you don't want something more exciting than

straight whiskey? I know you prefer gin. I can make you something."

She cocked her head to the side. "I appreciate you remembering that, but if you're having whiskey, I'll take it, too."

He nodded and walked over to the decanter sitting on his countertop. "Ice?" he asked.

"Yes, please," she answered.

She watched him as he got ice from the dispenser, certain now more than ever that something was amiss. The movements in his body weren't as they were last night. He was stiffer, his shoulders were undoubtedly tense, and heavens, the look in his eyes continued to trouble her. She wanted to walk over to him and wrap her arms around him. She wanted to kiss the heartbreaking sadness out of his eyes, guide him to the sofa, and run her fingers through his hair. She wasn't even sure it was serious, maybe he was simply knackered, but seeing him like this made her chest ache at unbearable levels. It concerned her profoundly.

His hands gently brushed hers as he handed her the glass, sending a flurry of butterflies loose.

She wanted to hold his hand.

He bobbed his head in a gesture for her to follow. His back garden looked like hers but with a roof over their heads. There were four chairs, a small table, and, from what she could tell, marigolds and dahlias growing off to the sides. There was a little shed with the door shut and a swing set. She wondered if it was for his nieces.

"The swing set is fascinating," she noted as she sat down and took a sip of her drink.

"Built it for my nieces," he replied. He eyed the shed. "And I'm afraid all you'll find in there are toys," he chuckled.

Violet smiled, wondering then what his sister was like. She couldn't recall seeing a photo of her. She imagined a child when he talked about her, but they would be close in age, so that was a silly thought. And then her mind trailed again, wondering what Ben was like as an uncle, what he would be like as a father. She had long abandoned the prospect of having children after learning that Dean was infertile. Another thing that wasn't in the cards for her, she had accepted.

Thunder roared above them, and the rain began to fall harder. She was itching to ask about his day. Maybe if she brought it up subtly, he'd vent about the things bothering him. Perhaps he'd loosen up. Or maybe he'd be frustrated with her for prying.

"Tough day at work?" she inquired—*subtle, real subtle, Violet.*

"No more than usual," he replied, taking a big gulp of this drink. Was this the second? The third? The fourth? "You should come by sometime. We're close to the school, you know," he added.

"Oh, I didn't realize that. I've been before, years ago. Does Florence still own it?" she asked.

"She does, yeah. When was the last time you were there?"

She thought about it for a beat. "Oh man, it's been ages. Maybe about twelve years ago. After Nan died and before I got married, I spent Christmases with the Henrys; I think the last time I was here was then. We went to Edinburgh the years before I got married because Simone had given birth to Phoebe, then later Colin."

She paused for a moment, wanting to know precisely when he moved here, but she was hesitant to ask. She dodged the thought every time it came to her: Was he here during that last visit? She didn't remember the older gentleman who lived here having anyone else with him.

"Were you—?" she started to ask, then stopped herself.

"I came here permanently eleven years ago after Dad's stroke," he said, thankfully comprehending what she meant to ask. He swallowed. "We used to spend the holidays up in Bristol with my sister's family. Change of scenery for him."

Violet unclenched her shoulders, not realizing she'd been stiff as a rock the past minute or so. "And how long had your father been here?"

"Maybe about eighteen years, if I remember correctly? He moved to Bath when my sister and I moved out. He hated the city."

Violet's breath hitched in her throat. The older gentleman was Ben's father.

Christ. All these years—he'd been so bloody close, and yet...

"I met your father, Ben," she admitted nervously.

He didn't say anything. Instead, he gave Violet a look that said go on. *How?*

"Aunt Helen had me take him gooseberry pie one year. I'd seen him around in the front garden; he always said hello. But that was my only close encounter with him." She shut her eyes, remembering it all—the look on the gentleman's face as he smiled and thanked her. He was a bit taller than Ben, certainly over six feet, and he was lean with greying hair, a neatly groomed beard, piercing blue eyes, and a defined bone structure.

Of course. Blimey, she should've known. But how could she have?

"Can't believe I'm envious of my dead father," he said with a playful huff.

"He was kind," she started to say. "Granted, Aunt Helen doesn't give pies to just anyone, but it was the way he spoke. He had a booming sort of edge to him and a gentleness all at once." She smiled at him, marveling at the man in front of her— grateful to have another piece of him this way.

"I see where you get it now," she finally said.

"I'm a bit amazed you remember such a brief interaction."

She laughed. "Cursed with a good memory, remember? It's quite awful most of the time. But in this case, I'm grateful for it."

They were quiet as they watched more of the rain fall. She dreamed of this. In the early days after her parents died, she'd comfort herself with thoughts of the future she wanted. A loving man beside her who'd sit with her as the rain came pouring down. She watched her parents do it all the time, and she'd fall asleep in one of their arms.

The house she and Dean lived in was spacious. Inside and out. They had the kind of massive garden people yearned for, plus the front porch from all her dreams, yet, she never went out there with him. She'd go there on the nights when he was working late, and she'd cry alongside the lighting. They'd never watched television together, and they hardly ate dinner at the same time. Violet was the house's lone occupant most days, and it never felt like home, no matter how much she tried to make it so.

She missed her flat with Simone constantly, and even during the first year when she and Dean could somewhat be considered newlyweds, she never felt at ease. She was playing a part on a familiar sort of stage from which she'd never have her swan song. Rather, she'd start over the following day until eventually running herself to the ground.

This wasn't even her home. It was Ben's. Yet, sitting with him underneath the night sky and boisterous thunder felt right. She felt safe and free.

He wasn't looking at the rain or her. He had his eyes shut for a few beats, and when he finally opened them, he turned to her. His gaze was so warm that it made her heart ache. The hard edges from earlier were a little less rough.

"When did he pass?" Violet asked. She couldn't remember if Aunt Helen had told her that detail.

Ben's eyes went elsewhere, even as he turned to her. "September 2nd marked three years. His mobility was never the same."

She smiled serenely. "I'm sure it was nice having you close by."

"He was certainly glad I left the agency for it," Ben remarked. "He and I...we were too damn alike; it was tough at times, but we were closer than ever in those last few years."

She gathered he didn't talk about his father much. Ben's reservations were both daunting and heartbreaking. She wanted to be a safe space for him.

She wanted to reach forward and hold his hand.

"I'm glad you two got closer. Having a chance to say goodbye is a rare, odd sort of gift."

He smiled easily. "So am I. He was the best man I ever knew, Violet. Truly. I don't think I would've ever forgiven myself if he and I weren't on good terms."

They were quiet for a beat. She continued to think of his father, saying a silent thanks to the heavens that he was granted the time to say goodbye. It was a chance she always wished she could have with her parents. Saying goodbye made mourning Nan easier. In her final few days, Violet constantly spent every day showering her with affection, begging her for stories she could hold onto and spending as much time with her as possible.

Ben sighed deeply. "I'm really glad you're here, Violet," he disclosed. The confession was so earnest that she could feel it. Her name was a benediction on his lips. The only thing stopping her from reaching over and taking his hand was the fact that she wasn't yet divorced. *Don't you dare feel guilty,* Simone had told her, reminding her of the number of women Dean slept with in the last two years while lying to her. *You deserve good things, Vi,* she would've said if she knew what was transpiring at this moment. It wasn't so much that she felt guilty, but she didn't want anything tainting even a single moment between her and Ben.

If anything were to happen with Ben, she wanted it untarnished. And yet, as she heard him say those words aloud, she wanted to throw every rational thought out into the storm. She couldn't reply to him. If she tried, she was scared she'd bare it all. But she couldn't stay idle either.

She suddenly felt wetness on her face, realizing in utter humiliation that it wasn't from the rain. For the love of all things wonderful, why were there tears coming out of her eyes?

Just say I'm glad to be here, too; it's that simple, she berated herself internally. Her body suddenly betrayed her, and she rose from her seat, walking the short step over to where Ben was still sitting. She gestured for him to get up, and when he stood, she did the unthinkable. She wrapped her arms around his frame.

You could've just held his hand, you bloody idiot. What are you doing? But that wouldn't be enough—not when she'd longed to do this from the moment she walked in and felt somewhere deep in her soul that he needed it.

His grip around her tightened, and a hand trailed to her head in a cradling manner. She could hear his heartbeat fight for regularity, and she heard him catch a colossal breath. She wanted to look at him, but instead, she clasped a little harder, loosening her grip only when she heard the thumping of his chest find its perfect cadence.

Whatever this was, whatever was happening, they might not need words to discuss later. Perhaps, they would forget about it tomorrow morning. But for now, she'd hold him until he forced her to let go or he broke the silence with words.

17

BEN

His world illuminated for the first time during this bizarre, achingly confounding day. One minute he was telling Violet he was glad to have her near, and the next, he was watching a tearful woman stand before him, gesturing for him to rise. He had no idea what was happening until moments ago when his heart started beating at a seemingly regular pace.

Violet was holding him with her arms wrapped tight around his back. It felt like a friendly sort of embrace, but he longed for it to mean more. Could it? If she divorced her husband, would he stand a chance? Could he hold her like this all the time?

Christ, why hadn't he visited his father during the holiday season more?

If he were the one to open the door that day, perhaps they would've been the married pair now. He took a deep breath and inhaled the scent of what he gathered must've been her shampoo—lilacs and something he couldn't name. It was intoxicating. He wanted nothing more than to turn his head and press a kiss to her temple—the same spot he had trailed his lips against sixteen years ago. He wanted to hold her face in his hands and ask her if a future together was possible, if not now, then perhaps someday.

He wanted to hold her like this forever.

He wanted to sit back down on the chair, lower her to his lap and watch the rain fall until one or both of them fell asleep to the lulling sounds of its melody.

Somehow, the weight in his chest had eased. It was still there but a little less heavy and demanding. His mind was quieter for a beat.

They stood in each other's arms for a few moments until he finally spoke with a low whisper in her ear. "Does this mean you're glad to be here, too?" he asked, smiling against her temple.

She looked at him then and smiled the shy sort of smile that wrecked his entire damned world and nodded, charting her fingers along his shoulder. She was looking at him with such reverence that it made him want to melt.

She sighed so quietly that he might not have noticed if he wasn't so hyper-aware of her. "I know you said you were just knackered, but I couldn't shake that there was something else bothering you," she noted. "I'm sorry. I just..." Violet exhaled again, heavier this time, before looking down.

He dropped one hand from her waist, still holding her steady with the other. He trailed a hand to cup her cheek, then stopped abruptly and put it down. Time seemed to have slowed. He was terrified of what he might do if he allowed himself to get closer than they already were. And he didn't want to cross any more boundaries than he already had.

"You're right. There is. And you've helped. Trust me. As I said, I'm glad you're here," he repeated, hoping she would realize that whatever this was, it was all in her hands. Ben imagined he was shit at hiding how much he wanted her, but he wasn't going to pretend he didn't either. He sucked at that sort of subtlety.

She smiled at him. "I like being here as well...with you," she affirmed quietly. An intense wave of sadness crashed on her expression then. "But I wish it were under different circumstances."

"What do you mean?"

"All of it. My divorce. The amount of time that's passed. I just...I wish it were different."

He could tell that this was hard for her to admit, and he didn't want to press her further. She was somehow still here, and that mattered more than anything. He'd take up all opportunities he could to spend time with her, so long as she wanted that. He wouldn't push.

Not now. Not ever.

He released the hand still resting against her waist, nodded in agreement, and sat back down. "I thought we were supposed to celebrate your job offer, by the way," he said, changing the topic entirely.

She held up her glass, took a final sip, and said, "We did," showing him both their empty glasses.

He chuckled as she continued to gaze straight toward the rain.

Her words about the quiet in-between often echoed in his head. He wondered if she had told that very story to anyone else and how they reacted to it.

Ben wanted to give her the world. He would find a way if she asked for it.

"I should get going," she said, turning to face him.

He wished she wouldn't. He wanted her to stay. He'd always want her to stay. He was sure of it now more than ever when nothing else made sense but the sound of her voice and the resuscitating jolts of her embrace.

"I'll walk you out," he replied, watching as she picked up both their glasses to take them inside. It was little moments like this that evoked contentment deep inside of him—the comfort of her in his space, all around him.

He watched as she walked out of his kitchen and swiftly put her boots on without bending over. He was certainly glad for that.

She was looking at him like she wanted to say something. Her lips were parted, and her eyes were searching his. "Ben, if you have a bad day, or if you...I don't know. If you need anything, I'm not going anywhere."

His lips pulled upward, and he nodded. "The same goes for you, then?"

She concurred.

~

It was two in the morning, and he couldn't sleep.

The art of asking a woman out felt foreign to him. But more than anything, it was Violet. He couldn't mess this up. He didn't even know what to do or how to make sense of the situation they were in.

He knew he could confide in his sister, but he didn't want to get her involved yet. Instead, he double-checked the time difference and picked up his phone to ring Edmund on a video call. The line on the other end continued beeping, and he really hoped Edmund wasn't busy. He felt directionless working this out alone, and there was no one else whose opinion he could trust.

"Mate!" Edmund bellowed on the other end of the screen. "I've been meaning to call you. Shit's been so busy here. I think this is the longest we've gone."

Ben chuckled. "It really has been, yeah."

"We just put the kids to bed. Nina's still there. You alright?"

"Good, yeah, I guess," he started to say. "I...I don't even know where to begin with what I have to tell you."

Edmund's eyes went wide on the screen. "Oh fuck. There's a woman, isn't there?"

"It's Violet," Ben blurted.

His friend blinked rapidly, furrowing his brows, almost like he was trying to determine if he heard correctly. "Violet, as in, the flight attendant? *That* Violet?"

Ben nodded continually. "The very one."

Edmund's mouth was wide open in a cartoonish kind of way. "What about her?"

Ben leaned back on the sofa and sighed. "She's my neighbor."

Edmund brought the camera closer to his face. "Brother, if my kids weren't sleeping, I'd scream. What the ever-loving fuck do you mean, she's your neighbor?"

Ben closed his eyes, biting the inside of his cheek. "Get this. You know Mrs. Henry, my landlord. You've met her a few times."

"Right, yeah."

"Violet is her daughter's best friend and has been since they were four. She moved to the house next door."

Edmund shook his head and sighed. "You're fucking joking me."

"Nope," Ben said emphatically.

Edmund's mouth fell open again. It was ridiculous. "I need my wife and booze to deal with what you're telling me. This shit doesn't happen in real life, mate. What the fuck?"

Ben huffed. "You're telling me. My damn head's all over the place. I don't know what to do about it."

Edmund pursed his lips. "I need to get Nina. Hold on," he noted before setting the phone to face his ceiling.

Few things gave Ben hope the way Edmund's relationship

with Nina did. The two had endured countless hurdles to find their calm, beautiful life. Everything felt possible when looking at them—even the prospect of him and Violet. It's why he needed to talk to him. Well, them now.

He faintly heard their whispers drawing closer before they picked up the phone and plopped on the sofa, setting themselves up in the camera frame.

Nina's smile radiated. "Ben! What on earth is this man trying to tell me?" she questioned, pointing to Edmund with her thumb. "The woman from Paris is your neighbor?"

"Hey Neen, you alright?"

"I'm flummoxed, is what I am."

Ben sighed intensely. "Yeah, she's my neighbor, and things are a bit complicated with her."

Nina tilted her head. "Complicated how?"

He licked his lips, biting down. "She's getting a divorce from her piece-of-shit ex-husband, who might make things difficult. What do I do?" he said, sounding small and vulnerable but not giving a damn.

Nina took the phone from Edmund and fixed her eyes on him. "Be truthful. Christ, I...I don't even know, but in a situation like this, all you have is honesty, Ben. How's it been? Have you been seeing each other, even as friends?"

"Yeah. A lot, actually. I've been taking her biscuits cause of this whole...long story with Simone, Mrs. Henry's daughter. And Violet was over at my place tonight. There was a moment. She said she wished things were different, her circumstances, us...time...I don't know," he shook his head, rattling his mind.

Edmund's jaw seemed to be stuck open. Nina's expression was joyous before she spoke. "I want details, but I almost feel like that's making you more confused, but look. You know our story. You know that this bellend said to me, 'If we weren't coworkers would you date me?' And I said, 'Sure.' And then he proceeded to annoy me until I changed all my rules for him. Ultimately, just be honest with her. Ask her if there's a chance for the two of you."

Ben listened intently.

Nina was examining the situation. She was silent for a beat. "Thing is, Ben, divorce is fucking hard. And trusting afterward is even harder. It's not going to be easy for her. But you're not a stranger, so maybe that will help. Hopefully, she felt the same way you did when the two of you parted. But you won't know that until you tell her you are interested in an actual relationship when she's ready." She shrugged her shoulders. "That's the best you can do. And then be patient with her, which we all know that you will be."

He bit the knuckle on his thumb and sighed deeply. "Yeah, you're right."

Edmund had put his head on her shoulder. A little less in shock now, seemingly. "She usually is. I stopped trying to argue that fact after our second date."

Nina rolled her eyes. "It was more like our twelfth, babe, but nice way of sucking up."

Ben smirked. "I fucking miss you both," he said after a beat.

"I don't think you understand how much I miss you, mate. To the point where kids can't wait til we're back during Christmas because I've been telling them stories about our job," he gestured the last word with air quotes.

Ben raised his eyebrows. "You've been what now?"

"Not all the details. We were computer makers who went on missions. They'll forget it in a few years."

"You're daft, you know that?" Ben said to his friend.

Edmund bobbed his head and winked.

"Everything good with you lot otherwise?" Ben asked.

Nina smiled. "Yeah, work is a bit wild, but other than that. Counting the hours til break."

"Aren't we all...I'll let you two go."

Nina moved closer to the camera. "Go sleep!"

"I'll try," Ben noted.

"Keep us updated, Ben Grant, or so help me God, I will fly my arse there and make this happen myself. I'm not about to spend another twenty bloody years watching you pine after this woman," Edmund said.

"It's been sixteen, mate. Not twenty."

He sneered. "Ah, same shit. The point is, it's been too long. You deserve to be happy."

Ben nodded. "Talk soon."

"Goodnight," they both said, nearly in unison; it was nauseating and adorable all at once.

18

VIOLET

"It's silly to think about how one person, after a short time, could become such an enormous part of you," Violet started to say, laying her head dramatically on the table. "Everyone I met after him paled in comparison; all I could think was, why aren't you Ben?" She sighed, holding back the tears begging to surge through. She was also still panting from the run she went on, thinking it'd relieve some of her pent-up emotions, only it made them far worse.

Helen, the woman who always knew everything before anyone told her, was genuinely stumped. She placed a cup of coffee on the table and stared. "What are you talking about?"

Violet raised her head and wrapped her hands around the giant red mug. It was one of her favorites, and Aunt Helen knew it, buying it for her years ago, stating, "Just like that lipstick you always wear."

She took a small sip of the hot coffee, a tiny bit of milk, just how she liked it. "Ben," she said, pointing toward the direction of his house with her thumb.

Helen Henry was looking at her like she was speaking a different language. "And what of him?"

Violet tilted her head and squinted. "Do you really not know the story? Aunt Helen, you figure everything out!"

"Apparently not *this*. Now spit it out," she declared, walking over to sit beside Violet.

Violet told Aunt Helen the entire thing, sparing details about the actual case, red lipstick stains on his neck, and heated kisses with their bodies clasped together against travertine limestone.

Aunt Helen's expression revealed a mixture of surprise and, perhaps, relief.

"I didn't even know him, not really anyway. I knew an MI6 agent. I wasn't even convinced Ben Grant was his real name, but every part of me held on to that look in his eyes. He saw me in a way no one else ever had. It was only a few days—one perfect kiss with gargoyles staring down at us, and I could never let him go." Violet paused, allowing tears to fall freely now.

"Gargoyles scream romance, don't you know?" Helen replied, reaching over to gently brush the tears from Violet's eyes.

She heaved a little. "There's no romance when you're in your forties and running from your ex-husband."

"Child, there's romance even if you're in your eighties. Enough of that poppycock."

Violet took another sip of her coffee and swallowed. She cleared her throat before asking, "Do you like him? As you know, a person?"

Helen's expression was stern. It concerned her, but not more than the look she gave Violet before she married Dean. There was disappointment in her eyes then and loads of sadness, too. She hated it.

Violet took a deep breath, her legs bouncing under the table.

Helen arched an eyebrow, sipping her coffee before she spoke. "Do you remember what I told you the day before you got married?"

"You said you wanted me to have the same kind of love my

parents did, the one you and Uncle Thomas have. You said you wanted me to find someone worth risking it all for, like Peter is for Simone." Violet repeated.

"And do you remember what you said to me?"

"Vaguely."

"You said, 'All the kind men are taken, Aunt Helen. This is the best I'll do.'"

Violet looked down, remembering the moment clear as day now. "You walked away from me then. You were so disappointed."

"I was," Helen said sternly. "I still am."

Violet made a small pout. "What'd I do now?"

"You still don't know how to trust yourself."

Violet protested. "Yes, I do."

Helen crossed her arms and stared.

"Oh, for Christ's sake, stop looking at me like that, Aunt Helen. Will you just tell me if you like the man?" Violet exclaimed fondly.

"Do you?" Helen asked matter-of-factly.

Violet threw her arms up in the air. "Well, I wouldn't be sitting here begging for your input if I didn't."

"And what do you like about him?" she asked.

"Aunt Helen, I know you love me, so I'm not going to question that, but why do you insist on torturing me? I'm not twelve anymore."

She took her coffee mug in her hand and wagged a forefinger before taking a sip. "Stop acting like it, then. And don't ask me a question before you've answered mine."

She sighed and set her head down again. "Everything," she mumbled.

"I can't hear you..." Helen singsonged.

Violet raised her head and looked Helen square in the eyes.

She let out another heavy sigh, trying to catch her breath from the torrent of emotions circulating in her.

"Everything, Aunt Helen. I like *everything* about him. I like how gentle he is and how he looks at me like every word out of my mouth is a new discovery. I like how kind he is, truly in every way. I like his whole face and his maddeningly perfect beard, and I like how he makes me feel safe."

Helen smiled then and took Violet's hand in hers. It was soothing and filled her with the kind of comfort that made Violet count her lucky stars. "That's because he is kind and gentle, and he's a lot like his father. He never remarried or anything of the sort, you know? He could have. He was younger than Ben is now when his wife died, but he loved her until his final breath, and he couldn't bear the thought of sharing his life with someone else. Ben is very much the same."

"He dated someone for a while before his father died," Violet said.

"I heard about that. But you know as well as I do that there are people in this world who would rather be alone than open their space to others. Frankly, you were a lot like that. I never quite understood what changed," she replied, a sad smile following suit.

"Being alone and sad got a lot scarier at some point. I started thinking I was the problem. And Dean wasn't bad, especially not at first."

Helen scoffed. "You were a trophy to him, love. He wanted you because he couldn't have you, and when he finally got you, all he wanted to do was parade you around to make himself look better."

Helen had always been transparent about not trusting or liking Dean, but those feelings escalated after she learned how miserable Violet truly was.

The older woman sighed. "I don't think I need to answer

whether I like Ben or not. He wouldn't be living here if I had problems with him. But you know deep inside of you that to a man like him, the woman he chooses to marry will be his greatest treasure, never a trophy."

Violet simply nodded. It was all she could do at this point. Helen was right. If Ben chose to marry someone, they'd be revered and adored. She wanted to be that someone, but she was scared—wholly terrified to risk losing him in any capacity. It could be better to hold onto the memories, to deem him as the one who got away and romanticize what they had then.

"Thanks, Aunt Helen. For all of it," she emphasized.

"You can thank me by taking Freddy in the afternoon? I have a check-up in London, so Tom and I will be making a trip of it before coming back tomorrow."

Alarms rang in Violet's ear suddenly. "A check-up? For what? Are you okay?"

"Oh, calm down. It's a routine check-up. You know I'm always on top of these things. I figured since you're here and available, we could leave him with you."

"But what if I wasn't free?" Violet laughed.

"Except you are."

Violet scrunched her nose and smirked. "Always and only for you, Aunt Helen."

"Good," she said sternly. "You can take him on your way home."

19

———

BEN

He had held Violet last night and gone into the following day fixated on the ease of being with her. The favorable experience made for a more productive work shift than the one before. After a successful run with pumpkin Welsh cakes, Billy's latest attempt was a seven-layer concoction he called the "stacked pumpkin cup." For as great as Billy was at managing the social media account along with his baking, he was shit at coming up with creative titles. He'd shrug it off and say, "I'm not a writer."

Still, as much as Ben wanted to protest the new additions, his mind was consistently elsewhere, spinning in circles as Violet consumed the very fabric of his being. When he closed his eyes, he could feel her arms around him—he could smell the lilacs, feel the velvety texture of her hair against his palms.

He was home now, fixing a loose nail on his floorboard, when he heard her.

"For the love of God, Freddy. Stop staring at the butterfly, and let's go!" She wasn't loud or commanding, but either their street was uncommonly quiet, or he was too focused on her. *Freddy? Mrs. Henry's dog?* Where were they going, he thought, wanting nothing more than to drop everything and go with her. He had delivered the biscuits to her bright and early again this morning but hadn't seen her when he got home in the afternoon.

This desperation to be by her side constantly was both exciting and agonizing. He couldn't keep doing this. He should be satisfied from her touch, and yet, all he wanted was to be in the same space as her.

He heard the jingling collar before they drew near, and he caught a glimpse of her. She wore a cognac long-sleeve, black denim jeans that sat above her ankle, and white trainers. Her hair was tied back in a loose bun, and a few wisps hung at the front.

Ben might've been able to get away with staying quiet without Violet spotting him, but Freddy was eagerly barking in his direction while wagging his tail. "First time he's stayed with me, but everyone else seems more riveting than I am," Violet said with a slight chuckle.

He tsked, knowing that was far from the case, but more the fact that he always had a treat for Freddy when he saw him. "Where are you two headed?"

She wore a shy sort of smile before saying, "Walking him along the skyline."

"May I join you?" he asked, hoping she'd say no, but wanting desperately to hear a *yes*.

She nodded keenly. "Of course."

He held up his forefinger to wordlessly ask that she give him a few seconds. "You've got to pull yourself together, man," he said aloud to himself in a low voice she wouldn't hear. He grabbed an extra house key he had so he wouldn't have to take the jumbled stack with the restaurant keys. He then quickly walked over to his cupboard, took the treats for Freddy, locked the door, and walked toward them.

The Goldendoodle nearly bolted from her hands in excitement, and while Mrs. Henry was certainly used to the reaction, it stunned Violet. He watched as she swiftly took control of the leash and stood her ground. "Will you wait for the man to get closer before you lose it? Jesus, Freddy," she retorted.

The statement and utter seriousness in her expression made him laugh. He instinctively put his hand on her bicep as if to apologize, then set it down even quicker. "It's my fault entirely. I've spoiled him too much."

"I've never known an eleven-year-old Goldendoodle with so much energy. He's too wild for his own good," she said. He could tell she watched intently as he bent over and played with the pup. Freddy looked up at her then as if hearing the comment. She looked him square in the eyes and changed her pitch, "Yes, I called you wild, you adorable little fur ball," she cooed.

After excitedly eating, Freddy led the way. A minute later, she turned to him and, with a big, glowing smile, asked how his day was.

He stared at her for a beat. "Better than yesterday. And yours?"

She jolted from another one of Freddy's sharp tugs. "Well, for starters, if I had known I'd be dog-sitting this tiny monster, I wouldn't have gone for a run at the break of dawn. I might not be able to move tomorrow morning. I'll report back if that's the case," she said with a little laugh.

"You run?"

"Yeah, and I hate it with a burning passion. You know how people say eventually you'd love it?" She grimaced and shook her head. "Nope, never. I've been running since I was twenty-two, and I *still* hate it."

"Why'd you start then?"

"Well, at the time, working out was a suggestion from my therapist—dopamine and all that. But I was so tired of reaching up and down at work that I couldn't be bothered to work out my upper body. So, I decided to run. She was right. It helps. I still hate it."

It took everything in him not to look at her legs at that moment. He remembered how they looked in the red dress. But at the same time, when he thought about that night, all he could focus on was her nearness and the feel of her body against his.

"Fair. If my mate Liam didn't own the local gym, I would've probably opted for outdoor exercise, too."

"It sucks when the weather isn't great, but I'm not one to move regardless when it's raining out. It's the best time for me and my books."

He chuckled.

"Was work really better today?" she asked warmly.

"I suppose so. Billy, my junior chef, was right about some of the pumpkin stuff. They're a hit with the customers."

She giggled and gasped simultaneously. "Don't tell me you gave in to something abysmal like pumpkin spice hummus, Ben."

"No. Fuck no. For now, just Welsh cakes and some sort of a six, maybe, seven-layer atrocity in a cup," he said with a shrug.

"I'm going to have to try them, aren't I? Look, as much as I hate it, the Americans were right about freaking avocado toast. They could be right about pumpkins, too. But wait, I have a question—where is he getting the puree?"

He smiled at the thought of learning another thing about her. She liked avocado toast. He'd be lying to himself if he said he didn't like it, too. But the idea of her wanting to try the desserts made them sound far more appetizing.

"I can't lose you to the other side, Violet. But come by tomorrow or whenever, and I've got you. And he's ordering them on the bloody web. He did it without telling me first."

She nodded in agreement. "I have to go get some supplies for the house. I will after."

His insides were in knots suddenly. The thought of seeing Violet at the restaurant did something inexplicable to him. Whatever this was, it was becoming more familiar and natural. She was staying in Bath, building a life right next door to him.

She made a mess of him, and every semblance of control he'd mustered through the years would go out the door in a second if she wanted him. And that was far more nerve-wracking than anything he'd done for the agency. If he somehow had to say goodbye to her again, he was certain he wouldn't be able to trek forward as he did before.

Even if she didn't want him, he wondered if it'd be enough just to be near her. Except, the mere thought of her finding someone and settling down made him recoil in anguish. That would be worse than a goodbye, he realized, shaking his head to invalidate the thoughts he didn't want to give attention to.

"Aunt Helen said she walks him all the way up to the skyline, then back down every day. Her spoiled little boy deserves his exercise, I suppose, though falling asleep on the ground sounds a lot more appealing right now," she said, pulling him out of his thoughts.

He chuckled and looked down. "Want me to at least run back and grab you a blanket or...three for comfort?"

"That'd be much appreciated," she joked. She smiled at him then, gazing a bit more intently than she had earlier.

It was killing him.

Freddy made a noise, prompting her to look away and at the leaf he'd suddenly started dragging under one of his paws.

"I can't wait until more trees turn and leaves fall," she said with a voice so small and so hopeful it made his heart squeeze.

She smiled and tilted her head a bit to look at him again.

"You know how when some people are upset, they picture a beach or a spacious place?"

He nodded.

"I always picture autumn, the vibrant trees, and foliage covering the earth. We had a park by the flat we lived in from age ten to when my parents died. Dad would take me there and throw me in the mountain of leaves. He did it til I was about twelve," she chuckled. "That's where I go when I'm upset—into the leaves, under a big, fiery red maple tree."

They walked in silence for a beat as he thought about her words and tried to picture her place of comfort. He imagined a little girl with the same laugh and quiet confidence.

"What about you?" she asked, her inquisitive eyes peering into his soul.

He cleared his throat and swallowed. Ben opened his mouth to respond, but she interrupted. "You don't have to answer if you don't want to," she added.

He thought about it a little harder. "No, it's just, I don't reckon I've considered it before...But if I did, it was always the inside of our home. Mum and I, in the kitchen, as I tried mimicking her every move. Dad watching a football game. My sister's first steps...those little memories."

"There's beauty in those little moments. I think I held onto autumn because my mum loved it so much that she always made sure it was memorable for us. And as the years went on, I understood why she adored it so much. There's a magic in the air that's hard to describe."

He wanted to stop them in their tracks and wrap his arms around her. He wanted to find every leaf in the city and bring it to her front garden. He wanted to plant maple trees all along her path. He wanted with such desperation that the desires alone scared him that much more.

"I wonder if that's why the restaurant is the only job I've ever fully liked," he returned. "My mum worked at The Auburn Cafe in London for years. She'd commute even when we moved a bit further out of the city."

She smiled at him. "I don't think you told me what your sister does; is she in the culinary world as well?"

"No, Emma's an obstetrician."

"Ah, that's lovely," she said.

As the rest of their short route followed with further silence, he continued to watch her marvel at their surroundings.

When they finally reached the top, she took a deep breath. Warm colors were finding their way into the edges where the city kissed the sky. The sun was beginning to set, with an afterglow sprouting gorgeous hues of pinks and oranges. Even the apex of St. Matthew's Church and the hills surrounding them felt more magnified. They were the only ones standing there at the moment.

He adored it here before, but it was different today.

He looked back at her, more mesmerizing than any view.

"My God, I'd forgotten what a beauty it was. I think..." she started. "The last time I was here had to have been before I started working as a flight attendant."

He smiled at the words. He felt them to this core.

"She is," he said, looking at Violet parallel to the skyline.

Other than the restaurant, it was one of the few reasons he hadn't moved after his father passed because coming to the skyline when nothing else made sense was restorative.

It suddenly dawned on him that though it wasn't a part of his childhood or adolescence, this was his escape—the skyline and now Violet. He looked over to the bench he'd often occupy, wanting to beg her to stay with him here and accompany him on walks every bloody day and night.

They could make this place their own and find the same languid serenity that they had in Paris.

She was still looking around, and he noticed that her fingers were more tightly curled on Freddy's leash than before. She was transfixing—the awestruck wonder in her eyes made his heart clench and release every coil that'd been there for years, all at once. He was a goner now. Bath never felt safer or more enchanting than it did right at this very moment.

He turned from her and closed his eyes, trying to catch and release his breath from everything stirring within him. When he turned back, she was wiping a tear from her eyes.

She smiled when she caught his concern and said, "I'm fine. I just... it's the first time I've felt at home here."

So did he.

He moved the short step over to her and placed his palm on the backside of her dangling hand.

He would only move further once she permitted him to—if she turned or initiated an obvious gesture.

Violet gently turned her hand, palm-to-palm, and slowly laced her warm fingers with his. He squeezed her hand, longing desperately to kiss it as he had in Paris. He felt selfish and horrible, yet he couldn't care less about any of those things.

He bit the inside of his bottom lip and felt his heart thud more ferociously in his chest.

Freddy was now standing between them, staring at him in a way that made him feel judged. He barked twice before they parted and looked down at him.

She bent lower and played with his floppy ears, saying things like, "Was I not giving you enough attention, you needy little fuzz ball?" Freddy was panting with excitement and far more pride than he should've had.

Dammit, he was jealous of a dog. *A dog.* He had to have known what he did.

And maybe it was for the best.

Violet rose back to her feet, and he was sure that if she didn't put on sunglasses or avert her gaze to hide that wondrous look in her eyes, he was going to explode. He swallowed and took a deep breath.

"Ben."

"Violet."

They called each other at the same time.

"Go ahead," he said.

"Go on," she said.

"No, you," then followed in tandem. They both laughed, and she shook her head. "Go on, please."

Please. The way she said it killed him.

He blinked.

"Violet, do we have a chance? After your divorce is finalized. I—I don't know if you'd ever want any of it again, but I figured I'd ask," he said finally.

The dazzling wonder in her eyes was replaced with another expression then—something sad and concerning with a hint of relief. *Had he said too much? Was this too soon? Was their time in Paris more haunting and beautiful for him than it was for her?* He'd be losing her, having had only less than a fraction of her to begin with.

She looked over at Freddy, who was playing with a lone dandelion growing from the grass. She stepped closer to him, curling the leash in her hand. Violet shook her head slightly as she flicked her eyes back to him and smiled.

She was biting her bottom lip, sending him into a torturous spiral with the uncertainty of what was going to follow.

She took a deep breath, a myriad of emotions cascading through her blue eyes, then bursting through her widening smile. She nodded subtly. "Yes. I...I want it to be done first..." she started. "Dean cheated on me frequently. He...uh, he doesn't know that I've drawn up divorce papers, and I don't want to be like him. I don't want to start something while he isn't aware that I've left him," she finished with a sad smile.

It was a piece of her puzzle that made him see blazing red.

How could he have her and cheat on her? How did the bloody moron not realize what a fortunate bastard he was?

Ben was certain fumes were releasing from every part of him because Violet suddenly cupped his cheek. Her sweet gaze tried to hold the humanity he was mere inches away from shedding completely. "He didn't break me, and he doesn't deserve my pity either, but I want a clean slate with you. Just as it was in Paris."

He nodded with understanding, extricating the breath stuck in his throat. "Was it obvious that I was planning to ram his head through the ground?"

She stroked his cheek delicately, fingers running carefully against his beard. "A little. I thought your eyebrows were going to pop off your face," she said with a small chuckle.

Freddy barked again, nudging her to move. She released her hand from his face and smiled at him one last time.

It'd be enough for now.

"Wait, what were you going to say? Earlier." He had to know.

She sighed, looking toward Freddy and then back to the skyline. "I was going to thank you for coming with me. It feels right here. Beside you."

He would go anywhere she asked. Whenever. Wherever.

He reached forward, moving the stray hairs that'd been blowing in front of her eyes. He lightly brushed her cheek and chin in their place. "Anytime."

He'd rein in his desires until she was no longer tied to someone else, and then he'd make sure every day of the rest of her life was full of the magic she deserved.

20

VIOLET

Violet spent the following morning, indeed, hating the fact that bodies weren't invincible. As predicted, her legs were killing her. She'd also spent the morning in her bed for minutes longer than usual because Freddy was nestled so closely to her back that she couldn't bear the thought of moving him.

While yesterday's biscuit delivery note read:

> *I've obliged and only given you three this time. This pains me, you know!*

Today's said:

> *Three for you and the rest for Aunt Helen when she returns. If you come by the restaurant after your errands, ask for me!*

Somehow, four days in, Violet was sure she would marry these biscuits if possible. It was deliriously inebriating to think of what else he could make, and if, at any point, the man brought sticky toffee pudding into the mix, she was sure she might actually "collapse and die." Simone's words, not hers.

There were few things in the world Violet loved more than sticky toffee pudding, and apparently, Jammie Dodgers biscuits had entered the equation.

It was a crisp morning, and though the high was thirteen degrees Celsius, the drop in humidity made the air feel much more delectably piercing. Remembering how nice it felt to wear the "Evermore Rouge" lipstick again the other day at her interview, Violet decided she'd put it back on today.

It'd been ages since she allowed herself to delight in the prospect of love—ages since she believed in its possibilities. Ben wanted a chance to be with her. He was still interested in her, as she was in him, making her dreams the night before steamier.

And though nothing had happened yet—nothing was set in stone, his kind, familiar eyes held her steady yesterday, turning to fury at the mention of what Dean had done to her. It was the very expression he wore in the plane as Agent Williams— commanding and minacious for justified reasons.

Yet, she wasn't anxious about seeing Ben again until she crossed Pulteney Bridge and saw The Crooked Branch on the other side. She was suddenly engulfed with anxiety, like a kid on the first day at a new school, but it made little sense logically. The Crooked Branch was his place of work. The people here knew him longer than she had—better than she did. What if they didn't like her?

She made her way to the steps, positively grinning at the exterior decorations once she got closer. Crooked branches, rightfully so, and faux auburn and rustic amber leaves hanging at their sides with muted greens intermingled in between. She wondered if The Crooked Branch was the type of restaurant to change their look depending on the season they were in or if they were a place reserved for perpetual autumn.

It was Christmas when she last visited, but she didn't pay attention to decorations at the time.

She walked in, and though her supposed great memory was failing her where decorations was concerned, she was certain Florence Miller had stayed the same since. She was a little older, but the fire was still boldly visible, and she radiated warmth in a way that reminded Violet of Nan.

"Hello, pet," Florence said with a giant smile curving up her mouth. "Table for one?"

"Hi! Yes, it'll just be me. I—uh, I'm a friend of Ben's," she mentioned, stuttering a bit as she tried to keep her nerves at bay.

"You're Simone Henry's friend, aren't you?"

Violet felt a bit at ease with that question. If Florence knew she was friends with Simone, then she'd certainly know she was acquainted with the Henry family, making her feel a little less awkward. She wasn't even sure why she felt discomfited. It was all so familiar and foreign at the same time.

"I am," she confirmed with an easy smile.

Florence's smile grew wider, and she gestured with her hand for Violet to follow. "Oh, I adore the Henrys. There aren't many families like them. Seeing them every Friday is always a highlight."

"I've been with them before—years back when I visited. I remember you, actually," Violet said.

"Oh, that's lovely. I wish I could say I remember you, dove, but I'm sure I will now," she said with an amusing wink. "Our Ben said you were a friend of Simone's who might drop by, but I'm certain there's more, and one of you will likely cave."

Violet choked on her own spit. "Oh, we're...not, this is... we're just friends."

Florence guided her to a table at the restaurant's corner, tucked next to a massive window overlooking the water. She looked at Violet with a glare that said both, "Sure you are," and "I wasn't born yesterday," but she settled with, "Very well then, I'll tell Ben you're here. And I'll see you again with the Henrys on Friday."

It sounded like a vague threat of sorts, just the kind of comment she'd expect from a woman who chose to run the front of the house consistently. If Aunt Helen and Uncle Thomas came here weekly, then surely it was for a good reason.

But now that Florence was gone and Ben would arrive soon, she was nervous again. Oddly, while some people had found going to restaurants alone a bit awkward, Violet was more used to it, taking quiet mornings to herself at The Rose House for scones before work. Still, she was nervous and fidgeting, with her heart doing one somersault after another. But Florence seemed to like her; maybe others would, too.

She looked down at her phone, wanting a distraction. After a few beats, she could see a figure coming up the steps through her peripheral vision, taking two steps at a time, if she had to guess.

Ben didn't look much different at work than when she'd seen him the last few days, though she found herself disappointed in his lack of uniform. He had to have taken it off before coming up.

"You made it," he said with a brilliant smile, turning her heart's somersaults more rabid.

She tilted her head a bit. "I did! I don't think Florence buys that we're just friends. I'm also pretty sure she's threatened me to show up with Aunt Helen and Uncle Thomas every time now."

Ben chuckled. "She'd do that. I figured if I didn't explain you were Simone's best mate, she'd spend too much time trying to figure out how I knew you." He shrugged adorably. "I suppose she's doing it anyway."

"It's quite alright. She's delightful," Violet replied.

He nodded. "She really is." He mapped out her face, and it did nothing to ease her nerves; somehow, nothing would calm the ripples in her chest. "Red lipstick suits you," he added.

She swallowed and blinked twice before realizing it was the opposite of what Dean would say. *You should try a more neutral color.* "Thank you," she managed to utter.

"So, what can I get for you?" he asked.

She squared her eyebrows. Shouldn't a server be doing this? "Chefs take orders?"

"On rare occasions—for specific customers, yes."

"I haven't gotten a chance to look at the menu yet; anything you recommend? Chef's specials and all that?"

"Forget the menu. Tell me what *you* want," he emphasized.

"Now that is absurd. What if I want an unattainable dish?"

"We'll attain it," he said matter-of-factly.

She chuckled. "You're ridiculous."

"Well, for starters, are you allergic to anything?"

"Shellfish."

"Noted."

They were quiet as he waited for her to order.

"You're really going to make me do this?"

He bobbed his head.

"Fine, let's see what you're all about. I'll have avocado toast," she started, suddenly remembering the pumpkin seven-layer concoction. "Oh, and I'll try that seven-layer pumpkin thing."

He rolled his eyes. "Can I refuse the second?"

"You can, but then I'm sure Florence wouldn't be happy to hear about it."

"How do you take your avocado toast?"

"Surprise me," she replied.

"Egg or no."

"Naw, not right now."

"I'll be back," he said.

When he was out of sight, she picked up her phone to text Simone. Violet was sure she'd love this bit of news.

> **VIOLET**: At The Crooked Branch. He's making me avocado toast.
>
> **SIMONE**: Good. I hope you feel an uncontrollable urge to pay him with your lips!

Violet had yet to tell her about the conversation the day before. In truth, she wasn't ready to face it, and talking about it with Simone would require every detail. It'd become much more real, and she wanted to keep some moments to herself to figure out what was happening before setting obscenely high expectations.

He was radiating when he returned to her, yet glistening beneath the smile she was now sure Ben reserved for special moments were the nerves she was certain he felt, too. But his presentation of the food was top-notch. If she were a critic, maybe she'd have more eloquent words.

The avocados were perfectly mashed and spread to every corner of the rye bread. At first glance, Violet could spot heirloom tomatoes and balsamic glaze. It seemed to be topped with poppy seeds, minced dried garlic, and sesame seeds.

He set it down for her. "I'll leave you to it. Please let me know if I can get you anything else, yeah?"

She nodded. "It looks great, Ben. Thank you."

"Let's hope it tastes as it looks then. We're still debating adding it to the official menu."

She squared her shoulder and gestured with the fork. "Well,

I do consider myself a bit of a snob when it comes to avocados. I'll be sure to let you know."

"Promise?"

"Cross my heart."

He dipped his head and walked back. And she was partly glad about it. The pressure of eating in front of him might suffocate her at the moment.

The avocado was spread so prettily that she tried to cut it as gracefully as she possibly could so as not to ruin her lipstick. She took a bite, managing to get everything in her mouth at once. Win-win. She could feel the same ridiculous moan threatening to burst out of her throat as it did the first time she tried the biscuits.

She was thankful to repress it, yet annoyed beyond comprehension that it was to be replaced with an audible *fuck*. If she thought Ben was dangerously fit before, then God above, she wasn't prepared for what he could do with his hands in the kitchen. She would spare her thoughts from venturing elsewhere. This was already too much.

He returned with another glass of lemonade for her.

She didn't even wait until he set the glass down before blurting, "What sort of sorcery do you perform when cooking?"

A hearty laugh struck out from him, and he looked utterly satisfied by the reaction. "I take it you like it then."

"It's so unfortunately great that I'll now be dissatisfied if I ever attempt to get it elsewhere," she said, hoping that she'd never have to now.

"I'll leave you to it then. And I'll bring by the pumpkin shi-," he started and groaned lightly, "thing, the pumpkin thing."

The sentiment made her giggle. Ben hating something with such intensity was a bizarre, oddly funny sight to behold.

When he left her alone again, Violet opened the Kindle app on her phone and continued reading her book. She shook her head at coincidently finding herself in a chapter where the hero and heroine gawked at each other over a box of pizza at the beach. She hated beaches, but she wouldn't mind it if pizza and Ben were involved.

After a few minutes passed, she was approached by a young Black man who had to be in his early twenties, with a brilliant, hundred-watt smile. He was holding a small tray that held the seven-layer pumpkin dessert. This must be the junior chef, Billy, she thought.

"Hi!" he said. "I'm Billy; Ben would kill me if he knew I brought this over."

"Violet," she noted, followed by an "Oh?"

"Violet," he repeated.

It took a few short seconds before Ben was next to them. "What are you doing?" he said with a subtle eye roll toward the boy.

"Considering these are my children," he replied, pointing to the tray, "I wanted to be the one to deliver them to our guest," he said with a sardonic cheerfulness.

"And how did you know she was the one who ordered?" Ben barked out in a low tenor.

Billy's smile was so massive that Violet understood precisely why saying no to the boy was so hard.

"Because you said someone ordered it, and you've been hopping up and down here for the past thirty minutes. I doubt it's for the Camden sisters, who order the same thing every day, or the Bowen clan, who are only here for their afternoon drinks."

"Maybe the Camden sisters wanted a change," Ben added.

Violet looked back from one to the other. "Ben, stop torturing the lad. I did ask for it."

Billy set the dessert down and gestured with his hands as if to say *see, I was right.* Ben was shaking his head at the both of them, which was more amusing than anything else. It reminded her of when he mocked her love for gargoyles.

She took a small spoonful and tried it, both the men standing beside her, somehow, a little less intimidating than before. She looked at Billy, then back at Ben sheepishly. "I'm so sorry, Ben, but it's good. It's actually *really*, really good."

He shook his head, a small flash of joy peeking through in his unamused expression. Billy let out a thrilled "yes" and blushed a bit.

"I'm sorry," she mouthed to Ben with a squint.

He huffed loudly, looked to Billy, extended his hand in a moment of truce, and said, "Fine, you win. Take the victory— add it to the page."

"Have you tried it, Ben?" she asked.

He grimaced. "No, I don't like pumpkins."

Billy made some sort of a noise that sounded like a chortle and said, "It's because he has no taste."

Ben shrugged, and Violet smiled. She caught Billy looking at the both of them. "Well, thank you for your kind words, Violet. I'm so happy you like it!" he commented enthusiastically.

"You're very welcome," she returned with a sincere smile.

When she was left alone with Ben, the place felt smaller again. Quieter. The somersaults inside prepared an attack. *Bloody hell, what was he doing to her?* He was simply standing there in that damned white t-shirt doing nothing, yet his bloody forearms were openly tantalizing her.

She reached in her bag hanging from the chair. "So, how much do I owe you?"

He shook his head to say no.

The stern teacher's voice came out in defense. "Ben."

"Violet," he mimicked.

She cocked her head to the side. "Come on, tell me."

"Nope," he said.

"Ben!"

"Violet!"

"I won't come back if you do this."

He winked. The bloody man winked. "You wouldn't break poor Billy's heart like that."

She sneered and furrowed her brows at him. "Don't bring innocent Billy into this conversation."

Ben shrugged his shoulders and crossed his arms.

"You're the worst right now," she said.

"You'll forgive me, I'm sure."

"And what if I don't?"

"Well then, we'll just have to find ways to make sure that you do."

He gave her a big, hearty smile. "I'm glad you didn't hate anything. You'd be honest with me, wouldn't you?"

"Of course, I would, which is why I couldn't spare your feelings in telling Billy the truth about..." She took it in her hands and examined it closely. "Whatever *this* is."

She took one more spoonful of it and then rose from her seat. "Thank you for everything, Ben. And thank Billy again, too."

"Anytime, Violet," he replied. "I'll see you soon, yeah? Get home safe."

"I will."

The Crooked Branch had a small tip jar at the entrance, she wasn't sure what it was for. Still, she put the twenty-five pounds she had in her possession inside before saying her goodbyes to Florence. "Thank you, sweetheart. I'll see you on Friday with the Henrys," she called out.

Violet decided to walk home instead of taking the bus. Her legs were no longer trying to start a war with her, and the weather was perfectly crisp without a drop of rain. Some trees along the way had been midway into their transformation, while others were just beginning.

The leaves on the ground were scattered in patches, but it was a delight, no less. She'd love this road even more when school was in session, and foliages covered the pavement. She also momentarily considered what barge living would be like while admiring the ones docked in the water. Good lord, the Kennet and Avon Canal path was as dreamy as the skyline. She couldn't believe this was her home, internally kicking herself for not noticing the tucked-away wonders of Bath when she was younger.

It was also reassuring to have met someone else at The Crooked Branch. And she was glad it seemed to go well.

The walk made her think of Ben's loneliness and how he must've felt in his darkest days.

They were kindred spirits that way, living far from the people they adored and not wanting to intrude upon their lives. He didn't have to openly disclose it for her to see. Nevertheless, she felt closer to everyone else here in Bath than she had in London. At least Aunt Helen and Uncle Thomas were close.

Ben was near.

It felt *right.*

For the first time in the last two decades, she didn't feel like a dried-up weed in the midst of wildflowers, growing accidentally in a place she didn't belong. Despite her uncertainties about Dean and what he'd say or do, she felt as though life could begin to make a little bit more sense.

She had almost reached her house when she got a text message from Ben.

BEN: Florence told me what you did. Bet you thought you were so sneaky with that.

It made her laugh to think of his stubbornness—to think that they could be like this, easy, fun, and a part of each other's lives.

VIOLET: I have no idea what you're talking about.

She'd leave it at that for now.

21

VIOLET

In a meeting earlier today, Abigail James had briefly gone over the curriculum while also mentioning the upcoming Autumn Festival. Aunt Helen was also aware of it, as The Wisteria Tea Room participated in it, too.

It made Violet slightly nervous, only because she wasn't nearly as creative these days as she wanted to be, yet excited to jump back in. Hopefully, it'd be like riding a bike. Now that she'd be teaching again as opposed to handling administrative duties, she wanted—no, needed, to flex her creative muscles.

She remembered a version of herself who was more fun—less reserved, willing to do whatever was necessary to make her surroundings brighter. She wanted that version back. She used to light candles all the time, host dinner parties, and decorate her flat according to the seasons. These little things were instant serotonin boosts while living in London. The person she used to be before Dean, before all the loneliness.

And everywhere in Bath was starting to feel a refuge—this house, this neighborhood, the *skyline* where it first hit her, Ben's house for crying out loud, The Crooked Branch, the streets—everywhere. It was all starting to feel safe and comfortable in a way that made her believe she could wake up every morning and feel alive again.

Sadness would always be a part of Violet's life. She knew the pain was unpredictable. But she could try to live fully again. She could believe that she wasn't meant to only suffer.

She was starting to feel like maybe, just maybe, she could live the life she always hoped she would. God never promised a perfect life; no deity did, but a good life, at the very least, was what people deserved. She knew every day wouldn't be rainbows or butterflies or brilliantly unique leaves falling from trees. She never expected that because it wasn't realistic.

Instead, she believed in the idea that when the world outside was drab and flooded, pillow forts and Queen's *A Night at the Opera* blasting through the record player would heal. Her father would sing "You're My Best Friend" obnoxiously loud to her mother while nudging Violet to join in.

When Violet was fifteen, she came home crying because of how touched she was by the lyrics in "39," sitting with her father for hours and talking about what they thought the song could mean. It was the song she had on repeat after her parents died, trying to hold onto them as she cried herself to sleep.

She believed that her parents would have wanted her to have a good, happy life full of enchanting moments that swept her off her feet, but she lost sight of that belief when the looming shadows took up permanent residence.

She was watching reruns of *Parks and Recreation,* and the show always made her crave waffles. She had ordered a waffle maker a few years ago but only used it on special occasions. It was one of the things she left back in London, which meant that she couldn't even walk to her kitchen to make some now.

She picked up her phone to order a new one because, with yet another rewatch, she knew she'd be craving them more often.

She remembered suddenly that she hadn't touched the biscuits this morning, going to her kitchen to retrieve them with a cup of tea. *Parks and Recreation* and Ben's biscuits—that's all she needed for joy if someone were to ask.

Her thoughts were interrupted by a call. "Yes, Aunt Helen?" she answered.

"Florence from The Crooked Branch rang. Your presence is requested during Friday night dinners now."

Violet laughed. "Yes, I'm aware. She was very insistent. But really, I'm sure you could make up an excuse for me."

"I will do no such thing. You *should* come with us. Simone would if she were here," she noted.

"Fine. But no funny business, please."

"What sort of funny business do you mean?"

"You know exactly what I mean, Aunt Helen," she replied with a chuckle.

"It's hard to take you seriously when you giggle like a schoolgirl."

"I'm not giggling like a schoolgirl."

The silence on the other end of the phone told Violet that Helen wouldn't back down. "Okay, fine, but in all seriousness, Aunt Helen—no conspiring from the two of you."

"We are not living in the Regency era. I don't need to meddle in your love life."

"You say that, but..."

"Enough with that. Any news from your solicitor?" she asked, reminding Violet that if her calculations were correct, they were officially approaching the one-month mark.

"No. I probably won't hear anything until the 21st of October."

"What would you like me to make to celebrate?"

This made Violet laugh out loud. Helen was so utterly

serious with the question that she probably hadn't realized just how so. "Divorces require celebrations?" Violet asked.

"They do when it means a woman is finally free from the prison she was in."

"In that case, then, I'd like to put in a special request for your Ghormeh Sabzi!"

"You got it, sweetheart. I can make it tonight as well if you'd like."

"Thank you, but I think I can wait. It'll make it all the more glorious when we're celebrating," she paused for a moment, thinking about the waffle maker again. "Aunt Helen, you don't have a waffle maker by any chance, do you?"

"I don't. What do you want with a waffle maker?" she inquired.

"I wanted to make some. Worry not; I've ordered one. And the second I get it. I'll bring some by for you and Uncle Thomas. You can freeze them and keep them for later, too."

"That sounds delightful," she said.

Violet had made waffles before, but never her mother's specialty, brown sugar waffles. It wasn't too different than the ordinary buttermilk ones she made, but it was one she had trouble perfecting. It wasn't the same when she was alone, and Simone was more of a pancakes woman.

Perhaps she could make them for Aunt Helen this week, or maybe Ben would like them.

Was he a waffles or pancakes sort of man? The answer to the question was imperative, and she desperately had to know.

She picked up her phone and shot him a text.

> **VIOLET**: *Waffles or pancakes?*
>
> **BEN**: Welsh cakes.
>
> **VIOLET**: Not part of the equation, sir.
>
> **BEN**: Is this a test?

> **VIOLET**: Answer a question before you ask one.
> Please and thank you.
> **BEN**: Waffles. Did I pass?
> **VIOLET**: Perhaps.
> **BEN**: I'll take that as a yes. Were the biscuits alright?
> **VIOLET**: Perfect as ever. Though, I really wish you'd
> stop trying to test my self control, even if it's
> because you're making up for upcoming your
> absence.
> **BEN**: I'm nothing if not thorough.

Thorough? He had to have known what he said, right? Nope. She wouldn't go there. She wouldn't think of that now.

> **VIOLET**: There are so many remarks I can make
> about that…but for now, I'll settle for thanks xx
> **BEN**: Haha! Cheers.

He'd probably pass every test with flying colors if he continued like this. It was getting ridiculous—the way he made her heart squeeze every time they interacted. This couldn't be healthy, could it? *Should hearts be put through this much thrill and excitement?*

Violet would also have to prepare her overnight bag to visit Yana in the Cotswolds tomorrow, marking the first time the women would see each other in four years. She couldn't wait to tell her about the agent living next door. Or, rather, the head chef.

22

BEN

He hadn't seen Violet in two days, wanting nothing more than to carry on every text conversation but forcing himself to stop. And now, he'd be going to Bristol to visit his sister's family. It was downright unbearable to think that he was *so* enamored with the woman that it felt like a part of him was detached because of the short distance.

While his sister's house certainly wasn't far from his, the girls always insisted he stay throughout the weekend.

He left Violet with enough biscuits to make up for his absence, and though they were nearing the end of the week, he had no plans to stop leaving them at her door.

She had a meeting at Knightley on Wednesday, then went to visit a friend on Thursday. She'd be returning Friday morning, and he'd be gone by then.

It could be healthy to put some distance between them. The days passed too quickly and not fast enough because he was counting the hours until she told him that the divorce papers were signed. He wondered which phone call he'd be, rightfully assuming that Simone would be the first, and perhaps she'd tell Aunt Helen in person.

He wished she'd tell him in person, too, but he could not guarantee that he wouldn't beg her to be his and fall to his knees to prove that he'd never hurt her the way her ex-husband had. He'd turn into some blubbering buffoon and scare her away forever.

Were there rules to how quickly you should date someone after ending a relationship? Especially if the relationship was unpleasant in the first place. Would Violet want to wait? He would if she did. He'd wait another sixteen years for her if that's what she needed from him.

He'd hate every agonizing minute of it, but he'd do it without question.

THEY WERE SEATED in his sister's terrace when he let his mind wander, Emma's words reeling him back to the present.

"You were awfully quiet at dinner today," his sister noted.

He missed Violet, and though the distraction with his nieces was lovely, knowing he'd be returning tomorrow brought back the emotions he was tucking in.

"Was I?"

"Mhmm," Emma confirmed, taking a sip of her beer.

"I didn't realize," he replied.

"Oh, come on, brother. I didn't hound you over the phone, but now that you're here. I know something is the matter."

"What if it's not a bad thing?" he proposed.

She lowered her knees from the position she'd been sitting in and hit him across the arm. "Bloody hell, it's a woman, isn't it?" she said with an unholy screech.

"Look," he began, positioning himself better to look his sister in the eyes. "Yes. But I don't want to talk about her right now or until I know there's something to tell. She has a lot going on. I knew her years ago, and now, we're neighbors."

Emma set her beer on the ground and nearly bounced in her chair. "I've been waiting for ages to hear this!"

Ben shook his head. Of course, she'd be thrilled, and a little too much. "Don't get too excited. Nothing's happened," he specified.

"Brother, women wanting to be with you was never the problem. It's been your decision and, of course, circumstances, but still."

He furrowed his eyebrows at the sentiment, though he knew damn well she was right. And he was slightly miffed that his little sister, of all people, knew it.

"Don't look at me like that. You know I'm right. You've never introduced anyone to Dad or me. You've never pursued anything, and the only reason Dad knew Hannah was because she was his nurse. At Edmund and Nina's wedding, you were paired with the most gorgeous maid of honor and you barely gave her the time of day."

He swallowed and sat back in his chair. She wasn't wrong. Molly, Nina's oldest friend, was indeed gorgeous, but he simply wasn't interested.

She was quiet for a moment and studied him intently. "I know losing Mum was different for you. You knew her. You watched Dad grieve her. You watched him lose his light. You also had a rubbish job that didn't allow any room for love, but I always figured that it was more so the fact that you were afraid to lose someone the way he did," she added. "On top of the losses, you're the kind of person who needs to feel safe enough to open up around people, and I don't think many people gave you the room to do so."

Ben couldn't even look at Emma because he knew she had a point. He was afraid of the loss. But he was also scared of the emotions he didn't quite understand until he met Violet, and his edges saw the matching cracks in her. Whether that was feeling safe enough to open up to someone or finding a true connection, he wasn't sure. In all his years of therapy at the agency, he'd addressed cases and crimes more than his own demons.

"I think you're also afraid of someone seeing the real you because it means opening that massive heart of yours and choosing to love instead of hiding away in the darkness."

He bent his thumb and bit it—a nervous habit he had held onto since childhood.

"How'd you do it?" he finally asked. "How did you get married and have kids and find happiness? Dad never loved anyone else after Mum. I don't think I could bear that kind of a loss."

She sighed deeply and took the beer bottle back in her hand. "For starters, I hid the bad parts from the two of you. Fear is the worst kind of demon. What happened to Mum was preventable, especially with our advancements in science and technology, but childbirth and pregnancies can still be risky. It was easier with Catherine, surprisingly, but before Lily was born, I started to freak myself out because my brain tried to convince me that I wouldn't meet her. Like our family was cursed with second children or something. It made no sense logically, but the thoughts would creep up."

Her eyes were tearing up now, and she bit her lip while holding back a smile. "The time came, I walked out of the delivery room with that firecracker safe in my arms, and then I wished so desperately that Mum could see her—that she could see *me*."

Ben's eyes were misting then because while he figured his sister dealt with grief in her own way, he never thought about how she must have felt before becoming a mother. He never thought of the fears that followed her.

"Amelia is the best mother-in-law anyone could've asked for. I'm beyond grateful every day that she's the grandmother of my children. And Aunt Bea did an extraordinary job helping out when I needed her. But I'll always wish I knew Mum, too. I'll have those days where I think of the what-ifs and the fears and the things I didn't experience."

She took Ben's hand in hers. "But that's the thing, brother. We have to push through even when we're afraid because sometimes, after crying yourself to sleep with seemingly ridiculous fears, you get a little weasel who asks too many questions and forces you to stay awake feeding her."

She smiled with such pride that he let the tears fall freely from his eyes. He felt so small for a beat; she sat before him, ten years younger, giving him better words of wisdom than he could've ever imagined. She was, in every way, their mother's daughter, and he hoped with everything in him that with the stories they told, she would know.

"Plus, love doesn't erase pain or grief, but finding someone who makes the aftermath of those dark nights bearable is the greatest gift. When I've needed him the most, Luke's taken the weight off my shoulders, and I've done the same for him. It's give and take in equal measures, and it's worth it. Every moment between us, the good and the bad."

He squeezed her hand back. "I'll always be glad love came easy to you. I would have hated for you to have felt a further absence in life."

"I'm fortunate for it, too. I know. But you know I could say the same thing about you, right? And I want the same for you more than anything else because as much as I love you, brother, I am so tired of worrying about you," she said with a hearty laugh.

He shook his head. "I don't recall asking you to?"

"Yeah, that's the bloody point. It's what people do when they care about you. Now, imagine that?"

"And now, I'd much rather prefer your husband return so we could stop talking about this."

Emma raised her eyebrows. "You realize that if I tell my husband to, he'll take my side, right? And we could both hound you about it? Funny thing about love, you get a permanent partner in crime who goes along with all your shit."

"You're becoming unbearable now."

"And that's why you love me. But look, in all seriousness, promise to tell me about her when you can?"

He smiled with contentment. He wanted to tell her all about Violet. He'd yell to the world about Violet if he could. "I will, yeah."

"Good."

Luke joined them a little later, and the three of them stayed up until two in the morning, marathoning the *John Wick* films, per Emma's request.

23

VIOLET

The past three weeks had been a dream of sorts. Violet spent every Friday at The Crooked Branch, familiarizing herself with more of the staff, the *actual* menu, and every vibrant corner inside. During her second visit with the Henrys, the new bartender tried to make a move on her when she walked over to the loo. Frankly, it made her chuckle at the prospect of the man not only realizing that she was probably a decade older than him but that if she were to date anyone, it would be Ben.

While nothing had happened between them, it felt like it should've been an unspoken truth that she was off-limits. *They both were.*

Billy, she learned, made the best chips in the building, and while Ben had perfected the battered codfish, the two of them working together was the kind of food heaven she would be happy to reside in forever.

In the short time that had passed, it had become easier just to *be*—when her waffle maker arrived, she made large batches to freeze for herself and attempted the brown sugar ones for Aunt Helen (who claimed they were brilliant).

So long as the weather permitted, she'd go on her runs every other day, and then she and Ben would take Freddy to the skyline on the days when she hadn't. After the first week, it had become a routine neither of them thought twice about.

She was to start teaching in two weeks, which would hopefully come at a time when she'd have a more concrete idea of how Dean was dealing with the divorce, leaving her mind to occupy itself fully on the Autumn Festival.

VIOLET WAS on her morning run when she got the call from her solicitor. She stopped in her tracks, breathing heavily from both the exercise and the nerves. "Amy, hi! I didn't expect to hear from you," she answered.

"Violet, you alright?" she asked.

"Yes, I'm well. It's been great here."

"That's good to hear, love," Amy replied. "Violet, listen, so I have a bit of good news."

Good news? Concerning Dean? The idea was too foreign. Her chest was closing up at the possibilities of what Amy would disclose.

"What is it?" she asked, trying to sound calm.

"Dean came home earlier than we thought. His solicitor notified me, we served him, and the next day, the signed papers were returned. With your permission, I could file them immediately."

Violet's breath hitched in her throat. *The signed divorce papers.* It felt too easy. Was Dean Colborne truly giving her freedom? He had to have ulterior motives of some kind. "Just like that? He's not requested to meet or asked where I am?"

"He did not. He's fully aware that I cannot disclose information to him. And I've only spoken to his solicitor, but it was nothing out of the ordinary."

"I realize that, but with everything I've told you about him, do you think he'd try to come find me?" Violet asked.

"I cannot say for certain, Violet. I hope not. He knows the law. I don't know him like you, but I cannot imagine that he'd pull something that would endanger you or his career. Take a beat. Try not to freak out. This is a promising start, but you give me a call if you have any questions or need anything, yeah?"

"I will. Thank you for everything, Amy."

"Of course."

"Talk soon," Violet said before hanging up. She hunched over, trying to calm herself as her head spun in circles. She took multiple deep inhales followed by intense, forceful exhales. The prospect of Dean finding her was probable, which terrified her the most. She thought about this over and over again when she left him that morning. Nothing would ever come easy with this man.

But she was finally close to divorcing him, really and truly. She supposed that she should feel some sort of sorrow, perhaps miss the idea of who she thought Dean was, but she didn't. She was going to miss his parents and his siblings. But she had already spent time missing who she thought he was when her world came crashing down.

She wanted to call Simone.

She wanted to run to Ben's house.

She didn't want to be alone.

She wanted to run to Ben's house. She hoped he'd be home. She wasn't even sure what she'd do or what she'd say, but it felt like she was granted a little more time than they thought. Two additional weeks where they wouldn't tiptoe around their feelings but get to act on them. She wasn't sure what any of that meant or how the reality would differ from the fantasies inside her head, but even if he stood at his front door and gazed at her, it'd be satisfying.

She ran back in the same direction she came. The jog was freeing now. The possibilities were gaining dominance against the fears.

She took in her sight. There were leaves gilded through her path, a delicious breeze traversing in the air. The crunching echoes of foliage crumpling below her feet and the satisfying scents of the earth's decay. It shouldn't be as sharply alluring, yet, nothing in the world could compare. Except maybe, *bergamot. Ben. All of him.*

Maybe, just maybe.

A run had never felt more keenly fulfilling.

She wanted to see Ben more than anything, but she should shower first.

She should figure out what to say. The idea of being with Ben worked. It felt right the moment she saw him again, but it felt even safer now that they'd gotten closer and found a rhythm —a friendship burgeoning through the dark clouds.

How would a person approach a situation like this? Should she wait a few more days to hear back from her solicitor? Should she wait until the papers were officially filed to the court? Dean signed them. He was aware of her desire to leave him, and he technically let her go by signing in return, despite his likely rage.

Why would she wait if she had internally mourned the end of her failed marriage for years now?

Why was she still contemplating it?

She wanted Ben.

It wasn't complicated anymore—it didn't have to be messy, miserable, or tainted.

Many people would've seized this opportunity and put everything on the line for a chance at love. Violet should do the same. These were the signs she'd been looking for. These were the cues to listen to. She sprinted into her house and straight into the shower.

It was still pretty early—only eight-thirty in the morning. She could text Ben casually and see if he was even home.

> **VIOLET**: Hi, do you work this morning?
> **BEN**: Hi, not until this afternoon.
> **VIOLET**: Come over for waffles and coffee, then?
> **BEN**: When?
> **VIOLET**: Whenever!
> **BEN**: I'll be there in about 20.

If there was a last page to one's life, Violet wanted to take a peek at it. She wanted the reassurance that this would be the thing to endure.

A career had an end goal—whether that meant a change or retirement. It was never meant to be a permanent thing. It was meant to be a period. But love was supposed to last. It wasn't supposed to end with summer or autumn or even winter—it was meant to carry through the seasons.

Stay.

And she wanted to, more than anything else in the world— she wanted love to stay this time.

She wanted to feel her heart pound in anticipation of seeing Ben after a long day of work.

She wanted to miss him when he wasn't around, and she wanted to fall deeper in love with every part of him.

But as she did the bare minimum of inserting frozen waffles into a toaster and brewing her favorite cinnamon hazelnut coffee that she'd ordered from a small resort town in the States, the emotions bubbling within felt right. She lit a clary sage and coriander candle on her coffee table and a balsam fir-scented one in the loo.

She was eager and excited, and the fears inside her were temporarily muted.

After a few short moments, Ben knocked on the door. And goodness, Violet found herself battling a rush of brassy nerves demanding far more attention than she would like to give them. None of that now. None of it for the rest of the week. *Please.*

She released the breath she was holding right before she opened the door. Ben stood there with a faint, half-smile, and his hair gorgeously tousled from the rain.

"Good morning. I didn't realize the rain had picked up," Violet said.

"Neither did I."

She grinned sheepishly, moving aside. "Come in."

"Anything I can help with?" Ben said while following her to the kitchen.

"Nope. We're good. Coffee or tea?" Violet asked.

"Whatever you're having," Ben replied.

She smiled at him standing in the middle of her kitchen, complementing the same fateful morning when they realized they were neighbors. The sight of him released a barrage of intractable butterflies loose inside of her.

She should merely rip off the plaster and tell him. The small toaster dinged, pulling her thoughts back to reality. She turned back to look at him as she took the waffles out and placed them atop the stove.

He gazed intently at her, mapping out every part of her in a way that she appreciated only from him.

"I have a bit of news," she said abruptly.

Ben's eyes widened. "Yeah?"

She nodded and made the short stride to face him more closely. "My solicitor rang."

She caught his Adam's apple bob at the words. His eyes

donned an expression of apprehension and intrigue. She hoped her smile would ease him a bit, but the look remained.

"Dean returned home early. He signed the papers," she paused and looked down before continuing. "They should be filed today." Violet inched closer to him. "It'll take months for the divorce to be finalized, but knowing he's signed it and that it's going to be filed soon makes it more real. And I—I don't want to wait anymore, Ben."

He gaped as the last words left her. "Say it again," he declared in a low whisper.

"I don't want to wait," she repeated, "If you still want to give us a chance, I don't want to wait anymore."

His long lashes fluttered up and down. The fine lines on his face were a little more pronounced, the crease between his eyebrows a bit more hollow as he pressed his eyes shut and gradually drew her closer with his arm around her waist.

He didn't have to say anything. His heartbeat served as a clear exposé, and Violet placed her hand right at the spot of its thumping. He looked at her finally, revealing a brilliant half-smile that made her heart soar.

"Darling," he whispered, faint gravel cobbled beneath his tender pitch, "I've wanted you for sixteen years," he affirmed.

The smile on her face grew wider as she drew closer before colliding her lips with his.

24

BEN

Violet's lips moved in slow, tantalizing strokes against his, gentle and pleading to foil the heated, intoxicating battle for control their first kiss was full of. He dreamed of this moment every day, agonizing to hold onto every memory while failing to grasp that nothing could come close to the real thing.

He marveled at the feel of her, wanting to etch every modicum of her softness into his being. She tasted like coconuts. It must've been some sort of lip balm. Her lips were brilliant and so achingly delicate.

She deepened the kiss, leaving the measured tugs behind for more heat and tongue as her hands roamed to his hair. Ben leaned back and slid further against the counter, parting his legs for balance as he brought her body to him. She was breathtaking and haunting and everything in between. His hand rose to cup her cheek, holding her steady as she parted from him, resting her forehead against his.

Violet opened her eyes and gazed into his—oceans of her dreams dancing through her effervescent blue hues. He could stay in her eyes forever, losing himself in every story tucked underneath.

One minute, he was standing in her kitchen, thinking about how nice her house smelled, and the next, she was kissing him. There was no rush now. He imagined it a hundred times over when he was alone—every second she was around. Yet nothing, not even the memories of her swollen red lips and eager hands trailing his body, could've prepared him for the intimacy of this moment.

This was the start. This wasn't temporary. They weren't racing against time trying to catch every piece of the other's touch and taste.

It could be slow and gentle.

It could be hot and heavy.

It could be everything they wanted, everything they needed —loud or quiet.

"It's hard to breathe when you look at me like that," he blurted, closing his eyes to take in her nearness. It was always hard to breathe around Violet, but her flushed gaze sprung contentment into every part of him he was sure had died.

He dipped his head to her neck. She carded her fingers through his hair, prompting a low chuckle to rise from her throat as he dropped a kiss to the spot. "Like what?" she whispered temptingly against his ear.

"Like you're looking into something worth seeing," he groaned. He lifted his head, placing a kiss at the tip of her nose.

She did it again, purposely deepening her gaze this time like she was trying to engrave the emotions into his brain. Violet reached for his face, the tips of her fingers brushed delicately over his beard, the corners of his eyes, and his forehead before holding him firm in her gentle hands and pressing her lips to his in a single, searing kiss.

"In that case, I have no plans to stop looking at you like

that," she said into his lips. "But I really want to eat those waffles," she replied, pointing to the stovetop where they sat on two plates.

He chuckled, kissed her quickly, and moved aside. This was madness and beauty and nothing he ever thought possible. He was captivated by her touch from the moment she entwined their fingers together, dazzled by her smile the second she showed it to him, and in love with her mind as soon she opened herself up.

Ben watched as Violet poured coffee into large mugs, mixing a tiny bit of milk into hers and holding the bottle up, wordlessly asking if he wanted it, too. He nodded. He took his coffee like his tea.

She poured it and then walked to the fridge. "Do you want maple syrup with your waffles or custard?" she asked.

"Syrup."

"More custard for me then!" she exclaimed, reaching into her fridge to pull them both out. He took the two mugs and set them on the table, walked back to her to take the two plates while she brought over the toppings.

He watched as she scooped an obscene amount of custard on her waffles, then took the maple syrup to drizzle faintly across it.

"So, your preferred form of waffles is a sugar overload like my six-year-old niece?"

She nodded profusely. "If I had biscuits, I'd crush them on top."

"That's a bit concerning, but I'm more than happy to bring you some—though there's a catch this time."

"Oh?" she said, taking a ridiculous bite.

"Biscuits in exchange for kisses."

She placed her elbows on the table and rested her hands against her chin. "Yes!"

He inched closer and kissed her. The taste of custard and Violet would be his very undoing.

He took a bite off his waffle. They were better than the ones he usually made.

She took another, licking the sugar off her lips. It drove him wild. How did he think she could handle any of this?

She reached over to take a napkin, passing him one too. "Do you want to know which friend I went to visit when I was gone?"

"A few weeks ago?" he clarified.

"Yeah."

"If you want to tell me. Sure."

"Remember Yana? The flight attendant."

"The one with you in the room, right?"

She nodded. "The very one."

He smiled. "You two are still friends then? How was it?"

"She's the only one from English Airlines I still keep in touch with. She couldn't believe it when I told her about you. She screamed so loud in the bloody pub I was sure we would get kicked out."

He laughed at the mere thought of it, watching as her eyes lit up in the process of telling the story. There was something about the way Violet recalled events that was so wholesome he couldn't handle it. "How's she doing?"

"Oh, she's mostly well. She's a romance author, which is hilarious and so proper considering that in Paris, we spent most of our time reading the same book over and over again. And she's got three little ones. She still looks the same; it must be those unfairly stunning Middle Eastern genes. A shame I don't have any from Nan's side of the family."

He looked at her with what he was sure were stars in his eyes.

"Anyway, she was bursting. Still calls you Agent Williams."

He choked out a huff. "Now that's a name I never thought I'd hear again."

"You know, I was sure you lied about your name, right?"

"My last name?" he asked.

"All of it."

The frankness cut him deeper than it should have. He never imagined that Violet would search for him. He would've made it easier, perhaps, and joined whatever bloody social media apps were necessary. He didn't think she cared.

"I have never and would never lie to you, Violet."

As though catching the faint shock in his voice, she reached over, placing her hand on top of his.

He turned his hand, entwining his fingers with hers and squeezing gently.

"Can I take you out on a proper date next weekend?"

She seemed stunned by the question. Not in a bad way, but in a peculiar sense that said she wasn't expecting it to be the next step. Did he misinterpret what all this meant? Did it only apply to clandestine meetings for the time being?

"In public?" she asked.

"Should we not be seen in public together?"

"I don't know, actually. I'd like to. But is that wise?"

He sighed, thinking it over. No one knew Violet here, not really. He only knew she was married to Dean Colborne because he searched for her. Bath wasn't some small town where everyone knew each other. Ben was hardly seen outside the kitchen at The Crooked Branch or the gym, and he could trust the few people who knew him closely with discretion. But if she wasn't ready for that, and if she wanted this behind closed doors only, then he'd oblige.

He'd do anything to keep her happy.

"I don't see why it'd pose an issue, but if you'd rather wait, we can do that, too."

"You're right. It's not like Dean has a hit on me or anything."

The mere thought of it made his blood curdle, taking him back to a place he didn't ever want to go back to, scaling shadows and watching his back. If the prick ever showed up here, Ben couldn't guarantee a modicum of control.

"I accept then," she said with a sweet curve rising on her lips and a faint pink coloring her cheeks. His breath caught in his throat.

People said he should find someone he wanted to spend the rest of his life with, but no one specified how to deal with the overwhelming emotions trying to burst through the barricaded parts of him.

She made him feel unscathed, effectively surrogating the shards of glass in his chest with delicately beguiling strokes.

He was sure he was staring again. He could stare for hours if he allowed himself to. So long as it wouldn't scare her away. "These are better than mine, by the way," he said, pointing to the waffles with his fork.

Her smile was sincere and a little sad. "It's my mother's recipe. Brown sugar waffles for autumn," she said with a soft drop in her pitch.

He took the hand he was holding onto and pressed a small kiss to it. "They're lovely."

He watched her expression change abruptly. She looked small for a beat, so unsure and desperate. "Ben—" his name a prayer, a form of armor, something she was trying to cling onto.

"What is it, darling?"

She shook her head. "It's not going to be easy. This. Us. I can't shake how sure I am of that. It's not over yet with Dean. It isn't like him to give in this quickly. And if it becomes too much for..."

He was certain he was shaking his head with violent disagreement at this point.

"Stop, Violet. Please don't continue that sentence. I let you get away from me once, then spent every bloody day since regretting it—I'm not here because I'm convinced it'll be some effortless jaunt to the park every day. I'm here for *you* and whatever comes our way. Good or bad."

She swallowed—the glaze in her eyes frightened him to his core. What'd the bloody arsehole do to make her mood oscillate so much? She was fine mere moments ago, giggling and flirting with fire flaring through her. Did any of it have to do with her mum, too? He could see the quiet place she went to.

"Okay," she replied, then quietly added, "The same goes for me."

"Good." He should change the subject and venture somewhere with hope.

He smiled, remembering his mum's words about learning a girl's favorite flower. "Will you tell me what your favorite flower is?" he asked, tracing her knuckles with his lips, refusing to let go of her hand until he absolutely had to. He wanted her to think of other things because the sadness in her eyes was making him want to set the world on fire.

A curve stretched subtly over her lips. "Tulips and mums."

"And your all-time favorite dessert?"

Her smile deepened. "You're so sure it isn't your biscuits?"

"Yes," he replied.

She chuckled. "It's a bloody cliché but sticky toffee pudding."

The response made him choke on a breath. "Violet, you're serious?"

"Yes, why?" she questioned.

He drew in a deep breath and closed his eyes. "I used to bake sticky toffee pudding with my mum every Sunday when I was a boy." He bit the inside of his cheek as her face dropped and settled to a place of profound comprehension. "It's...it's what brought me back to the kitchen a few years ago," he said with a low, sulking voice he would've hated to use in the presence of someone else.

She didn't say anything. She squeezed his hand, saying everything he needed to hear. She understood where he went— mere inches away, but years in the past. He didn't need to explain the sudden ache in his chest, filled with a longing that nothing could ever come to ease.

"I'm afraid to try it. I might have to attach myself to your hip once I do, then demand it every day."

"Should we switch biscuits to sticky toffee pudding, then?"

"No! You and Simone have created a monster. I'm not ready to part with the biscuits yet. Maybe *ever*," she said with a breathy laugh. "But wait, you've learned two essential things about me; what about you?"

"I don't have a favorite flower, I'm afraid."

"You've got to give me something here."

"You," he said, knowing with utmost certainty how that made him sound, but he didn't care. She had been his favorite thing in the world since the moment she sat beside him on a secluded bench and probed his heart and mind wide open.

She drew out a sardonic huff. "That's not fair."

Ben shrugged and returned to the waffle on his plate, popping the last piece into his mouth. "I stand by my answer."

"I'll figure out all the things you like, Ben Grant. I'm nothing if not observant and clever."

He arched an eyebrow. "Do share with the class once you've learned them."

She scowled, then a cheeky grin crossed her face as she looked down at her plate, took a giant finger full of the custard and smeared it in what he gathered was a straight line from his forehead to his bottom lip. She giggled, making a satisfied *hmph* sound before rising from her seat.

She took both their plates then and beelined to the kitchen, clearly proud of herself. He walked over to where she stood in front of the sink and boxed her in with one hand on each side of her, prompting her to wiggle her way around to face him.

She looked at him with a wide smile and prodigious amusement. Every version of Violet was perfect, but this captivating, incandescent glow made him feel like the luckiest bastard in the world.

"Clean it off," he ordered in a demanding, coquettish tenor, threading the command with a slight twitch on his mouth.

She lifted her hand to do so, but he stopped her by swinging his head. "Not with your hands," he clarified.

She raised her eyebrows, then got on her tip-toes, kissing and licking her way down from the fold in his forehead to his bottom lip, which she took in with a tug before gently biting down.

"All gone," she said proudly, like a kid who'd just been told they could have a treat once their plate was thoroughly cleaned.

"Except my face is still sticky," he countered.

She tipped her head to the side. "The loo is right over there."

He inched closer to her, smoothing his fingers along her arm, feeling goosebumps rise on her skin as she shivered slightly. Yes, good. He could have the win here. "One thing you should know about me, Violet Wedlake," he stopped mid-sentence to gently take her earlobe between his teeth, prompting a low moan to escape her. "I prefer to win," he said, a hair's breadth away from her lips, desperately wanting to kiss her again but holding off.

Her breath caught in her throat. "Good luck with that," she noted, turning her back to him with a quick chuckle.

This was going to be fun, he thought. As the trajectory of their relationship turned, he felt eons lighter—better and freer than he had in years.

He walked back over to her after washing his face and wrapped his arms around her frame, burying his head in her neck. She set the drying cloth down and repositioned in his arms, her heartbeat steadying. "We have to prep for inspections tonight. I don't know how long work will keep me. If it's not too late, can I see you after my shift?" he asked.

She turned her head in his direction and smoothed her thumb against his beard. "Yes, please."

He leaned forward, pressing a sweet kiss to her lips. Another at the side of her throat, lingering there for a beat. "This isn't a truce," he started, biting down gently. "But that lilac scent of yours kills me." He placed a kiss back at the spot.

"Oh, but I've already won this round," she said, shimmying in his grip to face him. She trailed her mouth to his jaw, right below his ear, and whispered. "Admit it."

He had to leave now; otherwise, he'd never make it to work. She pressed a slow kiss there. He lost it. "Fine, I really love the original Star Wars films. I'll watch any time they're on."

"Ha! I knew I'd win."

"You keep thinking that, darling," he replied, dropping another kiss to her lips before leaving. Of course, she'd win. He was too damn destroyed to do anything but bask in the glory of having her near.

"Will do," she called out once he was close to the door.

25

VIOLET

When she got off the call, Violet was sure Simone's wild shriek must have ruptured her eardrums. It was nice to have her best friend's support on this —wholly and with immense faith. Simone, like Aunt Helen, had good instincts about people, and Violet hated herself a bit for going against them when marrying Dean. To be fair, she knew Simone had a point; she just couldn't believe it.

Her fate had been signed, sealed, and delivered with a mediocre romance.

Except, the events of this morning still felt like an improbable fantasy. Ben, kissing and teasing her in her kitchen, uttering the words *I've wanted you for sixteen years*. It was euphoric and brilliant, and she couldn't wrap her head around how lovely it was.

She'd be officially starting at Knightley in one week, which would keep her busier and less antsy. She tried searching her mind for Autumn Festival preparations, but at the end of the day, creativity refused to flow when it didn't feel real yet. Violet always struggled to prepare for things in advance when she didn't have materials at her disposal. In this case, if she at least knew how her students were and what they liked, it could've helped.

So she used these quiet moments to do nothing but let her mind wander. She had finished the novel she'd been reading for a few days now while simultaneously staring at the library app, trying to will the ones she had on hold to become available quickly.

She should finally start watching *Fleabag*. She kept promising Simone that she would, but comfort show reruns and romance novels took precedence.

She made herself a cup of tea, curled up on the sofa, and turned on the TV. She had no plans to move except for maybe a shower at some point. She'd at least get through the show's first season.

SHE OPENED the door to Ben rather impatiently later that night, throwing herself into his arms. He lifted her from the ground, swaying their bodies for a beat.

A low chuckle stitched with a grunt rumbled out of him. "I might never get used to this," he replied, setting her down and taking her lips in a kiss that weakened her knees.

Violet laughed. *They were being ridiculous.* "We've been apart for less than a day and acting like it's been ages."

"It felt like ages," he rasped, peppering kisses along her neck.

"How was work?" she asked, not wanting to seem too eager to jump his bones.

He groaned in response. "Too long. Too much. You've wrecked me, darling. All I've done since this morning is think about you."

"Oh, and what did those thoughts consist of?"

He drew his forehead to hers. "You don't want to know."

"Except I do," she assured, placing her hand on his chest to emphasize the following words that came out of her mouth. "I really, *really* want to know."

He slid his hands, resting them against her hips. "What happens if I tell you?"

"Well, perhaps the thoughts become a reality."

"And what if those thoughts scare you away?"

"Try me."

He lifted his hands to cup her face. His voice came in like the first faint drops of rain—velvety and full of reverence at the same time. "I want you, Violet. I've wanted every part of you from the moment I laid eyes on you in that red dress."

She must've been scarlet all over; pursing her lips, she gazed deeper into his eyes, remembering that this was part of the reason she desired him so intently.

Ben never hit on her as overtly as others did.

He was never sordid or sly in her presence.

He didn't look at her arse when she walked by or leer at her as though she were up for auction. He only ever looked into her eyes. She smiled sheepishly, thinking of all he concealed to ensure she knew she was safe with him. "Yet, you were the only man in all my years of flying who didn't make me feel like cattle. I had hoped you were attracted to me because I was so drawn to you, and then you asked for permission to kiss me, for crying out loud. No man I'd met had ever done such a thing."

"Can I kiss you, Violet?"

"You can do whatever you'd like," she confirmed before colliding her lips with his in a staggering waltz. She pushed him against the door frame, the thud of his back extracting a satisfying sound from his throat.

They stayed there for a moment. Violet trailed her fingers to the collar of his jacket, sliding it off his shoulders with her lips glued to his. He wasn't the only one who wanted. She longed for every part of him, too—to see and touch and taste. She threw the jacket to the sofa, putting enough force in the movement to ensure it'd land there and not on the floor.

"I haven't been with anyone for about four years, and I've been tested since then," he said breathlessly after parting from her lips and drawing his mouth to her collarbone.

She swallowed hard, bringing her hands to his chin; she nudged him up to look at her. This part shouldn't terrorize her so much, and yet she didn't want to bring a morsel of Dean into this. But for transparency, she owed Ben the same truth he gave to her. "I got tested immediately when I found out Dean was cheating on me," she bit the inside of her cheek and looked down. "I haven't slept with him or anybody else since then."

Ben looked her straight in the eyes, gentle, warm, and so achingly kind. He nodded before pressing a tender kiss to her forehead. "Violet, I—I know words can be empty promises at times, but I need you to hear me when I say that I have no interest in anyone but you. And that's not going to change no matter how much time passes."

She ran her fingers along his beard. "I believe you."

He seized her mouth again in a deliriously wild cadence, darting his tongue forward and inducing a low groan of need to rise from her. She wanted every part of him, unclad and underneath her. Violet took his hand speedily in hers and guided him to her bedroom.

She could feel the pink in her cheeks burn as they stepped in—this was real. This was Ben. This was happening.

The clock wasn't ticking incessantly behind them.

They weren't racing against anything but their fusion-filled yearnings.

Her breath hitched as he drew her body closer, moving his lips from her jaw to her neck, where he sucked and tasted, elic-iting whimpers from the pit of her stomach. Her hands roamed his hair, trying to balance herself to his methodic movements.

"Tell me what you need—everything that you like and want," he groaned at the base of her throat. His lips darted down her neck toward her collarbones, every open space he could find scattering every corner with captivatingly intimate kisses that made her feel hypnotized.

She reached to the bottom of his shirt and roved her hands over his chest—she didn't need to see to know that he was ripped underneath. She felt the muscles clench as her fingers grazed his skin. He lifted the shirt and tossed it to the floor.

He was toned, remarkable, and scarred, breaking her heart into pieces when her eyes fell on the textured lines imprinted on his body. "My God," she whispered, pulling back to look at him. "Ben."

"It's alright—part of the job," he reassured, drawing a smile to counter the scowl she was sure she had donned. She traced the protruding line over his left pec and felt a tremor rise as his grip tightened against her waist. Violet leaned forward and kissed him there, grounding herself in his heartbeat, etching herself into this tattered piece of him, hoping it'd reach the corners where his pain hadn't yet healed.

She felt him tense against her and take a deep, harrowing breath that pierced into the far reaches of her heart.

His low grunt hit her bone deep. "Violet, darling, you're going to kill me if you keep doing that."

She rested her forehead against his. "No. You have to stay alive so I can take care of you more often," she proclaimed, wanting nothing more than to kiss every scar away, visible or not.

His hands refocused on the jumper dress she wore, reaching to the bottom and lifting it swiftly over her head; he threw it somewhere in the vicinity of his shirt. He mapped out her body with a treasuring regard that she wanted to pin to her memories.

He unzipped his trousers quickly and drew his lips back on hers, their tongues challenging one another in a familiar dance. He reached behind her, unhooked her bra, kissing her shoulders with each strap he lowered. He took in a lungful as he watched her chest rise and fall.

"Tell me what you like," he drawled against her ear, biting down gently as his hands explored her bare body.

Violet's breath fastened as his touch inched closer to her breasts. "*I—.*"

He pinched a nipple gently, drawing a murmur from her throat. His palm smoothed over the other—"Go on, use your words, darling."

"Your mouth," she choked out.

A low, hoarse grunt tumbled from him. "Lie back," he said, nudging her onto the bed. She was shivers and heat fighting for control in a way only Ben could elicit.

He joined her there within seconds, capturing her lips briefly before traveling down her body, his weight above her altogether pleasing.

His lips and tongue traced down her torso diligently, inching lower and closer to where she wanted him most, grating his teeth along the apex of her thigh. "You're so beautiful," he declared, making her feel desired in a way she had never imagined. "I've dreamed of this for years, losing all sense of control at the mere thought of it every bloody time."

She was in flames, and the sight of Ben dazzled her, hair tousled and sweat glistening on his forehead was a vision like no other—brilliant and spellbinding.

He took his time meticulously attending to her needs, understanding what she liked better than anyone before, *giving* and appreciating with his lips and tongue. Her fingers tangled in his hair and pulled; she was so close to collapsing.

"I need you inside of me," she managed to say.

"Let go, and I'll be right there."

With one long lick where she needed him most, Violet came undone, stars dancing in a glittering kaleidoscope around her.

She laid her head back and tried to catch her breath, reaching for the drawer beside her bed, she fumbled for one of the condoms she had seen earlier, certain at the time that Simone had slipped them when she was visiting. She located one, judging by the feel of the plastic, handed it to Ben before propping herself up.

She flipped him over, straddling him. They collided with heated urgency and desperation. Violet was atop him, taking control this time.

They were both burning for harder and faster, both begging the other for everything. He made discoveries in her that she'd not known existed—avalanches roaring to erupt in a surge. He was maddening like this, underneath her, flushed and bare, and hers entirely.

"*Violet—*" her name hitched deliciously in his throat.

They were downright, unreservedly adrift in each other.

Twisted limbs and wet kisses amidst rhythmic thrusts and groans.

He let her find release before him again, joining her the moment she fully let go.

Breathless and transfixed. She had never known pleasure like the feel of Ben's body entangled with hers. She had never known release this cathartic and satisfying.

They could be this way all night. They could be this way tomorrow and the day after that.

"I had forgotten that sex was supposed to be good," she said, her eyes frozen against the wall. She didn't want to utter the words aloud, but he should know. He deserved to.

"Just good?" he asked.

"Find every synonym in the bloody thesaurus for it," she answered breathlessly. His lips met hers again with a searing passion.

"Have I told you're perfect?" he said with a low, gruff whisper.

"I'm not opposed to hearing it again."

"You're perfect," he said into her lips, repeating the words over and over as his lips traced her jaw, her cheeks, her eyes, her neck. "You're so bloody perfect, darling."

26

———

BEN

Ben couldn't remember the last time he slept through the night. But when he woke up to Violet propped up on her elbow, gazing down at him with eons of warmth in her eyes, he was sure he had died, gone to heaven. There was no explanation for the idyllic sight of her like this.

"Violet," he mumbled, still trying to wake himself—absorb every line on her face and memorize how the sunlight from her bedroom window cast a breathtaking glow on her. How it lightened her hair and exposed the freckles on her cheeks.

"Good morning," she said, placing a delicate kiss on his forehead. He closed his eyes to her nearness, falling further into the daze he was in, denying the demons within a place to coincide.

The events of the night lingered on his body still. When he closed his eyes—she was above him again, underneath—once, twice, then enveloping him against marble shower walls. They had collapsed onto the bed with full force, and as he watched her eyes drift into slumber, he let himself go, too.

"What time is it?" he asked, realizing his phone was somewhere in her living room.

"Five past six. You should sleep," she replied, tracing the

lines near his eyes, sending him into a state of calming bliss as she let her fingers roam freely.

"Stupid inventory and health checks," he mumbled.

"How long do I have you?"

"Until seven-thirty. And after work, whenever you'd like."

She glowered, scrunching her nose in protest as she buried her head into the crook of his neck. Her hand traced his beard, the graceful pads of her fingers, soft and enamoring.

"Coffee then?" she suggested, hopping out of the bed more swiftly than he would've preferred.

He heard her start the coffee pot, and then she reappeared in the room before heading straight to the loo. "Aunt Helen apparently thinks I'm in a family of four; I have three extra toothbrushes here if you'd like one," she called out.

She didn't bother changing out of her pajamas, which he was selfishly happy about. The silky dark camisole, matching her black knickers, were driving him wild.

After finishing up himself, he walked over to where she stood in the kitchen, fully awake now, and kissed her with a sweltering passion. She swung her arms around his neck, and he traced his fingers over the muscled contours of her biceps.

She placed her mouth on the tip of his chin, roaming his jaw and scattering kisses all over. "I'm not at all chuffed about the fact that we had to leave the bed. Or the fact that you *have* to go to work this early."

"Don't tempt me to go back, or I'll throw everything out the window for you."

"Throw everything out the window for me, Ben."

He groaned at her admission. "Still not sure you're real. This must be a dream," he mumbled into her hair.

She looked at him with intent and then pressed a gentle kiss to the scar above his chest. He was glad he hadn't bothered with a shirt. "I'm real," she started to say, "I'm here," she finished, moving to his lips.

"And you'll stay?" he asked, hating how vulnerable the plea made him sound, yet not giving a damn because wanting her was bigger than his own blasted insecurities.

She let out a smoky laugh and tugged on his bottom lip with her teeth. "We're in my house. I should be the one asking you."

"Then ask me."

Her eyes were hazy, sparkling, and so brilliantly blue that it made his heart clench. "Will you come home to me tonight?" she asked.

He traced the stray strand of hair in front of her face and tucked it behind her ear. He smoothed his fingers along her natural waves falling in a fussy, gorgeous form. "Tonight. Tomorrow. Whenever you'll have me."

Violet tightened her arms around him. "Good, because now that I've seen it all, I'll never get over this side of you," she whispered into his chest. "Your laugh, your voice when it gets lower and catches, the way your shoulders ease and the lines on your face soften."

He wanted to engrave the delicate strings of her voice at this moment deep into his memory.

The coffee would be momentarily abandoned when they willingly started pivoting toward the rust-colored sofa. The sound of her breathing was as compelling as her laughter. He drew his hands along her back. "You're wholly responsible for it, darling. Every part of me that was dead, you've brought it back to life."

He kissed her hard and fast, limbs twisted in the small space in another round of give and take.

He rose then, hating the damned world for forcing him to. She gave him coffee in a takeaway cup. "Come by the restaurant for an early lunch? It'll be just the two of us for a bit before the rest get in at two."

"Us and Florence?" She asked.

"No. Just us. Florence detests inventory and has made it her mission to stay away."

She chuckled. "Will there be sticky toffee pudding?"

"If that's what you desire, then yes. What else would my lady like?"

She thought of it while he peppered her face with kisses.

"That, just, all of it. *You*. Who needs sustenance?"

The sounds she made were dangerous to every part of him. He'd never get to work now. "You have me. You have all of me," he rasped with his lips on her cheek.

And she did, in every way; Violet had pieces of him he hadn't ever come close to giving to others.

"Now, come on, tell me what you'd like."

"Surprise me with the food part. But make it light. I'd be lying if I said the sticky toffee pudding wasn't my top priority."

He laughed. "Ah, so that won you over, not the prospect of spending more time with me?"

"It'll go hand in hand if it's as good as your biscuits are," she declared, swinging her arms over his neck.

"Yeah?"

"What time?"

He kissed the tip of her nose. "How does noon sound?"

"Perfect," she noted.

He kissed her once more before leaving.

He loved Violet. He was certain of it—damned be anything else in the world because he knew enough to want to spend the rest of his life with her. But it concerned him because what if she wasn't ready for that? There were parts of her story he was still in the dark about.

There were pieces that she also cloaked when they first met, barricading herself beneath a tormenting need to be brave, even when her eyes propelled her pain forward. And yet, amidst a whirlwind of her own phantoms, she inched closer to him and gazed into his eyes like she wanted to understand every molecule that made him.

Ben knew he was somewhat of a decent-looking man. He knew deep within that if he weren't so anxious and if he showed the best parts of himself to the world, he could have love in his life. But she looked at him in a way that made even his bones feel seen. *Revered.*

As he watched Violet move and meander and question and sigh, he wanted only to know her further. As he got to that place where versions of her past and present coalesced, he knew he was a goner. It was difficult to let go of her then, but it'd be improbable now.

He wanted to wake up to her sweet kisses every morning, twist, and tether themselves to the bed every night. He wanted only her, always.

27

VIOLET

She really needed more clothes in her wardrobe. It'd been too long since she'd bought any new outfits. She had a few things for when she'd begin teaching next week, but nothing that screamed to be worn at this second.

She wanted to slightly dress up the light blue denim jeans and plain black t-shirt she was wearing. She shifted her velvet hangers back and forth a few times, idly grimacing before finally settling on an olive-green corduroy shirt slash jacket—"shacket," as the store websites were calling them now. This would do. If she didn't leave in the next five minutes, she would be late.

There was no time for makeup, only sunscreen, a bit of mascara, concealer, and lip balm—she'd go for the tinted moisturizing one that tasted like orange cream.

A knock on her front door rattled Violet while she was applying the balm. She grabbed the black bag hanging against a chair in her bedroom and double-checked to make sure her keys were in place.

Violet swung the bag across her shoulders and took her phone from the coffee table. It was probably Aunt Helen, she thought. Violet forced one ankle boot on when the person knocked again, harder this time, prompting her to call out, "Be right there."

When she opened the door, every muscle in her body recoiled. Tidal waves rose in her chest as she stepped back from the man standing on her doorstep. He looked like he hadn't been sleeping; his usual slicked-back black hair fell in his face, and rage boiled in his eyes.

Violet swallowed bitterly. "Dean," she managed to push out.

"You thought I wouldn't find you?" he asked, fury showing through his teeth as he shoved his way into the house; he closed the door shut behind him. "You thought drawing up divorce papers and hiring a solicitor would work in your favor?"

She gulped and backed further away from him. "Dean, please just let me go—move on, find someone new, be better," she begged, attempting logic and reason, wanting to give him the upper hand in a way that'd propel him to hear her for once.

He seized both her wrists and yanked her toward him.

She dropped her phone on the floor.

"What did I tell you about deciding who I'm with and what I do?" he bit back.

Violet tried twisting her wrists to unchain herself, but he tightened his grip harder.

A gross sneer formed on his mouth, and the rage in his eyes grew deeper. "We're married, and that's how it'll remain," he said with gritted teeth. "Pack your bags. We're going home. You're going to ring your solicitor tomorrow, and we're calling this entire thing off before it's filed in the court."

"Why? Why do you want to stay married to me? For Christ's sake, you don't even like me."

"Because no couple looks as good together as we do. The satisfaction of knowing I am the man beside you while others gawk at your fine arse," he pointed out roughly. "It's what every man dreams of."

The words repulsed her beyond measure. She pushed them on a back burner. If she was going to have her way, he needed to believe that she'd be the one losing in this. "The women you've been with are all better looking than I am. You can have any of them." Though she hoped that none of those women would find themselves permanently tied to him.

It's going to take a miracle for that man to change, his brother had told Violet. Matthew knew exactly what he was doing when he moved his family far from Dean, calling Violet to check in every so often. What changed men like Dean? Was it crossing a line they couldn't come back from, or did they feed the monsters inside of them until death came knocking? She didn't want to know, and she couldn't bear the thought of finding out.

He dodged the question by slowly repeating, "Pack your bags." He paused then and disregarded himself. "Or better yet, what you have now works. Most of your nice clothes are in our wardrobe anyway," he barked.

Violet shook her head. "Don't make this any more difficult than it has to be. I won't tell anyone you came here. I won't say a word. I won't make things worse for you if you leave me alone."

Her phone vibrated loudly on the floor, and she could see his eyes dart toward the screen. *Ben.*

Fury ruptured in his eyes. "Who the fuck is Ben?" he bellowed through his teeth.

She was quick on her feet in responding. "My landlord. He probably heard you. Keep your voice down. This isn't London."

He huffed a sardonic laugh. "You think I don't know that your landlord is Mrs. Henry? How do you think I found you, you lying bitch. I'll ask again. Who the fuck is Ben?"

"Fine. He's my neighbor."

He snatched harder at her wrists, trying to push fear into her. "You're lying to me."

She looked him dead in the eyes and repeated the truth

word for word. "You're hurting me. Let me go. As much as you're a disgusting bastard, even this is beyond you."

He twisted harder. "Answer my fucking question."

"He. Is. My. Neighbor." Violet said, enunciating every word.

"Well then, you can text him on our way out, tell him that everything is fine, and he can delete your number now. There's no need for him to have it any longer."

Violet's head was spinning. The ripples from anxiety and fear were colliding in a way she hadn't experienced in a while, scaring her for the first time in ages.

"No," she muttered, trying to stand her ground.

"And why not? Is it because you're lying to me?" He let go of her wrists, holding her face in his hands, crushing it.

She shook her head.

"Answer me!"

She finally squirmed out of his clutches and bit back the truth. "He's a friend, for crying out loud. I'm supposed to meet him for lunch. You're the one who repeatedly cheats on me, or have you forgotten that already?"

Dean picked up her phone and threw it against the wall. She flinched, hearing the hard-shell case hit the ground with a loud thud and fragments of shattering glass from what she assumed was a frame on the wall. With every word out of his mouth, he moved closer, forcing her to take a step back. "You do not have lunch with men who are not me. You do not look at men who are not me. And you damn well do not lie to me."

She fought back the tears as he grabbed her shoulders. Dean was slightly shorter in height to Ben, but holding her down with all his might made her defenseless. Everything she learned to defend herself abandoned her when she needed it most.

"Stop," she screamed, finally shoving him away with the strength she mustered. But he was too quick and seized her wrists again.

She could feel her skin crawl. She could swear her soul threatened to leave her body, not wanting any memory of this after the night spent with Ben—gentle and warm and so right. She tried to remember it, desperately wanting to hold on as she debated the next step.

Her head wouldn't stop spinning. Her focus blurred. Was her blood pressure dropping? Rising? Was it vertigo? She couldn't hold on. He was repelling.

"Or what? I told you, Violet, we're good together. I have a reputation to uphold, and you're a part of it. You don't get to leave me. Briar would've been penniless without my firm. On the outside, we're a perfect match, and that's how it'll remain. I'm sure the school would have no problem taking you back as head teacher. No one will have to know about this little stunt you pulled."

He crushed her wrists again, and she winced in pain.

"I'm not going anywhere with you," she tried to say, slurring the words. She kept drawing herself back, moving before she tumbled backward in a hazy disassociation, hitting her head against a picture frame and falling to the floor with a loud thud.

28

BEN

It wasn't like Violet to be late and unresponsive, but he tried not to make way for the scenarios running through his head. Maybe he should've left his car with her. Perhaps the bus was running late.

But when Mrs. Henry's name flashed on his phone thirteen minutes after noon, Ben's heart sank in his chest.

Something was wrong.

He could feel it now.

"Mrs. Henry, hi," he answered.

Her voice was shaking. "Ben. It's Violet. We're at the hospital. She may have a concussion."

His entire being crumbled.

"I'll be there straight away," he replied, turning off every appliance in such a frenzy he hoped he didn't miss anything. He sped toward the door with every limb in his body shuddering. He rang Florence to tell her that he'd be leaving, thankful that even if she'd be frustrated, she'd understand.

"Don't tell me you've burned my kitchen down before an inspection because that's the only reason you should be calling me now," she said.

Typically Florence was guaranteed to get a chuckle out of him, but not today. Especially not right now. "I need to go to the hospital. Violet's been hurt."

Her gasp was oddly comforting. "Oh no, love, I'm so sorry. I hope she's okay. I'll come down to the Branch now; don't you worry. Jeff and Billy are due in at two, anyway. Are you okay to drive?"

"I'm fine. Thank you. I just needed you to know."

"I've known you for years, son. You hide too much of how you're feeling. I'm in the right to be concerned, and I need to know that you're okay," she repeated, more authoritative in her tone while maintaining her warmth.

"I'm not okay. No, of course, I'm not. But I'm fine. I'll be safe."

"Alright. Keep me posted, will you? And I won't peep a word to anyone about this." He was glad he didn't have to tell her not to.

His vision went dark for a moment as his head spun through flames. He sat in the car and breathed deeply. He couldn't let panic rise.

He needed to get to Violet.

How Ben latched the panic out and drove to the hospital, he had next to no recollection.

Something—someone must've been looking out for him. He found a spot to park right near the entrance. As he approached the automatic doors, he spotted Helen Henry seated in a corner. She stood up when he approached.

"What happened? How is she?" he asked in a frenzy.

"They're doing tests now. I heard her door slam, and Violet is not one to slam doors. Freddy and I found her on the floor and that bastard running out."

Ben's insides were in knots.

"Was it her ex?"

"Must've been. I ran after Freddy, who bolted for her door

the moment I opened ours. I should've paid more attention to our surroundings."

As though she caught the rage and uneasiness rising in his chest, the older woman put her hand on his shoulder in the same reassuring manner she always had when he was especially quiet in the early days after his father died. "She's going to be okay. She's tough as nails, that one."

He closed his eyes and nodded.

After a short while that felt like ages, a nurse approached them. She looked back and forth to the two of them standing side by side. "Are you both here for Violet Wedlake?"

They confirmed in unison.

"The doctor should be by soon with the results, if you'd like to see her now."

Helen placed her hand back on Ben's shoulder. "I'm going to call my husband and fill him in. Go on in, love. I'm sure she'll be glad to see you."

The sight of Violet in a hospital bed compared to the vision he had of her from this morning was a punch in the guts far worse than any flesh wound he'd had. She looked so small that it was killing him.

He inhaled sharply as her eyes caught his.

He walked over to her and placed his hand on hers, rubbing his thumb gently against her fingers.

She said his name with a barely audible whisper.

"Yes, darling. I'm here," he coaxed, moving his fingers over the side of her face and to her cheeks.

She licked her lips, grimacing as she sat up even higher.

"How do you feel?"

She released a small sigh. "I'm fine."

He rubbed his palm against her forearm. She was trying to keep a brave face, and he hated it.

"Dean was here," she said in a low, exhausted voice.

"In the hospital?"

"No, at home."

He gulped convulsively, trying to keep his rage in check, but a disoriented Violet was making his vision red all over.

"Did he hurt you?" he asked.

"My wrists," she replied, turning them over; the one closest to him was a bit red, but the other was slightly darker. If marks with purples and blues appeared, he was sure he could kill the man. Revolt surged inside of him. He felt ill and horrified.

He gently brought her hand to his mouth, pressing her knuckles carefully against his lips. He held her there for a beat until a slight movement alerted him.

The last time he was in a hospital room, his best mate was in a coma, kept alive by machines, saved by miracles and twenty-six stitches. He watched as Nina wept in his arms, cursing and swearing that this had to be the end of it.

He watched Edmund hang up his badge a few days later, knowing they'd both be better off that way.

He didn't want to go back to the man he was, but every bone in his body demanded to rip Dean into shreds and give him back tenfold the pain he had caused Violet. The augmenting rage inside of him could frighten her. It could break her spirits further. She had to be safe with him. He needed to guarantee that, but he felt defenseless with her in this state.

"Ben," she called out.

He drew his attention to her face, and her eyes were glassy. "What is it?"

When her lips quivered and her nose scrunched, Ben's heart came to a precipitous halt. He'd seen Violet in tears before, and he was partly responsible for them sixteen years ago. He kissed them away and held her close. But when Violet turned her head and sobbed, he tasted death for the first time.

He sat on the edge of the bed and put his arms around her.

"Ssh. You're safe, darling. I promise. It's okay; everything's going to be okay." He soothed and let her cry in his arms.

"Men often get away with what they want," she sobbed. "What's the likelihood I'll be believed over him?"

Everything in front of him was red. *Fire.* Ben took a deep, excruciating breath as she inched closer to him. He hated Dean.

He hated his entire damned kind for having such an appalling reputation in this bloody world.

He pressed his lips to her head and carefully nestled her closer. "Please, try not to worry right now. You're not going anywhere you don't want to. I won't let that happen," he promised, hearing her sigh and calm and shift. He loathed how much she must've bottled up in the past.

Her head lulled back against him and stayed there. He was grateful she felt safe with him.

The doctor came after a few moments. "Ms. Wedlake, how are you feeling?" he asked Violet.

Her lips curved amiably. "My head and my wrists hurt a bit, but I'm mostly fine."

"You have a Grade I concussion but nothing more dangerous, and the small cut on the back of your head should heal itself. Your blood pressure was very low when they found you. Is this common?"

"It happens, yes, but it's rare." She answered.

"Hmm, alright then. It has evened out now, so you are good to head home if you have someone who can drive and monitor you for the next forty-eight hours."

"I can," Ben confirmed.

The doctor nodded and looked back at Violet again. "You'll need to rest, Ms. Wedlake. Ice those wrists if they bruise, and if the headache doesn't go away or if it worsens, you come right back."

"Okay," she said with a nod. "Thank you."

She squeezed Ben's hand tightly before slowly rising off the bed.

"Stay with me?" he asked.

A faint display of solicitude landed on her face. "You have to go to work."

She was mad to think that he'd be concerned with anything other than her right now. Work especially. "I have it covered. You're more important right now," he declared.

"I can stay with Aunt Helen, or she could come over," she countered.

"Are you saying that because it's genuinely what you'd prefer or because you think you're putting me out? If it's the former, I won't argue, but if it's the latter, I need you to understand that I can't bear the thought of being apart from you right now."

"Okay," she agreed. "Can we go to mine first so I can shower? Then we can stay at yours?"

He nodded.

They drove back home in companionable silence. Mrs. Henry was quiet in the back seat, undoubtedly just as scared as Ben. Her eyes had welled up as she took Violet into her arms. He knew she loved Violet as much as she loved her own daughter, but he didn't realize quite how much until he saw it. It broke his heart to think of all the tragedies she must've witnessed right alongside her. He imagined Simone's heartbreak at the news.

He gripped the steering wheel so tightly his knuckles were turning white. Violet must've noticed it because she set her hand on his thigh, gently nudging him to ease. He tried to shut his mind off, tried to set the fury at bay, focus solely on her and not what he'd like to do for her, but it was eating him alive.

He had to do something. *Anything.*

Thomas Henry was waiting outside when Ben parked the car and opened their doors. The older gentleman then wrapped

Violet in his arms. "You gave us quite a fright there, sweetheart. I'm so glad you're alright," he said.

"I'm sorry, Uncle Thomas," Violet replied, and Ben caught sight of the tears she tried to hold back. He loathed the fact that she felt the need to apologize, even if he knew she would've done it no matter the circumstances.

"You're okay. That's all that matters."

Thomas reached out for Ben's hand, shaking it firmly with wordless gratitude. He'd never get to meet her parents, but he was grateful to know Violet had the next best thing.

"You need anything at all, Violet, holler. We'll be right there," Helen said. Violet nodded and turned back to Ben. He smiled awkwardly, then gestured for her to walk toward her house.

She stopped at her door and reached into her bag for the keys. Mrs. Henry had noted it was around her body when they found her.

She gulped and stood frozen.

Her eyes went glassy. She looked frightened, making the blood in his veins surge. This was supposed to be her safe place, and Dean tainted that. Ben reached carefully for the keys in her hand, and she let go freely. He placed his hand at the small of her back and opened the door for her, stepping in first to ensure the front point was empty.

She kicked off her shoes, and he helped her remove her jacket, hanging it on the stand beside him. Violet placed her bag down on a small chair and walked straight to the bedroom. He followed her there, thinking of how the day could've gone differently. Hours ago, they were entangled in this bed, and now she was moving as though these walls were oozing with terrors.

She opened a drawer, took a few clothing items, and then walked to the shower. "I'll be quick," she said.

"Take your time. Call out if you need me."

Ben walked over to the living room and stood in the middle of the quaint space. His eyes caught a broken painting of wildflowers on the floor. Realizing it was where she must have fallen made his entire body shudder. Unspeakable rage filled him once more, hitting bone deep at the thought of how much pain she must've endured today and before this—the days where she had dealt with it alone.

Her phone was on the floor on the other side of the wall, beside a photograph.

He found her broom peeking through the cupboard near the kitchen and cleaned the glass off the floor, bending forward then to clean the small droppings of blood off the ground with a damp washcloth.

He took a deep breath and stilled himself against the TV stand. He didn't know how long he was standing there until he heard Violet's footsteps approaching him.

"You didn't have to do that," she said, leaning against the door frame.

"I wanted to."

She held her hand out to him, gesturing for him to come closer. Violet laced their fingers together, the same way she had when the sunset crept through that muggy July evening in Paris.

I wish you could stay.

Violet rested her forehead against his. "I wish I had asked you to stay in Paris. Perhaps our lives would've been different. But you're here now, and that look in your eyes is more heartbreaking than when we parted. What is it, Ben?"

"I don't know how to help you. I don't know what to do. And I hate that this happened to you," he answered.

He sighed into her wet hair—lilacs taking hold of him.

She let out a low whimper and drew closer to him. "I

promise I'm fine, and I know you're not going to accept that right now, but will you at least try?"

He placed a kiss on the side of her temple. He wasn't going to accept shit until Dean Colborne paid the bloody price for coming near her.

They walked out of her house together, with Ben scouring the perimeter for signs of anything that looked unusual.

29

VIOLET

She woke up on a bed that wasn't hers, and a faint thumping in her head.

Ben's. It's okay. You're at Ben's. She repeated to herself and took in the surroundings of his bedroom. He had a navy accent wall, two drawers, and a few hanging shelves with books and artifacts on them.

She noticed a paper airplane by his bedside table, *hers,* she realized, and it made her heart soar to know he kept it. His furniture was shades of mahogany brown, and a painting of a large forest hung on one wall. She hadn't done much to her bedroom; she wanted to wait—wanted to be sure, and now, she wasn't sure she ever wanted to go back despite how much she adored every corner of it.

She removed the blanket and sat up, taking a few deep breaths in and out. Her wrist might've ached more than her head at this point, but the worst of it all was the uncertainty of where this would all lead. She told Ben she was fine. She told him not to worry. But the truth was, she was scared stiff of what else Dean could put her through. The things he could possibly make up to tarnish her name at Briar as well as the district. What if it got to Knightley?

The anxiety made her feel more disoriented. She felt out of sorts for beats longer than she would've liked to. And much of it was blurring together now. She had to distract herself.

She rose slowly from the bed and walked to his kitchen, where she heard noises.

"Ben?" she called out.

He looked up from behind the counter, wearing a black apron with pinstripes on it. It delighted her to no end. Gomez Addams would approve.

"Did you nap well?" he asked.

She nodded to say yes. "What are you doing?"

"Dinner—amends for the lunch I had promised."

"You're an angel. Anything I can help with?"

"Yes, you can sit right there and do nothing."

She scowled. "But I want to help."

He lifted his eyebrows in protest. "You can help by resting. Doctor's orders."

"I have a minor concussion. It's not that serious." She wanted to argue further, make a comment about how she hated being coddled, but the look in his eyes noted that he wasn't in the headspace for any of it. He was scared.

"It's serious to me, Violet. I never want to see you in a hospital room again."

His concern was so palpable she didn't know what to do with it. She didn't know how to comfort him. Hell, she didn't even know how to help herself—she only knew how to deflect with humor.

She had to try and take both their minds off her situation. "Can I ask you a question then?"

"Of course," he replied.

"How do you plan on making me happy when I have to sit here and be useless?" she proclaimed with a huff, desperately wanting to nudge him out of the fear. She wanted to show that she was okay.

"There's sticky toffee pudding to compensate for your boredom."

"Ben, is there really?"

He confirmed with an amiable smile. "I promised it, didn't I?" It made her heart tumble and flutter.

"Okay, fine, another question then."

"Go on."

"Did you rob Gomez Addams' basement for that apron, or was it some sort of cosplay thing? Is there a hidden fanboy inside of you?"

He laughed. *Good.* This was what she wanted—the calm in his ocean blue eyes to return.

"My sister gave it to me. You're going to have to ask her whose basement she robbed it from."

"Noted. I'll keep this burning question in mind. I have much to thank her for. It's doing a lot for me right now."

"Is that so?"

"Oh, yeah," she reaffirmed.

"Good to know. We both know how to speak French, too. And I should've asked what you'd want for dinner, but I figured you'd be nice and say surprise me still. I hope tomato soup and cheese toasties will do."

Her eyes went wide. *The only downfall of not being in Los Angeles is missing out on the best cheese toastie they have at a place near the airport.* She had told him that during one of the nights they'd stepped out together. Had he remembered that? Or was this merely a coincidence?

She looked at him for a beat.

He pushed down on the top of the electric grill. "I know it probably won't compare to the one you told me about in Los Angeles, but hopefully, it's not rubbish."

Her mouth fell open. "You remember," she started, falling short of how to follow the fact.

He smiled. "I remember all of it, darling." The warmth in his confirmation was tangible. She could question plenty of things in this world, but Ben's sincerity was indisputable.

Her memory was also sharp, but goodness, how did he remember *that*? She'd nearly forgotten until he said cheese toastie. What else had she told him that he held onto with neatly tied bows?

They ate mostly in silence after she noted that she couldn't quite remember the taste of the ones in Los Angeles or even the restaurant's name. Was it Cheese Barn? Cheese and Barn? No matter; she was sure this would be her favorite now anyway.

He then presented her with the moment of truth. Was his sticky toffee pudding good enough?

"This could make or break us, Ben."

"To be fair, I don't think you can critique this one too harshly or any of this," he said, gesturing to the empty plates. "I was stress-cooking, so I wouldn't have to think about the hundred different ways I could kill your ex-husband."

She smiled softly and nodded.

"Somehow, I'm certain you're going to ruin me, and I'm not ready for it," she said. She took a bite, making sure she had a perfect layer, then moaned. *Yep*, just as she had with the bloody biscuits the first time she tried them. She moaned. She was beyond feeling embarrassed at this point. There was no way to hide it.

He chuckled at the reaction, and it made it that much better. "This is the best sticky toffee pudding I've ever had, and I'm not just saying that! The texture is perfect, and the taste is exquisite. I often find that the level of sweetness can be too much or too little in some places, but this is utter perfection. You're magic, Ben. What sorcery is this?" she exclaimed.

His enormous grin could ignite the sky. "Cheers. I'm so glad you like it," he replied, inching closer and placing a soft peck on her lips.

"I like mushy peas. I *love* this."

"Then I'll bake it for you whenever you like."

"Don't tell me that. How have you learned by now *not* to tell me these things? I'll take you up on them, and then you'll be sick of me."

He shook his head with a vehement frown. "Don't joke about that. I could never be sick of you."

His seriousness broke her heart. She was putting him through a roller coaster of emotions. She could tell this situation weighed arduously on his chest, and she wanted to make it stop.

She wanted him to lighten up.

She felt like she had a genuine partner for the first time, which made the pain worse—the concerns on his face, the hardened lines, the deep, penetrating sadness in his eyes—it was all too much.

She needed him to hold her, and, more importantly, she needed to hold him. He stood up, took their plates over to the kitchen sink, and began washing. She rose to help him, brushing aside the headache, knowing he'd try to argue against it.

"I'm helping with dishes," she started, and knowing he'd protest, she quickly added, "According to the internet, there's nothing that forbids any of this."

"The internet isn't a doctor," he replied dryly.

"But in this case, the internet is more helpful," she paused then gazed into his eyes, "Plus, I want you to hold me, and that'll happen faster when I help."

"Or, I could skip the dishes and hold you right now," he said, setting a cup in the sink.

"No, after. *Please?*"

He shook his head with a smile peeking through. "Fine, you can dry. If anything bothers you at all, stop. Okay?"

"Ben, we're two people. You didn't feed an army."

"It doesn't matter," he protested.

It didn't even last five minutes. And she valued his cleanliness. "Good as new," she said, folding the cloth thrice over; she set it on the counter and then looped her arms around his neck. Ben's arms encircled her waist.

"Thank you for taking care of me today," she said, tracing her fingers on the nape of his neck.

He shook his head and exhaled. "There's no need to thank me."

"There is."

He bit the inside of his cheek and clenched his jaw. A brush of fire flashed in his eyes, then subdued to a warm ember. "There's nothing I wouldn't do for you, Violet."

Ben placed a tender kiss on her forehead. It felt as though he was apologizing for the day, cementing his promises of the words said aloud into her.

"How did someone as gentle as you stay at MI6, Ben? That must have been so taxing," she finally asked, wanting to know, more than anything else, how his softness and sharp edges intermingled in a way that never once felt threatening.

"You want me to answer that in the middle of the kitchen?" he said with a low chuckle.

"Yes," she drew out. "Unless you've got somewhere better."

He smiled, then asked, "Sofa or bed," in a hushed whisper.

"Sofa."

Violet sat at the same edge she always had, the opposite end of where he preferred. He sat beside her and lifted her legs to rest them on his. He swung his arm around her back, and her head rested against the cushion. She looked up at him, eager for answers.

Ben drew in a deliberate breath. "From what I can remember, I was always a bit anxious and introverted, but when I was a teen, it got a lot louder in my head. I didn't know how to fit in, and while I wasn't slacking off in school, it was hard to grasp the material, so it started to make me feel useless. Dad said I was temperamental and would go days without talking to anyone. I remember thinking he'd have it a lot easier if he were only taking care of one kid."

Violet's heart shattered in her chest.

"The smart one who never misbehaved. The extrovert who could light up whatever room she was in. I didn't want to be a burden to them. My grandmother and aunt helped a lot anyway. Emma was in good hands," he continued. "I thought maybe I should join the Armed Forces or something equally reckless because it didn't matter. But Edmund suggested MI6, and I think I told you that part. Dad was against it for years, especially with his knowledge and experiences."

He sighed and leaned his head back. "It was the only time where I wasn't in my own head. I didn't think about myself or how I was feeling. I didn't care. I just wanted the restlessness to stop, and it allowed me to be more calculated where it mattered. I knew it wasn't going to be forever. Therapy here and there solidified that I needed to confront my grief, and before I could make the decision to leave and find a career more satisfying and less risky, Dad had the stroke."

She traced the pads of her fingers against his beard. "You would think it would have hardened you a bit. I'm so happy it didn't. It's what always stood out to me," she said.

She was picturing him as a boy, restless and withdrawn and unsure of how to push forward. She wasn't like that as a little girl; she was more fiery, loud, and active. It was later that darkness and trauma caught her in a snare.

But the voice inside of her noted that teenage Ben and Violet could've been great together, finding comfort in the silence of the other's company. The thought made her smile: her fire and his calm.

"It did where it had to, I think. I got a bit better at countering anxious thoughts with more level-headed alternatives. I don't know if I've ever considered myself gentle, but I suppose it makes sense. My mother was so warm, Violet. She was kind and soft-spoken. Perhaps a version of me always aimed to mimic that a bit. My dad, as you've met, was kind too but more assertive."

"I think we do that whether we realize it or not. The first time I legally ordered a drink, I asked for straight whiskey because it's what my father would order. I hadn't tried it before then. But I suppose it's our way of finding ways to be closer to them. To understand the parts of them that we didn't get a chance to when they were with us. Plus, Dad was a dentist, so I couldn't walk in his shoes the same way I could with Mum's."

He smiled with a serene gaze. She wanted to kiss him. She wanted to learn more. She wanted to know every detail about him that brought him to this place today. Did he ever have a schoolboy crush? Did she reciprocate? Was she kind to him?

"I'd never been more distracted on the job than I was the day we met," he blurted.

"Oh?"

"When you looked at me, something burst forward from the walls I'd built," he said. "And then, when I heard your laugh, I swear I felt drunk for a beat. I wasn't sure how to focus. You spun everything around me in circles."

His fingers traced idle rings against her legs. It was maddening.

A blush heated her cheeks. "On that note, when did you

know you wanted to ask me out? Because you say that now, but knowing you, you wouldn't have done it then."

He chuckled. "The third time when I came to get you, and we'd had a bad day with the case, do you remember that?"

"Yeah, I don't think I'd planned to come out that day, but you came to our door."

He nodded. "I briefly told you it'd been a tough day, and I don't know...It was the way you put your hand on my forearm. You steadied me," he paused, inhaling softly. "I don't think you realized it. I couldn't read your expression then, but the gesture stayed with me." He traced her jaw tenderly. "I thought about it all night while I tried to sleep, and I knew that, no matter what happened, I wanted the chance to at least see you away from that hotel. I wanted to take you on a proper date and make you feel as safe as you made me feel."

"You know I've never let another man kiss me on the first date—I would wait," she smiled.

"You're serious?" he said, his hand moving along her back.

"Yeah. You were the exception, and I didn't want anything to change that later either," she returned. She wanted to comb her fingers through his hair and trace the lines on his face, but her wrist was starting to ache again, and lifting felt like it'd require herculean effort.

They sat in comfortable silence for a beat. Violet's head cradled in the crook of his neck; his arm secured her close to him while his hand brushed her hair in gentle strokes.

"You're the best thing that's ever happened to me," he whispered as he shut his eyes.

It was at that moment where Violet realized she couldn't and didn't want to hide how much she loved him. Certain beyond anything else in the world that love was different with Ben because it was supposed to be.

She felt safe with him.

She felt strong with him.

She felt like she'd still be steady even if the world spun in a treacherous sphere.

She was about to blurt her feelings, and then he released a heavy sigh before speaking.

"I wish you took up my offer and emailed, Violet. I always hoped to see your name pop up in my inbox, but it never came."

Her heart split wide open. "I can't count how many times I drafted a note, even just a simple, "Hey, how are you doing?" But I never pressed send because I was worried. I could never find you on social media. You weren't even on LinkedIn. You were a ghost, Ben. What if you were married with kids, and it caused problems between the two of you? What if you never replied? I did come really close once while hammered, but my mate Eddie talked me out of it. Said if I still wanted to, I could send it in the morning. The morning came and logic returned. Plus, I could never actually take you up on those words. I knew you were sincere, but I...I didn't want to burden anyone. Half the time, I could barely talk to my friends."

"You could never burden me. Please tell me you know that now?"

She did know it.

She believed him with everything in her.

He was, in every way, her in-between beneath the sky. She thought it then, but she understood it entirely now. He was the anchor in her turbulent life.

And it scared her because losing Ben would hurt a thousand times more today than it did back then.

She looked at him then, tears brimming in her eyes. She wouldn't deny loving him any further.

She'd take the chance, stand square in his life, and maybe this time they could stay.

"I love you, Ben. I didn't want to say it too soon. I wanted to wait...I wanted," she shook her head and gritted her teeth, fighting the nerves foreboding inside of her. "I love you," she repeated. "I think I've loved you since you brought me two months' worth of gum, then held my hand at the restaurant, and I kept loving you even when I thought I'd never see you again. And now, this could very well push you away because it might be too much, but I need you to know that I've never felt what I feel with you."

She caught his breath hitch in his throat. "Violet," he started, his eyes misting.

He palmed the side of her face and held her there. He took a deep, ragged breath, "There are no words for how much I love you." He bit his bottom lip and closed his eyes, releasing a low laugh and an exhale. "How could you think that would push me away? You are everything to me, Violet—you're my whole entire heart—every part of me is yours. It's been yours since the day we met, and it'll be yours even if you decide you no longer want it." She felt the words cement into her soul—with every bone in her body, every bruise, every scar, she understood it.

He gently lowered her head to his and took her lips with tender tugs, inching closer only when she gave permission, careful not to push or pull too hard. They found themselves in a languid rhythm of contentment. A low, painful groan left her throat, compelling Ben to pull away despite her attempts to hide the discomfort.

"What is it? Is it your head?" he said, concern exposed so intensely in his eyes again that it hurt more than the physical pain.

"I'm fine. I promise," she said.

"Violet," he replied with an elongated pitch, looking at her with an urgency bleeding into his trepidation.

"My wrist. I moved it wrong."

He gently took her forearm, careful not to press weight anywhere near her hand. Drawing it to his mouth, he pressed a featherlike kiss to her pulse point.

"We'll ice it before you go to bed tonight," he said.

30

BEN

Ben was sure he'd never get tired of waking up in a bed with Violet—hair strands falling from the loose braid she put it in the night before, sunlight casting a brilliant glow on her face. In every way, sharing his space with her felt right.

Her soft gaze met his eyes shortly after he sat up in the bed.

"Morning," she said through a small yawn.

"Hi, darling. How are you feeling?" he inquired.

She blinked, then rested her eyes again for a beat as though waking up still. "Better. My headache waned significantly."

"And your wrists? Does any other place hurt from your fall?"

She slowly rose from his bed, sitting up to take a few deep, silent breaths before standing. Good, because the last thing she needed on top of a concussion was to feel dizzy because she got up too quickly.

"Only a little," she answered. But he wasn't buying it. When she sat up, he caught a glimpse of her wrist, purples and blues making their way onto her skin. He knew she was hiding the truth to get him to stop fussing, though he wasn't capable of that. If he didn't do it aloud, he'd dwell internally until it drove him mad.

"I'm going to go home and change, then pop in to say hi to Aunt Helen." He wanted to protest and offer to go with her, terrified at the thought of her being alone in that house. But he reasoned with himself that since he was home, he'd be there if anything were to happen. It would be a few moments anyway, and he didn't want to scare her away with his worrying. Not now.

"What would you like for breakfast?" Ben asked.

A curve formed on her pink lips. "You don't have to spoil me every day, you know? I'll have whatever you're having."

"Oh, but I do have to spoil you."

She scrunched softly and dropped her shoulders. "I'd give an arm and a leg for coffee, but I can't have that now."

He let out a low chuckle. "Soon. Come on now. What'll it be?"

"Surprise me."

He huffed, shaking his head playfully. He wanted her to be needy, loud, and demanding. He wanted her to tell him every little thing, including what she desired. He didn't even have avocados, so he couldn't make her toast.

His phone buzzed on the nightstand. His sister was calling. He answered as Violet switched out of pajamas.

"Emma, hey, you alright?"

"Well enough. You?" she answered on the other end of the line.

"I'm good, yeah."

"Listen, Catherine is reeling from a cold, so she might be crabby. You think you can handle it? We can have Luke stay home with the girls, but they were really looking forward to seeing you."

He was supposed to watch his nieces in two days. "Oh, fuck.

I'd completely forgotten about that. Of course, it's fine. You're bringing them on Thursday?" he confirmed.

"Yeah, everything, all right? You never forget."

"All good. Long story."

"Well, tell me when we get in then," she noted before hanging up.

He turned to Violet. "I forgot that my sister is supposed to bring my nieces for the weekend. They come on Thursday."

"Oh, that's lovely! Well, forty-eight hours will pass by then, so I should be back home," she replied eagerly. Her chipper tone at the idea of leaving saddened him a bit.

He was careful not to sound demanding, but he needed her to believe that he didn't want to exercise the thought of her being away from him when Dean's whereabouts were unclear. "Do *you* want to leave, Violet? Is that truly what you would prefer? Because I'm not going to oppose it if it's what you want, but I can't bear the thought of you alone."

She came to his side of the bed and stood closer to him. "I'm not a child. I've taken care of myself for years after my parents died. I know how to be alone more than I know how to be with other people."

I know how to be alone more than I know how to be with other people. And that's the part that scared him the most. They were both used to one way, consistently handling their problems on their own. They needed to learn a shared way of living. "I know you're not. I know you can handle it. Trust me, I know. But is that what you want? Do you want to leave? Because I'll go mad thinking only of you when I'm supposed to be responsible for two small humans."

She cupped his cheek and smiled. "Babe, I'm right next door, not miles away."

"Still. Is that what you want?"

"What if I stay with Aunt Helen?"

He shook his head. "Do you want to leave?"

"I don't, but..." she started to say.

"Again, unless you *want* to leave, I have no problem admitting to you that I'm far too greedy to let you go now that I've woken up beside you. I need you to stay, and I'll get down on my knees if you'd like me to beg. I'm not above it."

She chuckled. "You really are mad."

Good, he'd win this round. He had to. The thought of Violet anywhere except beside him weakened him.

"Don't I know it? Plus, I'm making almond cherry Welsh cakes and ice cream waffles. You and Lily could have a field day."

She scrunched her nose and threw her arms up in a dramatic gesture. "Why didn't you just start with waffles? How old are they?"

"Catherine's eight. Lily's six."

"Aw, Catherine is Phoebe's age."

He nodded with a small laugh. "I met Phoebe once. She's a sweet kid."

"Isn't she? She's her mother's daughter in every way."

He chuckled at the sentiment. It occurred to him then that Violet seemed like she would have wanted kids. Or maybe she didn't. If they were a bit younger, it could've been nice, he thought. "Hey, a bit of a personal question; tell me if it's too much, yeah?"

Her eyes broke him a little. Almost as if she knew. "Why don't I have kids?"

He nodded.

"I suppose it's my own problem for never outright asking him before we married, but Dean couldn't. He knew but failed to mention it, then claimed he was sure he had told me. I always wanted kids, but I don't know." She paused for a beat as though she were recalling the kind of life she could've had. "He knew I wanted them, but he'd hum and haw when I mentioned it."

Ben took a deep breath. "I'm so sorry."

"It's quite alright. I made my peace with it. We could've adopted too, but I'm partly glad we didn't. I would've hated to bring a child into this world with a father like him and all the issues he'd cause."

Ben sighed. The thoughts of what their past could have been haunted him once more. She should have never had to get used to not having what she wanted. The idea of having kids and a family was a foreign concept to him after a while—marriage, a shared future with someone else wasn't a life he pictured. Yet with Violet, he wanted it all.

Whatever she wanted—he'd make it happen.

She kissed his forehead briefly before stepping out.

"Call or scream if you need anything, alright?" he called out.

"I won't be long."

He walked back to his kitchen, trying to keep his nerves in check, suddenly remembering that Violet had yet to try his blueberry scones. He had a batch frozen a few days ago. There wasn't a way to make anything more glamorous with the ingredients he had in his fridge for something savory. He needed to go to the supermarket, but there was no way in hell he was leaving Violet alone for that long.

He would distract himself until she was back, but he hated this caging fear trying to lock him down. He couldn't stop his mind from imagining the worst-case scenarios.

It was only yesterday.

She seemed fine this morning. Truly. She seemed fine last night despite the pain in her wrist.

Still, he couldn't risk anything. He couldn't shake the agony he felt at the thought of her in any sort of pain or the prospect of Dean returning.

He couldn't shake that there was more to what Dean did that she wasn't telling him—more she was potentially afraid or unsure of. Yet, he didn't want to pry.

He already felt overbearing and hated himself for it.

31

———

VIOLET

After quickly changing her clothes at her place, she headed straight for Aunt Helen's house. Violet walked in while she was on the phone with Simone; they stopped in the foyer when Helen passed the device to Violet. Uncle Thomas offered to take Violet's phone to the shop to fix her broken screen.

A heap of concerns came from the other end. "Simone, I'm fine. I promise," she said into the phone.

"I would've been there in a heartbeat, babe, but Phoebe's ill."

"I know you would, and it's okay, I'm in good hands. And I have loads to tell you when we get a beat. Give my goddaughter the biggest hug."

"I need all the details when Mum's not hovering," her best friend declared with a chuckle.

Simone's support, despite not having the details, was the best stamp of approval. "I'll call you when I have my phone back. Love you!"

"I love you with my whole chest, you beautiful creature. Take it easy, yeah?"

"I will. Promise."

Violet handed the phone over to Helen and smirked at the quizzical expression she wore. "What?"

Helen raised her eyebrows. "I didn't say a thing."

Violet traced a circle with her fingers. "Yes, but your face is saying plenty."

Helen shrugged and crossed her arms. "My face is simply very glad you're okay and wants to know absolutely nothing about what you and my tenant are doing."

"We're drinking tea," she gave Helen a quick peck on the cheek and bolted out the door. "Okay, bye."

She preferred Aunt Helen when she was joking around or offering her honest advice—anything but the silence Violet experienced yesterday. She didn't want anyone to worry about her, especially not the woman who'd become like a mother to her. Violet knew Aunt Helen loved her deeply and understood how worrisome it must've been to be the one to find her.

Violet walked back over to Ben's, wondering how this situation would work out in the future. She would have to go home eventually, but if she was frank with herself, the thought of sleeping in her bed alone scared her now. It wasn't as harrowing to walk into the living area this time, but she wasn't sure she could stay there anymore. Her safe place had been tainted with Dean's intrusion.

She swung Ben's door open, and a buttery, sweet scent welcomed her. She trekked toward the kitchen, trying to guess what he was making.

"I hope you like scones," he revealed when he saw her.

"I *love* scones."

"Good because it's all I had."

Ben was now wearing a buffalo plaid apron and mixing what she assumed were the waffle ingredients for tomorrow. This was his most colorful yet, and he once again looked too unfairly fit. *Red buffalo plaid.* It looked so festive and cozy. Did he buy it for himself? Did someone buy it for him? It didn't look new; in fact, it looked very, very worn. "Oh no, that apron might have some competition with the pinstriped one," she announced, extremely glad they didn't have to hide any of these things now.

He let out a low chuckle. "Don't remember where it came from, unfortunately."

She walked over the short distance, brushed his bicep, and placed a kiss on his cheek. "I think you should wear this one in the winter too."

He turned his head and gently seized her lips. "You got it."

She batted her eyelashes purposely. "If we're feeling agreeable, I have another proposition."

He narrowed his gaze. "Let's hear it."

"Will you eventually swap out those greys in your closet for a color of my choosing?"

He tilted his head. "What color?"

"You'll know when the time comes."

He kissed her forehead. "Anything else?"

"Not at the moment. Is there anything you need?"

He picked up the plate he was setting up and slid it to her. "For you to eat."

"As long as they're scones. Yes. I will."

Ben's scones were unsurprisingly as good as his biscuits, but they didn't have her in a death grip the way his sticky toffee pudding did. In other words, the man's hands were dangerous in a kitchen. They were dangerous in other ways as well, for crying out loud.

The jam had to have been the same as the one he used for the biscuits. "So, question about the jam. It's what makes the biscuits so different than store-bought ones. Is it a family recipe?"

He donned a lovely smile. "It is, yeah. My mum learned from her grandmother. The only other person I've given it to outside of our family is Mrs. Henry. I'm always the one making it at The Crooked Branch."

"You gave your family recipe to Aunt Helen? That's so... comforting and sweet."

"She was incredibly kind to me when Dad died and checked in almost every day for months. It was the least I could do when she said that her daughter would not stop talking about the biscuits."

She chuckled. "Little did you know that someday I'd be just as obsessed with those bloody biscuits. Speaking of, I miss them," she declared.

"I'll have some for you by tomorrow."

She made a gesture with her hands under her chin and grinned enormously. "Yes! I finally get to crumble them on top of the waffles."

He threw a dish towel over his shoulder, laughed, and leaned forward to kiss her.

SHE HEARD enthusiastic chatter coming from the other side of the door after a knock. Violet was slightly nervous before Ben opened it, but Emma and Luke were both warm when introducing themselves to her.

And then her heart soared as she watched Ben stoop down and open his arms to two little girls running toward him with full force. She wanted to burn the image into her memory. It was a marvel to watch this side of him. Sadness was checked at the door, with full-blown boisterous joy replacing it.

"Uncle Ben, a big bee almost bit Lily!" Violet heard one of the girls say. Catherine she gathered.

He gasped dramatically, parting from the massive hug to look at Lily. "What?"

Emma rolled her eyes. "It wasn't a bee, honey. It was a beetle. And your sister was adamant about disrupting it while it did nothing to her."

His nieces both had dark brown hair like their father. Lily had piercing blue eyes, and Catherine's hazels matched her mother's.

Ben glanced at Lily a bit more sternly, his eyes still glowing with warmth. "Is that true?"

She giggled proudly. "I poked it until it flew, and then I ran away to the car very, very fast."

Violet smiled at the sight, and then Ben turned to her with a kind of brilliant smile that lit up his whole face. "Catherine, Lily, this is my friend, Violet; she's going to stay with us during the weekend, too."

"Hi," said Catherine with a shy smile, hiding a bit behind Ben's shoulder.

"Will you play outside with us?" Lily asked.

Violet stooped down beside Ben. "Of course, I will! Inside, too, wherever you two would like," she specified, looking to Catherine as well.

"Yay," Lily said, bouncing away from Ben and running toward the back garden.

Luke spoke then. "She means now, which is perfect timing because we need to head out." Catherine turned to hug her parents, prompting Ben and Violet to stand.

Emma brought her attention to Violet afterward. "So very sorry to leave abruptly, Violet. I'm excited to see you lot when we get back, though. Let me know if those knuckleheads don't behave," Emma said.

"Don't even worry about it! Hope the conference goes well," Violet replied.

They hurried out the door after Catherine gave her mum another big hug. "Cathy! Hurry up, you have to push me on the swing!" Lily shouted from the back garden. Catherine looked at Ben as if to ask for permission.

"Go on, duck. We'll be right behind you," he said.

Violet looked at him then. "This is great. They'll work up their appetites, and then we get to have all the waffles," she declared.

He chucked heartily and put his arm around her shoulder before they walked toward the kids. "You three are going to be a handful this weekend, aren't you?"

"Absolutely," she confirmed.

Catherine was shyer; a lot like Ben in many ways. Lily was a tiny smart mouth—outspoken and enthusiastic. They were parts of Ben's family, pieces of his life's puzzle, and everything their parents had endured to bring light and laughter into their lives. They were loud and charming and so adorably sweet.

Ben was always gentle, but she relished this side of him—he was warm and open, and the curve on his lips remained a constant.

The two days were delightfully wholesome, full of laughter and a whole lot of "watch what I can do," starting activities then abandoning them, and as promised, Welsh cakes and ice-cream waffles.

Catherine wasn't at all fussy, and she fell asleep in Violet's arms at one point. It was the kind of gift she cherished. When the shy kids liked you, they felt safe with you. Breaking through to kids like Catherine was one of the joys in Violet's life as a teacher.

EMMA AND LUKE returned to Bath at about three in the afternoon on Saturday. Aunt Helen had brought Freddy over to them, giving the girls the opportunity to play with him in the back garden.

Ben and Luke made a quick trip down to The Crooked Branch to pick up food, leaving Violet with Emma and the girls. Frankly, she was chuffed about it. They sat in the back garden, watching the kids in the yard.

Emma sighed, took a sip of her cider, and looked toward Violet. "You know he's never introduced anyone to us? I didn't even know his last girlfriend's name. I had to get it out of Dad, and he only knew because she'd been a nurse."

Violet smiled, unsure how to respond. She was hopeful it was a good thing.

"He told me a bit about you when he came to visit a few weeks back. That was the first I had heard, but he already seemed so different. So much lighter than I'd ever known him, Violet," she smiled with a massive grin. "I can't thank you enough for that."

The words stunned Violet. She wasn't sure what Emma was going to say, but it certainly wasn't the words that left her mouth. It was healing to hear, knowing that she'd been just as much of a light to him as he was for her. "Do you know how we met?" Violet asked her.

"Only that you knew each other years ago. Oh, please tell me. He'd never," she implored adorably. The glint of mischief and joy that flared in her eyes as she got excited matched a look she'd noticed in Lily.

Violet picked up her lemonade, wishing there was alcohol in it, took a sip of it, and then crossed her feet in the chair. "I was a flight attendant while he was working a case with MI6. There was a whole thing on the plane, then days in Paris, while information continued to come through. During that time, he'd offer to walk outside with me because the enclosed space was making me anxious," she said. How could recalling some of the most nerve-wracking days on the job bring *this* much joy? "When we were finally free to go home, he took me out to dinner. It was the most magical, most brilliant date I've ever been on, and then we went our separate ways."

"Jesus! How long ago was this?" she asked.

Violet gave her a half smile. "Sixteen years ago."

Emma humphed and bit down on her finger. "Blimey, it all makes sense now. That's why no one was ever enough for him. He knew *you*."

Violet's cheeks flushed. "The same can be said for me, I suppose. It'd been one date, but I'd never known anyone more kind. You couldn't even begin to compare him to my ex-husband."

"I'm not saying it because he is my brother, but he really is the kindest person. Dad never wanted him to join the agency, but even when he did, even when Dad gave him shit, he never fought him. He tried to reason," she paused. "He's a great brother too. I could call him at any time of day, and no matter where he is or who he's with, he'll answer."

She smiled and let out a sigh of relief. "I know he always thought he was too much—too calculated, too anxious, too quiet, too whatever else he convinced himself he was. He never said it aloud, but you could tell from the way he carried himself; he'd hold back and push aside all his feelings. He dropped everything to take care of Dad, and he never once complained. He would take care of the kids every weekend if I asked him."

His tendency to bottle his pain was more agonizing than anything else—Violet wanted to be the person he opened up to. He thought of himself as a man who was too much for everyone else, even while he was everything they needed.

Emma shook her head and gulped down another sip of her drink. "My eldest is a lot like him, which I'm sure you've gathered—quiet, shy, unsure how to approach people, and constantly thinking the worst. But once she warms up to someone, it's game over. Maybe if our parents knew what we know

now, they would've had him in therapy as a kid. Catherine sees one."

Violet didn't say anything; she was not sure what to say.

"He looks at you the way our dad would look at photos of our mum," Emma declared with a sweet, bright smile. "Except you're here, and that's what I meant about him being lighter—less anxious, less stiff. You brought out a side of him I've only ever caught the briefest glimpses of. He's a lot of fun, don't get me wrong—the kids adore him, but he's always carried more crosses than a person should."

"Thank you for telling me this," Violet noted, tears bubbling in her eyes.

Emma took her hand. "Of course. I can't tell you how much I've hoped for this day."

THE REST of the afternoon bled into the night too quickly. She wanted their time together to last a little bit longer. Violet had gotten along better with Dean's brother and sister than him, but it never felt quite as right as it did to sit beside Ben and his family during dinner.

Ben was so keenly aware of her presence, not because he wanted to check to see if she was putting on a perfect guise, but because he was consistently trying to ensure she was feeling okay.

She knew he was probably wondering how her head was faring with all the noises. She hoped she reassured him every time his hand came to rest on her knee underneath the table by placing hers atop his with a gentle clasp.

His nieces both insisted that she come over to their house to see the princess doll house where all their toys lived, including the superheroes. Emma concurred with the statements, joking that while she loved her big brother, she wasn't sure she ever wanted to see him without Violet again.

It felt nice and easy, and whatever else they needed to figure out would come in time.

"How's your head?" he asked once they were standing alone in the bedroom.

Violet turned to face him and placed a hand on his collarbone. "Perfectly fine. I've had worse head colds than this concussion."

He tucked a stray hair behind her ear and cupped her cheek. "Are you sure you're not just saying that to make me feel better?"

"I promise. The worst of it was the beginning, but honestly, all I feel now is a bit nervous for my first day at work."

He grazed his lips against her forehead, to her nose, then placed a small kiss on her lips. "You're going to be brilliant."

"How are *you* feeling?" she asked.

Ben released a tortured groan and enveloped her. His arms were tight against her back; his head burrowed deep in her neck. "I'm terrified to let you out of my sight, and I hate this. I feel so fucking helpless."

She didn't know what to say; frankly, there was nothing she could say. Logically, there was no way that Dean would've known about her job, but she understood Ben's fears. She was in knots every time Nan got in a car for years after her parents' accident. She understood the immensity of having to overcome the stunting pain she herself felt just sitting in a car at times. She hid it well, but often, in the streets of London, Violet would've rather walked miles than sit in a taxi when the tubes stopped running.

She didn't expect Ben to let her go without being afraid if even the mere thought of her alone next door made him uneasy.

Day by day.

She supposed it was easy to feel somewhat more comfortable with the situation because nothing terrified her more today than returning to the life she left behind.

"If it'd be better for you and convenient with work, you can drop me off and pick me up?" she suggested, with a softness in her tone she hoped would ease him.

She felt his beard prickle her neck with his nod, and a slow press of his lips sent a ripple of solace through her.

His grip around her tightened again, his hands trembling faintly at her back. His breathing was rapid, more intense than it was mere moments ago. She recognized the same light tremors and ragged gasps.

Violet entangled her fingers gently through his hair. The weight he carried bore a heaviness she could feel. Rounds of agony coursed through her bloodstream as she brushed her hand up and down his back. "Talk to me," she said slowly.

He lifted his head from her embrace and blinked rapidly. She traced the lines on his face, gently stroking the creases and hollows. Tip-toed to glide her lips against his weary eyes.

She rested her hands against his chest, hoping the touch would play a part in calming his heartbeat. "You're tired, my love. You've not slept normally since I came home from the hospital, and heaven knows how much you've been holding in before that. You're operating on fumes."

Violet threaded her fingers with his. "You've taken care of me since I got here. You were always by my side in Paris. Let me be your strength."

32

BEN

He didn't argue with Violet.

He was always knackered lately, but coupled with the events of the past few days, he felt powerless against his own body. Placing a hand on his chest, she nudged him to lie back.

He did so, but held onto her hand for a beat, willing himself to focus solely on her. The world wasn't a dark, cruel place with time standing still. Violet was beside him. He wanted to be brave for her. He tried to fight against it all, push beyond his fears to give her everything.

As though she could read his thoughts, she leaned down and placed a kiss on his forehead, traced his eyes with her lips— every line, every crease.

"You don't have to be brave for me," she pleaded. He said nothing. He closed his eyes to the touch of her soft fingers, then nearly flinched when she stopped.

She went to her side of the bed, sat down, then took one of the two pillows behind her and placed it on her legs. "Come here," she whispered.

He readjusted himself, laid his head on her lap, and looked

up at her. Violet began languidly carding her fingers through his hair.

He caught sight of her wrist as she rested her idle hand on his chest and gulped sharply. She'd been wearing long sleeves all weekend, doing a good job of hiding it that he'd almost forgotten about the purples and blues marring her skin. He believed her when she said it didn't hurt. She didn't seem to wince at any point during the weekend, but seeing it again was a further reminder of the darkness still looming ahead.

He took her wrist in his hands and pressed a gentle kiss to the shadows, onward to her palm. He kept it near his lips for a moment, wanting to see if she showed any signs of discomfort before placing it back down. She simply smiled down at him, closing her eyes in a way that exhibited contentment.

"I'll cover it up for work. Makeup does a lot these days," she said in an agile response.

He knew as much but hated the ordeal. How many women covered up horrors like this? How many men got away with their vile behavior? He knew he wouldn't rest properly until her atrocious ex-husband was either rotting behind bars or somehow paying a worse price. And he knew that Violet would hate these thoughts.

"Stop trying to figure out if I'm lying to you. Stop plotting murder in your head. For a moment, Ben, please. I would tell you if I was in pain. I promise," she paused and traced the indent in between his furrowed brows. "Sleep, my love."

"How do you know that's what I'm doing," he asked, genuinely curious.

She chuckled. "You're not subtle. You furrow your brows, and your pupils dilate. I also know you well enough by now."

He was running on fumes, tasting them all over. He had stayed awake far too many times and suffered the upshots of one collapsing morning after another, finding himself consistently buried deep underneath a rigid impediment against his chest. And he never believed he would ever truly be free from it.

Not until Violet and the perpetual light that followed her. Not until she took him by the hand and demanded that he stop in his tracks—the words *my love* echoing in his head.

There were things she was still hiding and carrying alone, pieces she was concealing somewhere in a guarded chamber far from his reach. Yet, amid her own sorrow, she spared herself for him, standing as his armor when he was stripped bare.

She was the first few drops of rain in the middle of a particularly dreadful night, lulling with its irrefutable serenade. The first brilliantly biting chill of autumn after too many days of grueling humidity—the first tree to evince its glowing shades of scarlet.

He closed his eyes, focusing his mind on the sound of her heartbeat above him. He forced himself to dwell only on this moment. His uncertainties could come back tomorrow. He'd mask it all again, but for now, he'd let her be his strength.

"Talk to me," he mumbled into the space between them, wanting to hear her voice again.

He didn't open his eyes, but he sensed her head tilt as she let out a deep breath. "What would you like me to say?" she asked.

"Anything."

She swallowed, and he opened his eyes to watch as she thought of something to tell him. She smiled when she caught him looking at her, using the moment to move her hand back to his face.

"I've never seen a fox in the wild. I'm convinced they're some sort of a mythical creature because everyone's seen them, but I've somehow never. I used to go running at dusk all the time, but the bloody things are never around when I'm there," she chuckled.

"Do you want to see one?"

Her eyes widened. "Of course I do. They're so beautiful to look at in photographs. It's a bit unfair that I've yet to."

There were foxes in the area at times. He'd be on the lookout now, determined more than anything to be the one beside her when she came across one for the first time. He might even add the seemingly silly request to his prayers. Violet deserved it.

"What else would you like to see?" he inquired.

"You. Sleeping soundly," she responded with a vulnerable tenor.

He closed his eyes again, wondering how on earth he'd been on the receiving end of her empathy—her compassion, her careful attention.

He smiled a little bigger when looking up at her again. "Keep talking then."

She arched an eyebrow. "So we're clear about my services, I'm hoping that means my voice lulls you instead of boring you, right?"

He nodded. "Darling, your voice is my favorite sound."

She seemed to accept his words with a smile that took his breath away.

"When I told my friends about you after I got home, apparently, I wouldn't shut up about how nice your beard was," she paused, brushing the backs of her long fingers against it. The sensation was delightful. "I'm glad you never shaved it off."

He let out a low chuckle. *How could he have? When she told him that very night.* He thought of her every time he debated shaving. "You told me then. It's nice to know you meant it," he replied.

She bent over and kissed his cheek, "Of course, I meant it," she confirmed, moving her lips to his forehead. "I've never fancied a man quite like you," she reiterated.

He hummed to her touch and lifted his hand to cup her cheek. She turned her lips and pressed a tender kiss to his palm.

Lord, she was brilliant and so devastatingly mesmerizing in her maneuvers. He wanted to sear every move she made into his brain—tattoo the words she spoke all over his skin.

His bones were weary, and his energy was fighting against him, but he would've taken her in a heartbeat had that not been the case. He'd *show* her how much he fancied her—how she drove him to perfect oblivion every time.

"You are the best thing that's ever happened to me, Violet," he said, briefly shutting his eyes again.

She was a marvel—a gift he could no longer imagine this world without. The soft strokes in his hair made his heaviness subside into a weight more docile.

He rose and moved to his side of the bed, extending his arm out to her in a plea to be the one who now held her. She did so, resting her head on his chest and laying her hand on the slope of his shoulder.

A hurricane could still be on the horizon, yet for a moment, the violent torrents inside him slowed and demanded less of his attention.

There was only Violet, shielding him from every calamitous aftereffect in sight with her tender and open adoration.

"Please be patient with me, Violet. If I—" the words caught in his throat. "If I seem overbearing...I don't want to push you away or overwhelm you. I'm trying not to replay that moment of you lying in a hospital bed over and over in my head, but it keeps coming back. The thought of how Mrs. Henry must've found you. The thought of something worse happening to you scares me to death. I've seen terrible things and been in horrible situations, but I have no sense of how to deal with this."

She moved her hand from his shoulder to his face, holding it there for a beat. "What if I text you an Emoji or a random word every five minutes to let you know that I'm fine?"

"You'd do that?"

"Okay, well not every five minutes because I'd likely get distracted and forget, but at least every hour? Every time I remember? Would that help?"

He exhaled and nodded. "I love you so much," he whispered in her ear as he held her closer. "I love you with every fiber of my being."

Her fingers smoothed the base of his jaw, and her smile made him feel ten feet tall.

Again and again.

As she had done in Paris.

"I love you, too."

33

VIOLET

Violet awakened earlier than him; the cool morning rain knocking on their window was a beauty she'd never get tired of witnessing. She looked at the man beside her and sent a silent prayer to the sky.

Ben was lovely like this—the lines on his face serene and steady. The gentle rise and fall of his chest becoming her favorite melody. She wanted to stay here, just like this, for a few hours and watch him. She wanted him to sleep. She remembered the scars she'd seen. She promised herself she'd kiss them all someday—she wanted to heal every broken piece of him.

He aged so well, too. The shades of grey in his tousled hair and his perfectly short beard were even more appealing than when they first met.

There was something statuesque about him—he commanded the room like a sea captain standing at deck, a maple tree spotted from miles away, with or without autumn's touch. Violet had known people in positions of power, but none had Ben's magnetism—an appeal he himself was utterly oblivious to.

He made heads turn with the kindness in his piercing eyes and stood in a manner that made the stars glisten.

He opened his eyes in a daze to her, the sunlight dancing along his face. "Morning," he mumbled, inching himself closer to her.

She smiled. "Good morning. How are you feeling?" she asked.

"Better now," he replied. "Come to the shop with me this morning?"

"Yeah, let's do it," she replied, preparing herself to rise.

He pulled her body back to him and held on to her firmly. "Not yet," he noted with a roguish grin.

Sundays would be a damn near dream if they spent it this way every time, a sitcom playing on the television, and Violet snuggled into Ben's embrace—the world was quiet here, still and comforting. She wasn't even in her home, yet she felt no difference.

That was until a phone call came in from her solicitor midway through the episode. Violet leaped out of his arms and stood up to pick up the phone.

"Amy, hi! How are you?"

"Well, love, and you?" she said on the other end of the line.

"As well as can be; any news?"

"A bit, yeah. Dean's solicitor, Daniel Flynn, has finally heard from him. He's laying low somewhere, working remotely. He's claiming that all he's done is talk to you, nothing more."

Violet was motionless, staring off into the living room with her eyes frozen. She could tell Ben was watching her through her peripheral vision. "What does that mean?"

"It can mean a few things, but he hurt you when he saw you, Violet; we can use this."

Violet sighed and shook her head. "No one will believe me, not to mention that I'm the one who fell back."

"Yes, but your wrists. The photographs you sent me can be enough."

"You know how respected he is. Daniel might have a moral compass, but he will still fight for Dean. And even if he doesn't, Dean could find someone new. It'll blow up in my face in the end. He'll resent me even more. It'll never end."

"Daniel doesn't seem to want to fight for him, judging by his tone. But I hear you. I'll see what I can do. I think you'll be okay, at the very least. I can't imagine he'll put his career on the line like this."

"I'll let you know if anything changes, but for now, I'll stay on the lookout. Thank you for all your help, Amy."

"Of course. Talk soon," she said as the line went dead.

Violet looked to Ben, whose expression had lost the warmth from the day. "Was that your solicitor?" he asked.

"Yeah."

He bit the inside of his cheek. "What'd she say?"

"Nothing new other than the fact that he seems to be working remotely. Amy thinks he could still be here. He told them that all he did was talk to me."

Ben swallowed hard and clasped his hands together. "Are you still pushing that you fell?"

He seemed a bit frustrated with her like he didn't believe her. Except it was the truth. "I did fall," she responded.

He scoffed slightly. "Violet, you walk with more grace than anyone I've seen on a moving airplane in high heels; if they ever hurt you, you never made it even the slightest bit obvious. You took karate and dance lessons when you were a child. You're not clumsy."

"That doesn't mean that I can't fall; my blood pressure was low, you know that."

His eyes grew more cross, but his tone remained steady. "Even if that's the case, look at your wrists. He hurt you. He instigated all of it. He threatened you, yet you're hiding it."

She shook her head. "I'm not hiding anything." She was hiding many things, but not this. This wasn't it. Hell, she wanted to tell him everything, but she was afraid of how he'd start to look at her and if she'd still be the same strong woman he loved.

He gulped, opened his mouth to speak, then paused. "I didn't want to push anything while you were recovering, but for Christ's sake, Violet. I was a spy. I know when someone's withholding information. If you want to continue keeping things from me, fine, but don't pretend it's one thing when it's not."

He barely raised his voice, but his eyes hurt her more than anything else because he was right, and she didn't want him to be. But she also didn't know how to approach the bloody situation without spinning a web they'd have to spend ample time undoing.

"I don't want to argue, Ben. Please let this go," she said.

"I'm not trying to argue. You sat on that sofa and told me you loved me, and I hoped transparency would be included somewhere in that declaration. Or am I just another man you love but can't find yourself falling in love with? Because if so, we're not on the same damn page. I am in love with you. There has never been, and there will never be, another you. I'm fully in this to the end, and that doesn't include keeping things from you."

She shook her head. "Of course, I'm in love with you. Of course, it's different with you. But I don't know how to talk about this. I don't want to," she said with her eyes misting. Her mind was taking her to places where she felt small and puzzled, drowning her in doubts that Ben wasn't responsible for.

"Then *say* that. Tell me you don't want to talk, but don't try to convince me that there isn't something more," he declared while walking out of the room.

She prayed that he wouldn't shut the door loudly and hoped that he wasn't the kind of person whose rage turned him into a monster. She listened carefully but heard nothing, figuring he must've left it open.

This wasn't how she wanted the night to end.

She wanted to tell him everything.

She wanted to forget most of her past entirely.

She wanted to go through it. She needed to.

She sat on the sofa for a beat and thought it over. How much would she tell him? What could she say to even ease his mind about it? She had to talk to Jane. She was a grown woman, but she needed someone to guide her through this.

She got up and walked over to the bedroom quietly. Ben was sitting cross-legged on top of the duvet. She knocked on the side of the door before stepping in.

She stood in front of him. "I'm not trying to hide the truth from you, Ben. It took ages for me to open up with Simone because I couldn't bear the thought of how she'd look at me. You know bits, but all of it—I. I don't want to take that risk with you."

He uncrossed his legs and slid to the edge of the bed. He wrapped his arms around her waist, pulling her close to him. He looked up at her. "Darling, what risk? What are you afraid of?"

"That you'll see me differently—that you'll stop seeing the bravery you supposedly fell for sixteen years ago."

"Violet, you watched me crumble just last night; should I fear the same?"

She shook her head vehemently. "Of course not! This isn't remotely the same, and you know it."

"I don't, because you won't tell me what *it* is," he said in an assertive yet warm tone.

"I will. I promise. Let me speak with Jane first. It's been a bit since I have, and I'm meeting with her virtually tomorrow."

He rose to his feet and placed a gentle kiss on her temple. "I'm not going to back down or pull away from us, Violet. There's nothing you can say that will change the way I see you or how deeply I love you. I'm here to the end."

She sighed into his neck. "What if I told you I murdered someone?"

He shrugged. "I'd take the secret to the grave with me then."

"You wouldn't look at me differently?" she asked curiously.

He replied without a second thought. "You probably had a good reason."

"I didn't murder anyone," she confirmed.

He held her closer to his chest and threaded his fingers through her hair. She believed him when he said these things, but opening up felt like it'd unleash an avalanche she wasn't ready to clean up after. She just wanted to be here in his arms, unbothered and safe.

34

———

VIOLET

"I t drives me wild every time you wear that lipstick," he said with a groan, holding the passenger's door open for her.

She could feel her cheeks flush. "Does it? It's my favorite shade. I was wearing it during our date in Paris."

"And the day you came to the restaurant," he added before closing her door.

She looked at him when he sat in the driver's seat, her eyes narrowed. "How are you so certain it's the same red? You know there are millions of shades, right?"

"I just am," he said with a wink, then started the engine.

She released a delighted *ha*, then looked ahead toward the road. "I'm thoroughly impressed. You are indeed correct."

"I've seen you wear another. But this one's more of a bright red. The other is maroon."

"I would've still worn it even if you hated it, but it makes me so happy that you don't."

"There's nothing about you I could hate," he confirmed with a gentle tenor.

"What if I steal all the food off of your plate?"

"Nope," he said with a gratified smirk, like he welcomed the sentiment, relished in it entirely.

Violet took a deep breath. One day, these simple moments might not seem so big, but right now, she'd continue to cherish them, like Ben dropping her off at work for her first day. Granted, the reasoning wasn't ideal, but it was lovely, no less.

"You know I'm not always a morning person? Some days, I won't say a word until I've at least had breakfast. I might not even want to look at you."

He chuckled. "Seems fair. Some days, I don't want to look at myself either."

She rolled her eyes playfully at him. That one might not be the case anymore. She couldn't imagine *not* looking at him, even if she was too tired to speak.

"What time are you going to work today?" she asked.

"We're closed on Mondays, remember? I only went in last week because of the inspection and inventory preparations."

She remembered immediately after asking the question. "What about the rest of the week?"

"Mornings. I'll go in as I drop you off, then leave when you do."

"Do you get to make your own hours?"

"Ideally, I should be there from the afternoon to night rush, but I told Florence that for the time being, I'm going to be coming in the mornings."

He was doing this entirely for her sake, and she wished he wouldn't. She also knew that if she voiced her concerns about burdening him, he'd be adamant it was how *he* wanted it.

This wasn't a winning game for her. "And she's okay with that?" she simply inquired.

"She is. I don't need to be there for the kitchen to function."

She turned to look at him. His expression was still and...hot.

For once, could he just not look so bloody fit? "Humility looks good on you. But I'm sure the team loathes it."

"You're right. Billy's probably gutted he can't get on anyone else's nerves."

Her lips quirked up, and she looked onward. The maple trees lining the school's entrance were more vibrant than they had been when she visited to meet the staff a few weeks back. Where the leaves fell, they created dazzling tapestries on the grass.

She was positively giddy.

Ben parked the car at the drop-off zone and turned to face her. "Have the best day," he said merrily.

These ordinary moments with the man she loved—crisp mornings, colors all around, the indescribable magic of autumn —how could they be anything but the best?

She leaned forward for a quick kiss. "Thank you."

Violet knew Ben wouldn't leave until she was inside the building, so she didn't take her sweet time walking in. Still, she was grateful it was quiet in the area because students hadn't arrived yet, and she could hear the foliage crunching underneath her ankle boots. She could swear that the birds up ahead must've been as jovial as she was because their song sounded different today.

She turned back when she got to the door and waved, catching Ben's hand rise from the distance; she walked straight into the teacher's lounge that Abigail had shown her. Four teachers were already there: Claire Jones, the Year 2 teacher; Patrick Dalton, the Year 5 teacher; Lucy Williams, Year 3; and Jack Carver, another Year 4 teacher like Violet.

Knightley was half the size of Briar, with two classrooms for each year to contrast Briar's four. It was the type of school that, according to Abigail, was far more involved in the community and present throughout the various festivals during the year.

Though at the moment, they were focused entirely on the Autumn Festival.

This particular teacher's lounge was different from Briar's. Its quaintness felt more comforting. The furniture wasn't all brand new, with top-of-the-line appliances. They were quality, yes, but it was somehow livelier. There was a mustard-yellow velvet sofa at the end of the room, wooden chairs matching the oval tables, and the fridge, best of all, had photographs attached to it. It must've been of the teachers she gathered, promising herself she'd take a closer look once she got more situated.

She would miss having her own office to work out of, but she could adjust well, given that it already felt like the room was imbued with personality.

Patrick mentioned something about a dance number for his students when Violet walked into Claire, opposing the idea. "You can't modernize everything. In my day, we were carrying on traditions that had been around for centuries," she said.

"I love Austen as much as the next guy, but I'm not making my Year 5 students dress up like they're from the Regency era. Plus, the Jane Austen Festival happened last month. They want to do what they see their older siblings do on social media apps. I think we should let him," Patrick protested.

Jack shrugged his shoulders. "I'm with whichever option gets you two to stop talking for five minutes so I can take a bloody nap."

Patrick caught her presence then. "Violet! Good morning! Please weigh in on this," he started, "a modern choreography number with all the kids wearing some shade of orange or a traditional quadrille in the middle of the park? Which sounds better?"

Violet grimaced with a sardonic smile. "I don't want to get involved."

Patrick countered by throwing his hands in the air. "You're

part of the staff now. You're involved. Come on, don't be as quiet as Grace was. You were the head teacher; you have to have more to say."

Lucy laughed. She, Jack, and Patrick seemed to be the youngest teachers here. They had to have been in their thirties, at least. And Claire seemed to be in her sixties. She was a stunning Black woman with dark brown hair, and she had the same motherly affection in her eyes that Aunt Helen did. It was easy to tell she was everyone's go-to here.

"It's the girl's first day. Let her breathe," Claire noted from her seat.

Jack let out a muffled groan. "Why is there only *one* bloody lounge in this place?" he mumbled.

"Did you get to bed late last night?" Lucy whispered.

"My flatmate's new puppy was barking until four in the morning. An adorable thing, but it was pure torture," he responded back to her. For an instant, the two of them disappeared in their conversation—like they were the only people in the room.

Patrick was looking at Violet for a response then. "Modernizing things doesn't hurt. How about a best-of-both-worlds situation? You either have a modern choreography in traditional clothing or a modern ensemble of sorts while still keeping a quadrille for a modern song," she suggested. She was a little proud of herself for the quick response.

"Problem solved. Now five minutes of silence. I'm begging you lot," Jack muttered.

Patrick's lips formed a massive curve. "Oh, this is going to be fun," he tittered.

"Any ideas for what you'll be doing for your class?" Claire asked Violet.

Jack grunted and got up. "Well, I'm napping in my classroom."

"Should've thought of that earlier," Patrick snickered with a loving bark.

Violet smiled as he walked by her—poor thing. A good nap could do wonders, even if it were just five minutes. She looked back at Claire, who was sipping her coffee.

"I was thinking of having them each make their own wreaths to sell at the festival. But I'll have to coordinate with Jack when he's a little less knackered," she remarked.

"That's a beautiful idea," Lucy said enthusiastically, and the best part was that Violet was sure she meant it. There was a sincere warmth in her eyes, and during their first meeting, Violet determined she was the kind of teacher who adored her job. They all seemed to. And she was certain that while there'd be many complaints and frustrations with the job when she was more acquainted, it was comforting for the time being.

"Lucy is right," Claire confirmed. "That does sound beautiful. And I'm sure Jack wouldn't be opposed to sharing the idea with his students when he's a little less narky."

Violet smiled at the older woman. A rush of joy washed over her. Patrick was right. *This was going to be fun.*

She already felt like a better version of herself with the opportunity to use her creative streak.

HER FIRST DAY couldn't have been better. While her students were sad to see their former teacher Mrs. Wilson go, they adjusted pretty well to Violet; a few even made her "Welcome to Knightley" cards.

Ben was already waiting outside for her when she walked out. He was leaning against the car door, and he had changed out of the clothes he was wearing when he dropped her off. He now donned a red buffalo plaid flannel shirt and dark denim jeans. The shade of red complemented her lipstick pristinely. *God, they were cute*, she thought to herself.

Who was she kidding, thinking she could get used to this? The days wouldn't bleed into a normal rhythm and become less magical, it'd become even sweeter—more thrilling. She was going to ensure that one day, she'd see him in a white cable-knit jumper because nothing was more alluring while simultaneously cozy.

And then she would explode into motes of dust.

He extended his hand to her when she got closer and enveloped her in a brief embrace. "How was your first day?" he asked, opening the door.

"Go—," she started to say before she spotted the large bouquet of flowers on the passenger's seat.

Striking orange and maroon chrysanthemums, bright shades of coral roses, and a few gerberas dispersed with ruscus leaves, all wrapped in brown paper and a twill string.

Her eyes flicked back to him. "What's all this?"

"I've been wanting to get you flowers since you told me what your favorites were. But then everything turned pear-shaped," he paused and pressed his lips to her temple. "Congratulations on finishing your first day, darling."

She sighed deeply. "*You. I...*thank you," she replied.

In all the years she'd been married to Dean, he never once bought her anything but simple red roses. Twice a year, once on her birthday, excluding her fortieth, and the other on Valentine's Day. And while they were lavish bouquets he likely made his assistant order, she'd off-hand mentioned her favorite flowers to him, but he never bothered to remember. And all her previous exes were the same in that regard. It wasn't a fact she was ever adamant about correcting people.

Since she was born in May, Aunt Helen and Simone would send tulips on her birthday, but no one was sending her flowers during the autumn season. She could always buy them for herself, she did sometimes, but this—this was everything.

It was reassuring and lovely because Ben heard her in ways no one ever had. He went out of his way for her, breaking the barriers she'd put up to protect herself by refusing to hope for better.

He was doing things she'd only ever dreamed of, set on the firm belief that men like him simply didn't exist outside of fictional worlds.

But that was the thing about Ben. He was proof that decent men existed. He came to her like a dream, making the conventional feel profoundly beguiling. Memorable. She wished she kept a personal journal because these would be the kind of things to write along the lines, set it in a place for safe keeping, and hold onto for dear life.

People didn't appreciate the consoling fragrance of mums nearly enough, like a warm, secure blanket.

Just like Ben.

And every moment they shared together.

35

BEN

Ben was delighted to see Violet's eyes soften at the sight of the flowers. He could feel his mother's pride at his actions, knowing he remembered her every word.

Not everyone loves roses, my sweet boy.

He'd remember tulips and mums for the rest of his life, and if she suddenly decided she liked sunflowers tomorrow, he'd remember that, too. The only reason he had mixed the flowers was because the florist didn't have enough mums.

Violet had insisted they keep them at his house since it's where she was staying the next few days, which brought him a sense of comfort, knowing he wouldn't have to beg again and again and again.

She went back to her place for the next hour to speak with Jane, and he stressed-baked sticky toffee pudding to get his mind off it.

Aunt Helen had invited them both over for dinner later for Violet's favorite Persian dish, Ghormeh Sabzi. Ben would supply the pudding.

When Violet returned, she had changed out of her work clothes into another oversized jumper dress and removed her makeup. She seemed to have quite a few of these, and he liked seeing them on her. Warm enough for the weather, with her legs bare enough to drive him wild.

"You alright?" he asked as she approached the kitchen.

She walked over to him and wrapped her arms around his frame. "Brilliant," she replied after placing a kiss against the line of his jaw. "We'll talk after Aunt Helen's?" she suggested as a question.

"If that's what you want," he answered with a smile.

BEN UNDERSTOOD IMMEDIATELY why Helen's Ghormeh Sabzi was Violet's favorite, and frankly, it felt nice to have someone else cook for once. And for it to be someone like Helen Henry made it all the more delightful because he got to share it with Violet.

"Has The Crooked Branch decided what they're serving at the Autumn Festival?" Thomas asked.

Ben wiped his lips with a napkin. "My junior chef is determined we add in our 'pumpkin parfait enchantments,'" he paused and turned to Violet. "They have a name now," he confirmed. "But as far as dishes go, we can't seem to settle on one."

"Does it change yearly?" Violet asked.

"Yep. We try to offer varieties."

Helen chimed in. "The Wisteria Tea Room would get far too much flak if we dared to do anything different than the cucumber sandwiches. We once served only the cakes and tea, thinking perhaps a change would be nice, but we were met with only disappointed customers."

"Can you blame the people? Cucumber sandwiches are the Lord's greatest creation," Violet remarked. "Next to sticky toffee pudding, of course," she added to Ben.

Thomas smirked and raised a silent glass. "She's not wrong, Helly. There's a reason I make you bring some back for me after every shift."

Helen chuckled. "And I concur. We learned our lesson, I suppose."

"You know what you should serve, Ben?" Violet asked with a massive grin framing her face.

He knew exactly what she was going to say—avocado toast.

"Avocado toast?" he retorted.

She nodded gleefully and put a big spoonful of rice and meat in her mouth. She was so damn adorable like this; it made his heart sink.

"Now, wait a minute," Helen bit back. "Since when is avocado toast on the menu? I have that thing memorized front and back."

Ben chuckled. "It's not."

Thomas nodded with understanding, and Helen furrowed her eyebrows at him.

"You know you two get off-menu items, too. Don't give me that look," Ben said.

She doubled down on the very look. "Well, good. Then I'm ordering it the next time I'm in. And yes, for dinner. I'll hear no judgments."

"Cheers," he said with a low chuckle.

"Tell us about your first day, Violet," Thomas added.

Violet smiled and started speaking enthusiastically with her hands. She clamped them together and rested her elbows on the table. "It was quite lovely. There's actually a Year 2 teacher there, Claire Jones. She reminds me so much of you, Aunt Helen."

"Well, of course, she does. Claire is one of my favorite people in this place. We went to secondary school together. She moved back here around the same time I did and started teaching," Helen responded.

Violet sat up straighter, a sweet joy nestling itself in her expression. "Oh, I adore that."

Helen raised her glass, prompting everyone else to do the same. They clinked them together. "You're in fantastic company there, sweet girl. I think you'll enjoy Knightley."

"I genuinely believe so," Violet voiced eagerly. It elated Ben to see her like this—full of hope and joy. She was the same wide-eyed beauty he left behind in Paris that night, only braver, better, and full of more heart than he could've ever imagined.

They talked for another hour or so, discussing the festival and trying to get Ben to bring in avocado toast to the festival even though it wasn't on his menu and probably wouldn't be quite yet. He agreed with a solid "maybe."

He liked the fact that the avocado toast was an exclusive on the menu, meant only for Violet and their loved ones. It made it better. Plus, he was still honing the recipe despite her insistence that it was perfect.

It felt nice leaving Helen and Thomas' house with Violet, breaking bread with the closest people she had to family, and seeing a side of her that came out around them.

He liked hearing the wild stories of how she and Simone tried to sneak out of the house one time and then walked back in to apologize because they couldn't bear Aunt Helen's disappointment. Helen let them go after that, knowing she could trust them in anything together. He liked hearing Thomas mention that Violet's father was better at playing football than he was at grilling.

He liked how Violet would tilt her head and listen to the stories while looking at Ben to see his reactions. And he loved that he was her partner through this. They trusted him with her, and she confirmed as much on their way back to his house.

She turned to him when they got to the door. "You know, I asked Aunt Helen if she liked you, and she had said, 'He wouldn't be living here if I didn't.' And she's entirely serious. She told Dean she didn't trust him on our wedding day. He thought she was joking," she said, nestling herself in the crook of his arm. "Thank you for coming with me. I really wish Simone and Peter were with us, too. It would've been the perfect end to what's the only good Monday anyone will ever have."

They took their shoes off as they walked into the house and turned to each other in surprising unison. Violet's mouth curved upward, and it damn near wrecked him. How on earth did someone look at her and not realize what a treasure was beside them all along? He could never grapple with this idea. "I'm really glad she does," he responded.

"I know I have things to tell you. And I think I'm ready to, but I don't want to spend a night like this digging up the past. Can we talk tomorrow?" she asked.

How could he ever say no to her? He suddenly understood with full conviction why George Bailey was so adamant about lassoing the moon for Mary. She could ask him for anything in this world, and he'd jump to it.

"Of course," he answered, pressing his mouth to hers in a searing kiss.

She chuckled into his lips, her husky laugh drowning out the noises in his head.

He broke his lips from her. "What are you laughing about?"

She narrowed her eyes and dipped her chin. "I like it when we're on the same page," she revealed, grazing her lips over his jaw and down to his neck.

He smoothed his palm along her hair, releasing a low groan of need. "I'm thinking I need to skip to the page where I take you to bed then."

"A bit needy, aren't we?"

"Achingly," he admitted with a low grunt. Ben helped her out of her coat, hanging it on the stand. He turned back to her swiftly. "We should probably discuss you moving here on a more permanent basis."

Violet arched her eyebrows, a subtle line running along her lips. "You want to discuss that now?"

He wrapped his arms around the curve of her bottom and lifted her. "After," he mumbled as her legs circled him. Ben led her to his room, set her down on the bed, and hastily removed her clothing, following promptly with his.

She was transfixing in every way, and the bare sight of her in his bed made his head spin. In all its loud, riotous glory, the world would always find a means to exhaust him, wear him down, and make him bleed, but Violet staring back at him would be perpetual emancipation.

Shadows of the past loomed over them, difficulties were obliged to follow, and every day was sure to bring another shitty nuisance. Yet, none of that would trouble him if she were *beside* him, *underneath* him, *above* him.

Her touch would continue to reignite embers and burn like wildfires.

He wanted this to be a permanent arrangement.

They already played neighbors, paper airplanes in and out.

He never wanted to lie in this bed without her. Or any bed, for that matter. Sofas, picnic grounds, wherever their trajectory would lead, he wanted, *needed* to be beside her.

Replacing her clothes with his hands and skin torched him at every point of contact. He wondered if he'd ever get used to it all, come to a place where it'd be a natural shared bliss instead of lightning strikes of passions all at once.

He was curious about the calm, but he'd bask in the intensity a little more—hold onto it tighter.

Her fingers grazed delicately against the scars on his chest, and another jolt charged through him. "I want to know the story behind each of these," she said, flattening her palm against his drumming heartbeat.

Violet positioned herself on her knees and drew him closer to her, kissing his lips, his jaw, along his neck.

She peppered kisses on the moles dispersed along his chest. His knees grew weaker with every movement she made, requiring immense effort to continue standing.

As though sensing his undeclared agony, Violet pulled him closer, motioning for him to lie down.

She climbed atop him, losing herself in a decadent rhythm of the cartography she was determined to master. She'd glide her fingers along a scar, then follow with the press of her lips. She repeated the art once, twice, three times, a dull phantom ache pursuing in desperation to thread itself to her.

"I wish I was there when you got these. I wish we stayed together after Paris," she whispered, kissing a mark on his pec brought on by a knife wound in Berlin.

She sighed and looked into his eyes. "I wish we met before Paris. Somewhere in London, maybe. So much time wouldn't have passed." She drew herself lower to the wound on his ribcage—the spot he'd been impaled in London, only nine days after leaving her in Paris.

The painkillers made him dream of her—ache for her.

She was here now, her lips hovering a hair's breadth away from the circular-shaped scar as her fingers roamed over the rest of him. He closed his eyes, allowing a single ensnared tear to fall freely, releasing his heart from the barriers he'd put up.

She was here now.

She was his.

She would be beside him tomorrow, too, the demons less brash and numbing, his ever-growing love for her would be the new chief in command.

She finished by pressing her lips firmly to the soft juncture of his pulse point, remedying with achingly soothing blows and kisses. She would be the only one to scar him.

He looked up at her over him and traced the three vibrant orange poppies inked on the side of her ribcage. One after another. "Is there a story here?" he asked.

She smiled serenely. "Since the flowers ultimately represent remembrance. I got the first two after Mum and Dad died, then the third for Nan."

"They're beautiful. The artist's line work is lovely."

He'd make a mental note to thank the heavens for how the tracing glow of moonlight haloed her form and illuminated the brilliant curves of her hips.

Later, he would feel the crescent moon marks deliciously along his back. Where she would dig and leave an emblem, she would do so with immense reverence, passion, and sweet frenzy.

He'd been internally magnetized to her since the moment they met, but it was physical now, too, binding them closer than ever.

Her screams with him weren't battle cries; they were signs of catharsis.

If she spent a few glorious moments showing him her adoration, he'd spend the rest of the night giving in tenfold, unraveling new discoveries in what she liked and needed. He would leave no part of her untouched, without his kiss, or left wanting.

They'd tangle together in an intoxicating haze. Scars and aches and terrors would take nights off, leaving them alone to the sounds of the other's pleasure. Where they'd end and begin didn't matter—they were nestled somewhere warm and safe— an intimacy that would only ignite and grow.

36

VIOLET

She tossed and turned since three a.m., accidentally waking up Ben twice. When she realized she wouldn't be sleeping around five, she got up and went to the living room.

Violet had done this a hundred times over back in London, trying to escape from the agitating thoughts in her mind. A living room was less overbearing than a bedroom at night. But it was different this time, she wasn't running from Ben, she wanted to sprint toward him fully, while fighting the thoughts that her past could push him away still.

His dark-heather hoodie was still hanging on a chair from last night, so she put it on and lounged on the sofa. She should really bring some more clothes from her place, at least a dressing gown for mornings like this. Though the hoodie was far more comfortable, with the scent of his musky bergamot cologne lingering in the threads still.

It felt like home—just as every corner of this house and Bath —all of it.

She couldn't keep putting this conversation off. It had to happen today after they got home.

She distracted herself by reading until he got up. Ben came to her a couple of hours later. She had a feeling he'd been awake the entire time, but she imagined he was giving her the space she needed.

He walked over and placed a gentle kiss on her forehead. "You okay?" he asked.

She nodded and sat up. "Thinking about everything I have to tell you today. A little nervous about it. But I can't keep dragging my feet," she said.

He put his hand on her shoulder. "I can be patient, my love —you don't have to say anything until you're ready. If it's bothering you that much, I'd rather you sleep than be this anxious about it," he answered.

She kissed his cheek. "I know, but I think I'm ready. So, that's probably why my head's been so muddled. I should go to my place and get ready, though. It's a shame I can't walk in like this," she said, pointing to herself in his hoodie.

He chuckled. "I'll have coffee ready when you're back."

She smiled wistfully and walked out the door.

VIOLET WAS thankful that no part of the day had been stressful, so she wouldn't have to postpone this conversation any longer. She switched back into his hoodie from earlier this morning, sat on the sofa, and tapped the space beside her for him to sit.

She took a deep breath and steeled herself. "First, regarding the other day, I wasn't lying about falling, at least not from what I remember. In trying to free myself from his grip, I lost balance as I tried to bend farther back. I felt dizzy before it all happened, too, and I couldn't tell if it was my anxiety or blood pressure, as the doctor said. I didn't feel as though I was completely there, like I had an out-of-body experience of sorts. The point is, I can't say he pushed me when he didn't."

He gave her hand a tender squeeze.

"Dean's words were always far more vicious than his actions. This is only the second time he physically hurt me. The first happened after a particularly hard trial. The Granger case changed him entirely, or perhaps it brought out who he truly was, but regardless, the differences in his personality were massive. I used to try taking dinner to his office, offering to stay, and keep him company, but he'd push me away. Eventually, I stopped trying. The case ended, he lost, the firm bounced back, but he sort of just...I don't know, stayed in that pit. I told him about Jane, about everything she'd done to help me, and he laughed. 'You still pay that chit to jot some notes in her journal and nod?'" She mimicked his tone.

"I really lost it at that comment. I started yelling about how I wouldn't be standing without Jane and that I felt insulted by him mocking everything I'd been through. I was already on edge the entire day because of work and that was my breaking point. He grabbed me by the wrists and yanked so hard that it caused a sprain. I immediately told him I wanted a divorce the following day, and he sobbed, apologizing and begging me to forgive him. He said he'd die without me." She shook her head, remembering the pitiful side of Dean she didn't quite understand.

The look in Ben's eyes broke her, but she had to continue.

"I was too fucked up to add another thing to my conscience. So, I forgave him. But the verbal abuse didn't stop. He'd also been drinking more. He'd come home even later, and his compliments were always weaved in with some backhanded insult. 'We look pathetic as a couple when you wear heels and are taller than me.' 'That lipstick is nice, but you should try a more natural color.' 'Your brain is brilliant, Violet, but how I wish you had bigger tits.' We were on our way to a children's charity event when that one came out of him," she huffed.

She bit the inside of her cheek, willing herself to continue. "And then the cheating happened. I felt like such shit. To think that you're not enough for someone who constantly belittles you —it made me feel so...worthless. I rang Jane sobbing because I didn't know who else to tell. I couldn't burden any of my friends with the pain I'd been feeling. Dean's brother, Matthew, was the one who told me."

She took another deep breath. "When he came home that night, I confronted him and told him I wanted a divorce again. He said if I brought up divorce one more time, he'd tell the school staff that I slept with him for donations before we were a couple. He said he'd tell everyone I did it again and again for all the promotions I'd later get. I never asked for that money, Ben. Not a single dime. He made those contributions because I rejected his initial offer, and he thought that would get me to comply. I still didn't. He continued to make them after we were together because it looked good for him. He then promised that if I tried to leave, he'd sully my name, so I could never work in those districts again."

Her eyes welled up. She hated every part of this story, but she especially hated the night at the pub. "I only ever got with him because he happened to be at the same bloody pub on a day I was feeling especially down, and I mistook it as a fucking sign."

She sighed heavily. "He'd say things like we're staying together because we're both respectable and threatened to make my life hell even when he was cheating on me. But we stopped talking altogether unless we had an event to attend where we'd put on a show. I moved to the guest room. And here we are today. The moment I saw a way out, I took it."

She was fidgeting with her fingers then. "You once asked me

why I married him if I didn't love him, and I briefly told you that I got tired of feeling lonely. But at the time, it felt so much bigger than that. All my friends lived far away, and I really wanted what could maybe be my safe place—my last phone call at the end of the night—someone to come home to. I don't know. I had my dream job after years of working toward it, but I had no one beside me. So I mistook his persistence in asking me out as his fight to be worthy of me when I was only ever a trophy. He wanted me because I didn't give in right away, and that was it. I put up with it because I was terrified of what he'd do if I left. He even made a remark about having nude photos of me that he'd blast. Logically, I know it's a bluff, I never sent him shit, but what if they were taken without my awareness? I would have no way of knowing. My defenses were always down. I couldn't fight back, or he'd somehow use it against me. I quite literally had nowhere to go in London if I wanted to keep my job because I was never sure what he'd say or do to get me fired."

She released a large, painful exhale at the memories.

"There was a decent version of Dean. Maybe. I believe it only because his family is full of incredible people, but I can't be the one to bring that out of him. There was a moment when I thought I was meant to help him. I had to learn the hard way that no one could change another person. I'm not the first, and in the disgusting world we live in, I won't be the last woman who's been in this situation."

Ben had one of his hands balled into a fist, so she reached forward and took it. He relaxed at her touch. "I didn't deserve what happened to me. I know that, but I'm still peeling back the shame that I chose to settle with him. I was better than that. I didn't let Simone get back with her sleazy ex, fought like hell to ensure she knew her worth, and thankfully months later, she met Peter. I was always everyone's go-to for advice, and I mucked up my own future because I wanted love so desperately that I gave in to the belief that

Dean was the best I could do. And admitting that out loud, saying I was scared to be by myself, giving in to all the pressures because my friends were married, and I wanted it too..." she paused, letting another weary breath out. "Anyway, I should've known better."

He must've gathered that she finished because he slid closer to her and took her in his arms.

She could feel a slight quiver in his body, sensing that he needed this more than her. He held her for what felt like a few minutes, without any movements but the gentle brush of his hand against her hair.

His eyes were damp and full of rage when they parted. His jaw was clenched so tightly that she reached up to stroke his cheek in an attempt to relieve the stiffness.

"I don't want to have to talk about him again after we figure out what he's doing and how to end it. I want to move past it. We're a lot harder on ourselves than we are on other people. It took years to work through this with Jane to realize that I wasn't weak or stupid for going against my better judgment. But with everything that's happened with us and his return the other day, so much of that came rushing back, so the thought of telling you scared me more than anything."

He brushed his fingers against her temple and brought both his hands to cup her face. "Violet, listen to me carefully, please."

She blinked rapidly, swallowed heavily.

"Even if you got with him believing that he was the one or some incredible person worth fighting for, you shouldn't have to carry an ounce of shame for any of the things he's done to you. You shouldn't have to look back on your emotions or the choices that led you there because his actions are his responsibility and his alone."

She heard him. Fully. Still, everything in her ached a bit. "I meant it when I said he didn't break me. Some of my demons were there long before him, but he makes me feel so small, Ben. I've gone my entire life trying not to burden people after my parents died, even Nan; I tried to be strong for her. But my strength feels fragile when he's involved, and that's what shatters me. Not knowing how to end it, once and for all, so I could fully put him behind me."

He took a deep breath and looked at her quizzically. "Is there anything of his we can use or exploit? A weakness, some sort of a massive wrongdoing? I can also contact some people in the agency and have them dig around," he suggested.

She shook her head multiple times, sending a wave of fear to every bone in her body. "I can't let you do that. This is my mess. I can't have you or anyone else get involved."

"Violet, your mess *is* my mess. If I can help you, why would I sit back and do nothing? Seeing you like this is killing me. That bloody arsehole is lucky I wasn't home when he came."

"Because I can't predict what he'll do or how bad it can get. He has resources and people, too. If you're involved, he'll find a way to exploit you, too. Dig up stuff from your past. I don't know. And I can't have any of that. You, your family, the Henrys, anyone at The Crooked Branch. I can't have anyone fight this for me."

He sighed. His hands were shaking again as he took hers and held them against his heart. "Violet, there's quite literally nothing he could find on me that the agency isn't already aware of. I've led what might single-handedly be the most boring life since then. If I remember correctly, I've once been a day late on my phone payment because I mixed up the dates, but that's about it. I've never even gotten a bloody parking ticket, which is a bit odd, but we won't question that for now."

She continued shaking her head vehemently. "Ben, no. Your sister, Luke, your nieces. He'll find *something*. I can't risk any of that. Please don't make me," she said, her eyes burning with the tears threatening to pour out.

"I'm not going to do anything until I have your full permission. But Violet, darling, I know you believe this is your fight and yours alone, but you are the love of my life, and I can't sit back and watch you take this on by yourself. Let me be your partner. I'm not trying to swoop in like some knight in shining armor, but I have the resources to not only help you, but to potentially make sure this fucker understands that he cannot pull these stunts and get away with them with anyone else. Please let me at least try."

The plea in his voice was the catalyst that her tear ducts were waiting for. If she allowed Ben to try, it'd feel like she was using him. And yet, deep down, she knew that if their roles were reversed, she'd do the exact same thing for him. Ben wasn't Dean. She knew as much sixteen years ago. She knew it today with even more conviction, but it scared her no less.

She got herself into this mess. She should be the one to get herself out. "I hear you, Ben; I do, but I'm terrified. I can't let you do this."

"Terrified of what? Violet, I promise you there's nothing he can do to me or my family. I might not be in the agency, but there's much I've not forgotten. He's the one who should be terrified of me. I have very little remorse for arseholes like him. And *if* something comes from this, he never has to find out where it came from. It'll never come back to either of us."

She sighed deeply. She hated every part of this, and she hated that she couldn't argue further.

She had no other option. "If it gets too dangerous at any point, please promise me you won't proceed further."

He nodded. "I promise. I'll make the phone call in front of you if that helps ease you."

He got off the sofa, went to bring his phone from the

bedroom and came back to sit beside her. He found the contact and then put it on speakerphone, allowing her to hear every word. With every ring, she grew more uneasy.

"Ben! Mate, it's been a while! How are you?" said the man on the other end of the line.

"Isaac, hey. I'm well, yeah. How are you? How's the family?"

He chuckled. "Oh, man, Lizzie's already walking, and she's so chatty. It's a ball."

Ben smiled easily. "Ha! That's incredible, man. They change every day, don't they?"

"Oh, it's wild. Every bloody day, I swear, she looks different from the night before."

"Get used to it, mate. You'll be running her off to school before you know it."

"And now I'm begging you to change the subject so I don't have to think about that," Isaac said.

Ben inhaled a lung full. "Sure, yeah, I actually have a massive favor to ask you."

"Of course. Anything for you."

"You're still working in the agency, right?"

"Unfortunately," he answered.

"Would you mind looking up a chap for me? Anything heinous you can find in his record, I'd take it all."

"You alright? That's the last thing I thought you'd ask me."

"It's a long story. He's my partner's ex-husband. Been causing some shit."

That word again, *partner.* It was strange how quickly they fell into this routine, forgoing all conversations about labels in such a way that she genuinely forgot that was part of the whole dating process.

"Of course. Give me anything you've got on him. I can have the information for you ASAP."

Ben's sigh of relief was palpable. "Dean Colborne. The barrister."

"Ah, I'll have a look, mate. Let me call you back."

She closed her eyes, trying to ease the tremors in her leg that'd been shaking convulsively since the men started talking. She needed to go buy supplies for the wreaths anyway. Perhaps that could take their minds off it all.

"I owe you," Ben assured.

"You forgot about that training shit, old man. I've been owing you since then. Finally get to pay you back. But also, the next time we visit, I expect every pudding on the menu to be complimentary," he said with a laugh.

"You get that for life. Not just the next time."

"Keep that thought until I've got concrete proof for you," Isaac noted.

"Cheers."

When he hung up, Violet rose and stood in front of him. "Want to go get supplies with me for the festival? I can't just sit here and wait, or I'll spiral."

He took the hand she was holding out. "Let's go."

37

VIOLET

The phone rang at a quarter to nine p.m. Violet and Ben had barely managed to get through their late dinner. Ben answered immediately.

"Isaac, yeah."

"Well, this man's a fucking disaster. I wouldn't even know where to begin. But mate, he has eight bank accounts with far more money than a damn barrister should. There are multiple overseas funds, various accounts under the name Dean Parker. There's some very dodgy stuff in here that I got to send down for further investigation," he noted.

Violet's eyes grew wide. What the fresh hell?

Ben huffed—not the least bit shocked, it seemed. "Well fuck. Do what you have to do. But uhm, just don't mention me?" Ben noted.

"Yeah, of course. Look, there's a lot of shit in here. I can't imagine how he's getting away with it, which would probably worsen the outcome if someone covered for him in the past."

"Add domestic violence into that equation as well," Ben added.

"Fucking hell. Yeah, well, listen, I'll keep you posted if I hear anything, but if it's as bad as it seems, you'll see it in the news before I even get to you."

"Complimentary meals for life, mate. And whatever else you might need from me. Thank you," Ben said.

"I'm holding you to it," Isaac remarked with a chuckle.

The men hung up, and everything inside Violet was recoiling. Could this have happened during the Granger case? Were they linked in any way? Frankly, part of her didn't care. Wherever this led, she was concerned for his family more than anything, but she wanted this man far in her past where he belonged. Away from all women, not only her.

She sighed deeply. "What now? Do we tell the solicitors?"

"Nope, no one. Whether you want to use the photos of your wrist or not, that's on you. But everything that Isaac told us should be enough to send him away. Did Dean...uh, ever know about me in any way?" Ben asked.

"No, the only person I ever told in detail was Simone. And I didn't even tell her about the case—just about you and us. I would trust that woman with my life, so I hope that's okay. I would've exploded if I had to keep it in. Yana, of course, because she was there. I later told Nan while she was very ill. As I imagined, she adored you for being kind to me after the anxiety attack. Lastly, a few of my closest, most trustworthy friends know that we met in Paris during that time, but I never mentioned you were an agent. Other than them, no other person in this world knows about you. Dean only knows your name because he saw the caller ID that morning, but I told him you were my neighbor, and that was it."

Ben nodded. "That's fine. He has no way of tracing it back to us. He'd need some very powerful resources if he dares to even try. And in that case, someone on the inside would have to be helping, which wouldn't work in Dean's favor."

"So, we just sit and wait?"

"Yeah. I know this part sucks. A lot, actually. But he's going to be behind us one day, and until we know more, I'm happy to keep going with the routine we've got right now." Ben looked at her with a mixture of pride and pain. It wasn't pity. It was profound empathy, and she felt every ounce of it piercing through her. He took her hand in his across the table.

She nodded, interlacing her fingers through his.

He rubbed her thumb and lifted her hand to his lips. He placed a tender kiss on the back of her hand. "You were afraid that I'd look at you differently through this, but Violet, it only proved that your strength is unmatched. You went through all of that, yet your capacity for love is still limitless."

She sighed into the warmth of his lips on her fingers and then rose to where he was seated. Ben turned in his chair, settling her onto his lap.

"Thank you for fighting with me," she said, tracing her lips along the lines on his forehead.

"You know I still owe you an official first date," he hummed.

She chuckled. "Is that so?"

He captured her lips in a quick, searing kiss. "Yes."

"First thing after all of this is done?" she suggested.

He confirmed.

"At least the Autumn Festival will keep us busy," she said.

His eyes widened. "Bloody hell, how do I keep forgetting, even when we just came back from the shop?"

"Wait till you start helping me with wreaths. Then you won't forget, but you'll loathe me for roping you into crafts. We'll have the sweetest display but it will pale in comparison to Patrick's dance number," she said with a satisfied smile.

"I'm actually quite good at crafts," he returned, biting gently into her bottom lip.

She melted into his kiss. "Is that so?"

His grip around her tightened, his lips trailing her exposed collarbone, up toward her neck. "Oh, yeah. But crafts will have to wait until after I'm done with you."

38

BEN

"Remind me to thank Violet about twenty times at the festival tomorrow, boss. I'm pretty sure her reaction to my pumpkin parfait enchantments is where half my confidence comes from," Billy retorted.

Ben sighed and swung a cloth around his shoulder. "Will you at least call them something else?"

Billy squared his shoulders. "Nope, Emily from The Wisteria Tea Room thinks they're delightful."

Ben rolled his eyes. "Well then, she has questionable taste as well."

"Please. If Violet said the name was sweet, you'd agree in a heartbeat."

He was absolutely right. If Violet thought so, he'd agree.

These months had always been synonymous with grief for him, but Violet brought warmth into every corner. She made his world feel lively. She was sunrise and sunset simultaneously—incomparable variations of an afterglow.

"You don't get to talk about my relationship at work," Ben retorted.

Billy, Jeff, and Leo all chuckled at the same time. "Yes, we do."

He grimaced and squared his shoulders. "If you still want Friday off, you, of all people, should stay quiet, Jeff."

Billy chimed in again. "You know what people on the internet say when they watch a fictional couple interact? They say they ship it."

The point was entirely lost on Ben.

"What the bloody hell do you want me to do with this information?" he asked.

"Nothing. I simply wanted to be the first to say I ship the two of you."

"Oh, that's a good one. I'm with him on this one, Chef," Leo remarked.

Ben rolled his eyes. "Did you all forget you have jobs to do?"

"You know, this might be worth losing the day off. I think my wife will understand. I ship it too," said Jeff.

"I'd expect this behavior from Billy but not from you lot," Ben responded.

"The boy keeps us young, Chef. Embrace it."

"I'm not embracing shit," he barked, growing more and more frustrated, even if he didn't completely hate all this.

"You better be embracing Violet; otherwise, what kind of a man would you be? Your father raised you better than that," Leo noted.

"Once again, my relationship is no one's business in this kitchen." He looked at Jeff. "And you? Kiss that day off goodbye."

The man chuckled. "I'll give it a few hours; you'll see Violet and forget all about your threats to us."

Florence walked in mid-argument. "A child spilled chips at table five. Someone please make a new batch immediately. Also have you lot decided what we're offering at the festival?" she said.

Leo got right to the chips. Billy looked at Ben as if he was supposed to make the announcement.

Ben patted the boy's shoulder. "Go on then, Billy. Fill Florence in."

Billy shifted in his position and stood up straighter. He folded the cloth he had on his shoulder then cleared his throat. The kid was a wreck around Florence, and he was her bloody favorite in this kitchen. "The pumpkin parfait enchantments are doing really well with customers, so we're considering adding them along with the Jammie Dodgers. And as far as savory, our fried halloumi sticks and chips."

"That's a bit dull, isn't it? Simply fried food?" Florence asked.

Ben watched as Billy gulped down hard. "Yes, but since they're customer favorites, we figured it'd be nicer than the smaller versions of battered cod. It's worth a try. Plus, three more restaurants have signed on this year. There's going to be far more food than ever before."

Florence nodded her head quizzically. "Oh, hmm, well, alright." She turned to Ben then. "You'll be holding down the fort throughout the morning, yes? We're closing early, but not until three."

Ben bobbed his head. "That's the plan. Leo will be with me. And so will Haley and Paul," he replied.

"Oh, good. Very well, then. Carry on," she flickered with her hands, then walked out of the kitchen.

Billy's shoulders slumped, and the tension in his body eased. Ben let out a low, sincere chuckle. "You know Florence adores you, right? No need to get all tongue-tied with her," he said.

His lips curved into his usual enormous grin. "Does she really? It's hard to believe that. She's just like my Nan. You know they do, but man, you can never be sure."

"You can be sure," Ben responded swiftly.

As an order came through for sticky toffee pudding, he

wondered if it was Violet. Yet, he knew that she'd be at work, so that couldn't have been the case.

It felt nice to be at ease and know that Dean was out of the picture—to be at work without thinking of him disrupting Violet's day. Her solicitor had called after Isaac's discoveries, stating that she received confirmation that Dean had been working from home in London all along. The bastard merely intended to freak her out. It made Ben want to wring his neck. He'd also heard from Isaac that the overseas funds were indeed fraudulent, and an investigation against Dean was underway. His divorce would be the least of his problems now, with legal cases stacked against him.

He and Violet could move forward with their lives, taking everything day by day—hopefully under the same roof.

They really, *really* needed to figure out this homing situation since things felt more settled. He knew Violet liked her space and many of the pieces in her house that Aunt Helen had chosen, but he selfishly wanted her with him.

He wanted them to live in the same place, to leave it and come back to it together. One house over would feel kilometers away if he were to lie in bed without her. They could find some semblance of normalcy now, gliding into a rhythm where glimmers of joy could be unveiled in the mundane.

As he added custard on top of the warmed pudding, he lost himself in the memories of her sheer bliss as she first tried his.

39

VIOLET

Preparations for the Autumn Festival had gone too well during the past two weeks. Jack Carver was a grump on the surface, but he was a team player and quite kind when he wasn't knackered. However, he was certainly always kind to Lucy Williams. Violet would bet everything that they had feelings for each other, yet they both believed it was unrequited.

She'd been sitting at the school's booth for about three hours, surrounded by the gorgeous wreaths the children had made. But she was feeling a bit superstitious, so she began over-thinking and imagining all sorts of possible catastrophes.

What is anxiety if not a persevering little shit that has no concept of a day off? She'd rationalize. She'd combat.

She knew there would be no surprise visits from Dean or anything awful of that sort. And thankfully, there would be no rain damage with the quality of booths the city donated this year.

Holding such events outdoors meant leaves dancing on the ground with a chill delicately wheedling in the air. And the weather was quite proper—tailor-made for her to admire the white cable knit jumper she bought specifically to ogle Ben in.

There was far too much grey and dark heather in his wardrobe, which was *hot,* in every way. She'd never complain.

But something about a man in a white jumper sent her heart off waltzing. He had promised that there was nothing he wouldn't do for her, so she knew he'd oblige. He would be arriving after his shift at the restaurant, and the thrill of seeing him made her feel so giddy she could explode.

This would also be the first time they would be out in public together outside of quick trips to the shops and The Crooked Branch.

Violet was used to charity events in cocktail dresses and gorgeously expensive gowns. She was used to heels, high-end jewelry, and bejeweled clutches. It'd been too long since she'd gone to an outdoor event with children running in every direction and people cozily walking by.

Life had passed her by with such intensity she couldn't even remember the last time she had gone to the farmer's market in Notting Hill. Four, maybe five years ago? Too long.

It'd been too long since she felt free.

It'd been too long since she felt happy.

It'd been too long since she felt loved.

To be incandescently revered and deeply cherished was a profound wish she had never even uttered aloud.

Jack leaned over in his seat and positioned himself similarly to Violet, one hand under his chin, leaning against the small table in front of them. "Are we daydreaming over there?"

She blinked twice and tilted her head. "Oh God, did I have some sort of a goofy grin on?"

Jack chuckled. "Yep. You're also crushing one of those fake leaves in your hand."

She looked down at the crumpled plastic. "Oops."

"Don't sweat it. I'm sure I look the same way, occasionally."

She arched her eyebrow as if to ask if he wanted to elaborate, knowing that he likely wouldn't. She was going to pry it out of those two at some point. One of them was bound to crack.

"That's all the information you're getting from me today," he confirmed with a small grunt.

She huffed. "Noted. We can talk when parents and Lucy aren't approaching."

She watched as Jack squared himself and rose to his feet, the glint in his eyes reappearing. Oh yeah, he liked Lucy. *A lot.*

Lucy walked back into the booth to stand with the two of them, and the parents introduced themselves before asking which wreath belonged to their child in order to purchase it. The students adored the wreath-making process, making it more rewarding to see their parents' reactions.

It was also lovely how quickly she fit in with everyone at Knightley.

Lucy spoke first when the set of parents left. "Patrick's dance number is actually pretty cool, guys. I can't believe he pulled it off."

Jack rolled his eyes.

Violet smiled. "Well, I, for one, can't wait to see itty bitty waltzes to a strings cover of Taylor Swift's 'Love Story.' It's going to be adorable."

"It is! My cheeks hurt from grinning so much while watching them rehearse behind the stage."

Violet looked to Jack to see how his reaction would change with Lucy's excitement. His lips twitched slightly, but there was no denying the warmth in his eyes.

This was the beginning of something special. Watching two people continue to lose themselves in each other's eyes. *This must be what Simone meant when she told their friends about her behavior with Ben*—the little things she wouldn't notice herself that outsiders looking in would observe.

There was nothing but beauty in every fraction of these moments—the uglier sides included, and the troubles that could come. It was going to be worth every minute because here, in the winding streets of Bath and underneath the canopy of gorgeous trees, she found the pieces of her she used to dream of. New friends she was growing to care for immensely. A love she believed in with full conviction.

In every regard, the quiet realizations of the day made sense in the same way that only grief had. She knew with unwavering conviction that it was never a feeling she would fully understand, but a constant measure of the love living deep inside of her. The very love she'd barricaded and tucked away.

It was all on full display as well as the freedom to be herself again.

Just as grief was a part of her, today, her agency would be, too.

Claire joined them at the booth as well, walking in while Lucy was telling Jack about the local band getting ready to perform some song covers.

"They call themselves The Tower Wolves. They're quite good. They sound a bit like if Fleetwood Mac and The National had a baby. Their lead singers are a man and a woman, and goodness she can *sing*. I caught a show once accidentally because they were performing at St. James Wine Vaults," Lucy said.

It was then that Violet spotted Ben walking toward her from the west, the sun and its array of light casting an intoxicating glow on him. The white jumper was everything she wanted to see on him, and she was tickled by the thought of also being the one to take it off.

He smiled when he spotted her and sped up slightly. How

Ben Grant entered a space would always floor her. He was a vision—a bloody kaleidoscope, fitter than anyone she'd ever laid eyes on, with his gaze permanently locked on hers.

She told her colleagues she'd be back and walked right over to him.

She leaped into his arms, circling hers tightly along his neck.

"You wore the jumper!" she specified excitedly.

He chuckled and spun her around. She could dissolve into pools of liquid heat with his arms capturing her like this. There was no place safer than Ben's embrace.

His reverence was home.

For a woman who used to loathe public displays of affection, even this moment felt right. He placed a quick kiss on the side of her head when he put her down. "Of course, I did. Can I steal you from that booth for a bit?"

"Yes. I've been here all day. I think it'd be okay if I left for a beat."

He interlaced their fingers together. "Good. Take a walk with me."

They walked in companionable silence before he asked how it'd been going.

"Smashing! Did you know Billy's pumpkin parfait enchantments sold out in two hours?"

Ben rolled his eyes lovingly. "Of course, they did. I'm never living that down."

"Let him have the win, babe. His excitement was precious. He came to find me just to let me know."

"Alright, yeah. I'll take the gloating if it makes the two of you happy."

"I promise not to always conspire with him to torture you with more pumpkins, but on occasion...maybe?" she noted, scrunching her nose while smiling at him.

He swung his head lovingly, eyes sparkling right alongside his comforting smile.

The cheery sounds around them, the lines of colorful trees encircling their sights, falling leaves moving with the wind—it all made her heart swell.

She gazed at Ben again—the jumper stretching perfectly on his taut muscles was a thing of beauty. The rolled-up sleeves, baring his forearms should have been illegal. She wanted to hold on to this memory forever, vaulted into the most sacred hideaways of her being—as far as they'd reach.

He turned to her, stopping their jaunt. He ran his fingers delicately against her shoulders, up her neck, landing at the base of her jaw. "I have a surprise for you that I'm hoping might make today a little better," he declared.

Her eyebrows rose in question. What was that supposed to mean?

He smiled, and she caught his eyes going over her head. She wanted to turn, but she took a pause. *What was he doing?*

"You can turn around," he whispered, nudging gently at her chin.

At which millisecond she went from shocked to teary-eyed she couldn't place. Phoebe and Colin were in her arms, chattering loudly in her ear. A squeaky voice declared she missed her, and another said she smelled nice. And then they let her go and moved aside.

She was at a loss.

Simone's arms were then wrapped tightly around her, jumbled conversations blending together.

This was home.

This was safe.

This was everything she wanted and more.

How was Simone here? How was Peter here? How were the kids here? When was this arranged? *Did Ben do this?* A great day turned to the best. Her favorite people left on earth, all in one place.

This was real.

This was *everything*.

Somewhere in her blurry peripheral, she saw Ben and Peter shaking hands. He inched lower to talk to Phoebe and Colin. Simone took Violet's face in her hands and looked into her eyes. She didn't need to say anything for Violet to interpret.

I love you. You're not alone anymore. You've got us all.

"This is very real," Simone answered. She must've asked it somewhere during the muffled "What is happening," she repeated through her tears. "All of it, babe," she emphasized.

When she could see clearly and take it all in, it was better than anything she could've hoped for. Better than her wildest dreams, prayers, and every wish she must've made during desperate nights alone. It was an ordinary day no more.

It was magic.

"HOW ARE YOU?" Simone asked, her voice soft and assertive, enunciating the syllables to signal the safe space for the truth. She wiped a bit of the mascara that ran down Violet's cheeks.

Violet exhaled eagerly. "Can a person explode from happiness?"

"Do you remember what you said to me the night before my wedding?"

"I wrote you a three-page letter, babe. Which part?"

Simone laughed, nestling further into Violet's side as they walked. "You told me I was glowing in a way you couldn't put into words. You said there was something in me that felt ethereal —untouchable. And right now, you have that same glow. It killed me that you didn't before. It killed me that you weren't *this* happy."

Violet bit the inside of her cheek. "The first time he and I spoke, and I mean really spoke back then, I felt lighter with him. And in a way, that scared me because my defenses were completely down. I don't know how I allowed that, but I couldn't help it. He makes me feel safe, Simone. I love everything about him, and I'm sure I'll eventually want to murder him for being too bloody chipper in the mornings, but it feels surreal to know that he was mine all along." She shook her head in disbelief, stunned by her own happiness. "I love him in a way I didn't know was humanly possible."

Violet looked back at Ben and Peter playing a game of croquet with the kids.

"He's everything I wished for. I was so lost, Simone. I wasn't broken, but I was lost. I was scared and unsure while I fought myself. But he sees it all and holds me steady. I didn't know it was conceivable to feel this much—I don't know where to put it all."

Simone looked over with a wink. "On top of him? Underneath?"

Violet laughed aloud, hitting her arm playfully. "You're the worst."

"You love me for it."

Violet shut her eyes for a beat when they stopped, far enough from the men where they wouldn't hear but close to see them still. "How did this happen?"

"It was all that man of yours. He got my number from Mum and told me all about how he was sure us being here would make today better for you. We spoke for a while actually, loads of chatting about how much we adore you. And here we are. We've actually been here since yesterday, hid it from you pretty well."

Violet licked her lips and shook her head. "He really is wonderful, isn't he? He did that?"

"You've never believed anyone would ever be fully good enough for me, and you're right, the same goes for you. But just as you said about Peter—Ben comes pretty close. He'd give the bloody world for you, Vi. I knew it. I did. But this proves it."

Violet placed the back of her thumb to her eyes, trying desperately to stop the tears.

"If you'd just move here, life would be great."

Simone chuckled. "You and Mum are going to start a campaign, aren't you?"

"Yes, exactly."

Softened and subdued, the daylight grew dimmer, and shades of oranges and reds enveloped them. One conversation at a time, she tried to hold onto it all. Ben's hand wrapped around her waist. Phoebe and Colin bouncing along. They would only be here until tomorrow night, but it was everything, still.

The sounds of their laughter—every word, every look—it all felt like a dream.

In all her years of planning and coordinating, this was the first time a day ever worked so well.

The kids clearly had a blast with Patrick's choreography, and the crowd cheered more enthusiastically than any of them anticipated.

The Tower Wolves played an acoustic cover of Fleetwood Mac's "Everywhere," and somewhere in the surprising and dazzling chaos of a solid performance, she was encircled in the arms of a man who loved her ardently—the home she'd been missing, needing, and searching everywhere for.

"I don't know how I'm ever going to thank you for this," she said, looping her arms around his neck.

He held her close, running his hand up and down her back. "I'm a selfish bastard, Violet. I'd do anything to see that beautiful smile on your face."

She looked up at him and rested her forehead against his. "I love you more than I can bear sometimes."

He captured her lips in a desperate frenzy as if to show his own inability to grasp the adoration. "I'm going to spend the rest of my life trying to find ways to show you how much I adore you. And it's never going to be enough, but by God, darling, I'm going to try."

She smiled at him, inching closer to clutch his lips again.

The man of her dreams she'd left behind in Paris was meant to be hers all along.

Sixteen years later—somewhere in Somerset, with floating leaves swaying all around them—they'd find the foundation of their second chance beneath the most gorgeously encompassing afterglow.

EPILOGUE

1 Year Later - Violet

They'd just returned from an unmarred, wondrously mending week away in Paris, revisiting and unreservedly exploring the city where they first fell in love. It was sort of an anniversary trip, but more so a celebration, for this would be Violet's last week off before starting her new position as head teacher of Knightley Primary School after Abigail James' transfer to Oxford.

She hadn't expected the promotion to arise when she first started, nor did she think she'd get the job when she interviewed. Yet, it was all she hoped for. She adored teaching, but working to ensure all students, not just her own, were in good hands was the job she favored most.

Violet rummaged through the post as Ben showered, organizing the essential documents from the miscellaneous, when she came upon a card from Yana.

She set the remaining stack on the marble countertop and slid her nail through the seal on the back. She expected something book-related, or maybe she was getting an early start on Christmas cards this year.

She briefly caught a glimpse of an old, familiar wall with the miniature mirror where she'd touched up her lipstick. It teleported her back to the place they'd just visited—the new paint job and renovations liven the hotel up plenty, but the wistfulness of those four walls and the rusted door were etched in her memory still. They didn't set foot in the actual room—813 was still a distant memory, but surely it would've also been fine-tuned.

Her heart was pounding in a way it hadn't when they first walked into the hotel, for old times' sake.

She pulled out an old 35mm photograph of herself—deep brown hair falling in waves, purposely donning a trifling expression, her tongue sticking out at the camera, wearing *the* red dress. Standing in the middle of their hotel room at L'Hotel Lavande, it all came rushing back to her. Again. She'd entirely forgotten that Yana had taken a picture.

How did she forget that? Violet remembered everything.

She took out the paper from inside the envelope and unfolded it. Before she began to read, she dragged her fingers against the edges of the photograph.

Violet,

About seven years ago, I found batches of undeveloped film in a box from my move. One of them was from Paris. I wanted to send it to you so many times—to ask if you'd like it or just, I don't know, surprise you. But I was always a little unsure if you wanted that part of your life dug up. You once said you regretted that day, jokingly, because you said Ben ruined all other men for you. And I guess I didn't want to remind you of a time that might upset you while you were married or dealing with heartbreak. So, I kept it. It's a stunning photo, isn't it? The sun peering through that measly window. You were glowing that day. No wonder he couldn't keep his hands off you. I'd known you for almost three years at that point, and I'd never seen you cry. It broke my heart to see you walk out with this wild joy to return with a tear-stained face and straight into my arms, where you told me how it'd been the most magical night of your life. I'm sorry, Vi. I tucked it away for safekeeping and remembered its existence again about a week ago when I caught the news in the paper about that shithead ex of yours. Charged with multiple counts of fraud? Have fun rotting, wanker. Anyway, my friend, you deserve a tangible memory of that day—along with the man beside you forever. I have digital copies of all the other embarrassing photos we took. I'll send you those later. I hope you forgive me for not sending it earlier. Love you xx

P.S. I get to write the romance novel about your lives someday, right?

Violet snorted, swapping the envelope for her phone to text a response. She was leaning against the counter, the photograph next to the stack of papers.

I'd trust no one else to do our story justice. This was a perfect surprise, Yana. I have no bloody words. And I think you were right. Seeing this before might've broken me. Hell, even I'd forgotten, and we just got back from Paris! So your timing is oddly spot on. How are you both such a stellar photographer and a brilliant writer? It's unfair, woman. Xx big, big love!

"Darling?" Ben called out, walking toward her.

She perched up and smiled at him.

He placed a kiss on her forehead. "Is there a lot to weed out?"

"Huh? Oh, I lost focus, actually. Look what Yana sent me," she said, handing him the photograph.

She heard his breath drawback in his throat and watched his eyes emit something entrancingly warm and reverential. "Can we frame this?" he asked, his voice so muted she wasn't sure he meant to say it aloud.

"I look like a bloody buffoon. You want people to see that?"

He tugged on his bottom lip and moved the photograph to the side of Violet's face as if he were comparing. "There were so many moments during our time in Paris that made me want you, but I knew I was wrecked when you stood your ground and started yelling at me about gargoyles."

She rolled her eyes fondly. "I didn't yell at you. I scolded you."

"You squared your shoulders like you were about to karate chop me, and then you called them art," he said, demonstrating the presumed position she'd been in. He inched forward, closing the space between them. "This is the look in your eyes when you get excited about something. So, yeah, I want it framed."

She was sure now that she must've been making the same face because she didn't think twice about winding her arms around his neck and kissing him like they hadn't spent days and nights entangled in each other's arms.

~

October 24

TYPICALLY, Sunday was the one day out of the week neither she nor Ben worked. In autumn, it involved maple brown sugar waffles and cinnamon hazelnut coffee. There were usually reruns of *Parks and Recreation*, but today, a new series called *Ted Lasso* was playing.

Shortly after last year's Autumn Festival, Violet had moved to Ben's house, and Aunt Helen put her place up for rent again.

She got to keep her brick-red colored sofa, thankfully, Ben wasn't too attached to his grey one.

They would never need separate spaces again.

They spent lazy afternoons on said sofa and had sticky toffee pudding after dinner.

Scars persisted in healing, and tears fell more for blissful occasions. It was hard to believe it had all been real. It *was real.*

This was their forever.

Violet was sprawled in his arms, acutely invested in the show's fictional football match, when he looked down at her and brushed the hair back from her face. She had lightened it again, blonder than she'd ever been. He sighed, thick with contentment and whispered in her ear. "Take a walk with me?"

She hummed, leaning further into his embrace. "Where to?"

His fingers trailed indolently against her cheek. "To the skyline."

"Okay. After the episode ends."

AUTUMN WAS AT ITS PEAK—AMBER hues all around, glowing yellows and bright dazzling oranges. Both crisp and damp leaves brilliantly charted the pavements with ineffable vibrancy.

When they got to the tip of the ever-growing beauty of Bath, Ben wrapped his arms securely around her from behind and kissed her cheek. She inched back a little, leaning her head against his shoulder.

He took a deep, hearty breath. "When I pulled you into my arms that very first time and heard your laugh gust straight to my chest, everything in the world made sense," he tipped her face to kiss her lips. When their mouths pulled apart, he averted their gazes to Bath's sprawling splendor—*home.*

A chill pierced her rapidly when his arms unraveled from her body.

She turned back to hold onto him again, but Ben Grant was on his knees before her.

He exhaled and beamed at her, his eyes misting. "Violet, my love, you are my one definitive treasure—my whole entire world. You brought meaning back into my dull, achingly hollow life, and I want to spend the rest of my days beside you, doing everything in my power to ensure you're happy, cherished, and adored as profoundly as you deserve. I want to spend all our Sundays fighting over what to watch next, only to end up kissing through it all until you yell at me because we aren't paying attention. I want to keep building a life with you, to bake sticky toffee pudding and biscuits whenever your heart desires. I want to continue seeing the world through your eyes. I want to be the safe place you come home to every night."

He paused and bit his lip. She was fully crying. "I didn't ask you in Paris because...well, I figured it'd be obvious, but even though that's where we met, and it's where our story began, our lives were changed here in Bath. You said we'd have a chance right here, on the skyline, and I want to keep making promises that we plan to keep. What do you say, darling, will you be my wife?"

This was the place where she first felt at home—the words she said aloud to him, wiped tears from her eyes and watched as he drew closer to her, asking if he had a chance.

He was the only one who ever did.

He was the one she wished for without realizing it—before she had even met him. He was her whole world. She traced the curve of his jaw and nodded rapidly.

"You're the only man I've ever wanted any of this with, Ben— of course, I'll marry you."

He slid the diamond ring onto her finger and brushed his thumb delicately along it.

This was real.

He rose to his feet and kissed her tears away. More memories of Paris flashed through her mind, only this wasn't goodbye. It was yet another beginning—another piece of their life's puzzle to make up the shining afterglow of their in-between.

"I love you. I'm *in love* with you. And I still have such a wildly massive crush on you and the way you look and sound when you laugh," she said through lingering kisses.

He dipped her in his arms, kissing her lips with what felt like every fiber of his devotion descending like a decadent downpour. "I'll find a way to give you the skyline, seize it all—something grand and unbelievable to show you how deeply and fervently I love you."

"You've already given me everything. The magic in autumn feels infinite with you," she proclaimed, her voice smoky and spiked with gratitude. "It's all I've ever dreamed of."

In a field of green, speckled with shimmering autumn leaves, they kissed with promises brimming in every move they made—*I love you.*

This is real.

This is home.

You and me and the skyline.

THE END

ACKNOWLEDGMENTS

I wrote this book for every person who's ever felt like time wasn't on their side—the people who've spent too many lonely days, crying themselves to sleep and wondering when their moment would come. Whether it's in a job or in love, as lonely as you feel, I hope you can find comfort in this fictional story.

Dad, as mentioned in the dedication, this one's for you. Thank you for teaching me the importance of putting pen to paper. I was always scared to walk in your footsteps, but when you passed, it was the only way I could work through the pain grief brought on. You were the biggest fan of my writing, and I miss you always. I hope a copy of this is sent to Heaven somehow, and I hope you're sitting on a park bench with falling leaves as you read it.

To my family, thank you for your tireless and immense support while dealing with me throughout this entire process. I'll spend the rest of my life trying to thank you, and I love you all more than I could ever put into words.

Jenna, it's not hyperbolic to say this book wouldn't exist without you. You virtually held my hand through the entire journey, listened to all my anxious thoughts, ramblings, and every wild idea I had with the utmost patience. I'm floored by you. You pulled the weight at Marvelous Geeks when I needed you most. And then, you gave me the cover of my absolute dreams. You are as much a part of Ben and Violet as I am. Thank you forever. I love you to bits!

Kate, sharing this story with you has been a tremendous highlight and a big help. I can't imagine where this book would be without your touch as an editor. I got through the hardest parts because of you. Your insight and wisdom have been irreplaceable. There are truly not enough words to express my gratitude for you. Thank you x infinity. Forevermore. All of it. And here's to our angsty ghost boys and the girls who bring light back. I adore you to the moon!

Sarah, in more ways than one, my writing career changed entirely because of you. You introduced me to a little show that I sincerely believe changed my life and, more importantly, my journey as a writer forever. I owe so much to that day. But above all, to our friendship, which means the world to me. Your perspective in this book is one I cherish deeply. Thank you immensely for taking the time to edit amid all the chaos and busy days. Love love love you forever!

Annie, you already know that you're entirely responsible for so many of us getting into the romance genre, which I'm now certain was your goal all along. I'll be thanking you always for introducing me to this beautiful, wholesome, and happy world. Thank you for your feedback with this book baby and believing in me. Big, big love!

Maneh, Marian, and Arsik, if I loved you three less, I might be able to talk about you more. You've been with me during the best and worst days. You believed in me even when I didn't believe in myself, and I'll spend forever saying thank you!

Lizzie, Jeanette, and Lyra, thank you for keeping me sane at work during edits, and for supporting me during every anxious spiral I had. I don't know how any of this got done with everything we were going through, but I sincerely couldn't have done it without you!

Amy, you were the first person to beta-read the roughest draft, and I'm so grateful for that. Your support and our friendship have meant so much to me. Thank you for loving these characters and rooting for me. You're one of the bravest women I know, and I adore you!

Erin Langston, thank you for reading the first four chapters when I was wrecked over my abilities. Thank you for answering every little question I had, and more importantly, thank you for your kindness and belief in me. You're such a brilliant writer and an even more brilliant soul. How'd I get so lucky to call you a friend?!

BK Borison, friendship aside, I'm such a massive fan of your work, so having you encourage me has meant a ton during this journey. Thank you so very much for patiently answering every single question I had about the field and for talking me out of the negative thoughts. You rock big time!

Iris, my resident British babe, sunshine friend. A little ship brought you into my life, and then you played a role in my book by answering every question about British culture and words while simultaneously rooting for me. Meeting you and frolicking around the streets of London will always be one of my favorite memories. Let's do it again soon!?

And finally, to every reader who picks this book up, I've tried writing something profound too many times, but I just can't find the words. Thank you simply isn't enough. Please know that your willingness to give this story a chance will always stay with me!

ABOUT THE AUTHOR

Born and raised in California, Gissane Sophia (pronounced Geese-Enny) is a hopeless romantic who ceaselessly champions that vulnerability is a strength. She's a fan of complex characters, found families, her bright, brilliant family and friends, coffee, forests, and all things autumn. When she isn't dabbling in writing romance novels, she's reading them. And when she's doing neither, she's devouring fiction through TV and film, working full-time as an entertainment editor and writer.

 x.com/gissanesophia

 instagram.com/gissanesophiawrites